LEAVE THE GRAVE GREEN

DEBORAH CROMBIE

SCRIBNER
New York London Toronto Sydney Tokyo Singapore

SCRIBNER
Rockefeller Center
1230 Avenue of the Americas
New York, NY 10020

Designed by ERICH HOBBING

Manufactured in the United States of America

ISBN 0-684-19770-7

For my dad,
whose creativity and
enjoyment of life
continue to inspire me

ACKNOWLEDGMENTS

I'd like to thank Stephanie Woolley, of Taos, New Mexico, whose beautiful watercolors provided the model for Julia's portraits. I am also grateful to Brian Coventry, head cutter at Lilian Baylis House, who took time from his extremely busy schedule to show me LB House and introduce me to the mysteries of Making Wardrobe; and to Caroline Grummond, assistant to the orchestra manager at the English National Opera, who was kind enough to show me both front- and back-of-house at the Coliseum.

My agent, Nancy Yost, and my editor, Susanne Kirk, provided their usual expert advice, and thanks are, as always, due to the EOTNWG for their reading of the manuscript.

Last, but by no means least, thanks to my daughter, Katie, for helping our household run smoothly, and to my husband, Rick Wilson, for his patience and support.

LEAVE THE GRAVE GREEN

PROLOGUE

"Watch you don't slip." Julia pushed back the wisps of dark hair that had snaked loose from her ponytail, her brow furrowed with anxious concern. The air felt dense, as thick and substantial as cotton wool. Tiny beads of moisture slicked her skin, and larger drops fell intermittently from the trees to the sodden carpet of leaves beneath her feet. "We'll be late for tea, Matty. And you know what Father will say if you've not done your lessons in time for practice."

"Oh, don't be so wet, Julia," said Matthew. A year younger than his sister, as fair and stocky as she was thin and dark, he'd physically outstripped her in the past year and it had made him more insufferably cocksure than ever. "You're a broody old hen. 'Matty, don't slip. Matty, don't fall,'" he mimicked her nastily. "The way you carry on you'd think I couldn't wipe my own nose." His arms held shoulder-high, he balanced on a fallen tree trunk near the edge of the swollen stream. His school haversack lay where he'd dropped it carelessly in the mud.

Clutching her own books to her thin chest, Julia rocked on the balls of her feet. *Serve him right if he caught it from Father.* But the scolding, even if severe, would be brief, and life in their household would return quickly to normal—normal being that they all behaved, to quote Plummy when she felt particularly exasperated with him, "as if the sun rose and set out of Matthew's backside."

Julia's lips twitched at the thought of what Plummy would say when she saw his muddy bookbag and shoes. But no matter, all would be forgiven him, for Matthew possessed the one attribute her parents valued above all else. He could sing.

He sang effortlessly, the clear, soaring treble falling from his lips as easily as a whispered breath. And singing transformed him, the gawky, gap-toothed twelve-year-old vanishing as he concentrated, his face serious and full of grace. They would gather in the sitting room after tea, her father patiently fine-tuning Matthew on the Bach cantata he'd be singing with the choir at Christmas, her mother interrupting loudly and often with criticism and praise. It seemed to Julia that the three of them formed a charmed circle to which she, due to an accident of birth or some inexplicable whim of God, was forever denied admittance.

The children had missed their bus that afternoon. Julia, hoping for a private word with the art mistress, had delayed too long, and the loaded bus had rumbled by them, splattering dark freckles of mud on their calves. They'd had to walk home, and cutting across the fields, had caked their shoes with clay until they had to lift their heavy feet deliberately, like visitors from a lighter planet. When they reached the woods, Matthew had caught Julia's hand and pulled her, slipping and slithering through the trees, down the hillside to the stream nearest their house.

Julia shivered and looked up. The day had darkened perceptibly, and although the November afternoons drew in early, she thought the lessening visibility meant more rain. It had rained heavily every day for weeks. Jokes about the forty days and forty nights had long since grown stale; now glances at the heavy sky were followed by silent and resigned headshaking. Here in the chalk hills north of the Thames, water leached steadily from the saturated ground and flowed into already overburdened tributaries.

Matty had left his tightrope walking on the log and squatted at the water's edge, poking about with a long stick. The stream, in ordinary weather a dry gully, now filled its banks, the rushing water as opaque as milky tea.

Julia, feeling increasingly cross, said, "Do come on, Matty, please." Her stomach growled. "I'm hungry. And cold." She hugged herself tighter. "If you don't come I shall go without you."

"Look, Julie!" Oblivious to her nagging, he gestured toward the water with the stick. "There's something caught under the surface, just there. Dead cat, maybe?" He looked round at her and grinned.

"Don't be disgusting, Matty." She knew her prim and bossy tone would only fuel his teasing, but she was past caring. "I really will go without you." As she turned resolutely away she felt an unpleasant cramping sensation in her abdomen. "Honestly, Matty, I don't feel—"

The splash sprayed her legs even as she whipped around. "Matty! Don't be such an—"

He'd fallen in, landing on his back with his arms and legs splayed awkwardly. "It's cold," he said, his face registering surprise. He scrabbled toward the bank, laughing, shaking the water from his eyes.

Julia watched his gleeful expression fade. His eyes widened, his mouth formed a round *o*.

"Matty—"

The current caught him, pulling him downstream. "Julie, I can't—" Water washed over his face, filling his mouth.

She stumbled along the bank's edge, calling his name. The rain began to fall in earnest, big drops that splashed against her face, blinding her. A protruding stone caught her toe and she fell. She picked herself up and ran on, only vaguely aware of the pain in her shin.

"Matty. Oh, Matty, please." Repeated again and again, the words formed an unconscious incantation. Through the muddy water she could see the blue of his school jacket and the pale spread of his hair.

The ground descended sharply as the stream widened and turned away from her. Julia slid down the incline and stopped. On the opposite bank an old oak teetered precariously, a web of roots exposed where the stream had undercut the bank. Here Matthew's body lodged, pinned under the roots as if held by a giant hand.

"Oh, Matty," she cried, the words louder now, a wail of despair. She started into the water, a warm metallic saltiness filling her mouth as she bit through her lower lip. The cold shocked her, numbing her legs. She forced herself to go on. The water swirled about her knees, tugging at the hem of her skirt. It reached her waist, then her chest. She gasped as the cold bit into her ribs. Her lungs felt paralyzed from the cold, unable to expand.

The current tugged at her, pulling at her skirt, shifting her foothold on the moss-covered rocks. With her arms held out for balance, she inched her right foot forward. Nothing. She moved a few feet to one side, then the other, feeling for the bottom. Still nothing.

Cold and exhaustion were fast sucking away her strength. Her breath came in shuddering gasps and the current's grasp seemed more insistent. She looked upstream and down, saw no easier crossing. Not that access to the other side would help her—it would be impossible to reach him from the steep bank.

A little moan escaped her. She stretched her arms toward Matty, but yards separated them, and she was too frightened to brave the current. Help. She must get help.

She felt the water lift and drag her forward as she turned, but she plunged on, digging her heels and toes in for purchase. The current slacked and she clambered out, standing for a moment on the muddy bank as a wave of weakness swept over her. Once more she looked at Matty, saw the outline of his legs twisting sideways in the current. Then she ran.

The house loomed through the dark arches of the trees, its white limestone walls eerily luminous in the dusk. Julia bypassed the front door without thinking. On around the house her feet took her, toward the kitchen, and warmth, and safety. Gasping from the steep climb up the hillside, she rubbed at her face, slick with rain and tears. She was conscious of her own breathing, of the squelching sound her shoes made with each step, and of the heavy wet wool of her skirt scratching her thighs.

Julia yanked open the kitchen door and stopped just inside, water pooling around her on the flags. Plummy turned from the Aga, spoon in hand, her dark hair disheveled as always when she cooked. "Julia! Where have you been? What will your mother have to say . . . ?" The good-natured scolding faded. "Julie, child, you're bleeding. Are you all right?" She came toward Julia, spoon abandoned, her round face creased with concern.

Julia smelled apples, cinnamon, saw the streak of flour across Plummy's bosom, registered in some compartment of her mind that Plummy was making apple pudding, Matty's favorite, for tea. She felt Plummy's hands grasp her shoulders, saw her kind and familiar face draw close, swimming through a film of tears.

"Julia, what is it? What's happened? Where's Matty?"

Plummy's voice was breathy now with panic, but still Julia stood, her throat frozen, the words dammed behind her lips.

A gentle finger stroked her face. "Julia. You've cut your lip. What's happened?"

The sobs began, racking her slight body. She squeezed her arms tight to her chest to ease the pain. A stray thought flickered disjointedly through her mind—she couldn't remember dropping her books. *Matty. Where had Matty left his books?*

"Darling, you must tell me. What's happened?"

She was in Plummy's arms now, her face buried against the soft chest. The words came, choked out between sobs like a tide released. "It's Matty. Oh, Plummy, it's Matty. He's drowned."

CHAPTER

1

From the train window Duncan Kincaid could see the piles of debris in the back gardens and on the occasional common. Lumber, dead branches and twigs, crushed cardboard boxes and the odd bit of broken furniture—anything portable served as fair game for Guy Fawkes bonfires. He rubbed ineffectually at the grimy window-pane with his jacket cuff, hoping for a better view of one particularly splendid monument to British abandon, then sat back in his seat with a sigh. The fine drizzle in the air, combined with British Rail's standard of cleanliness, reduced visibility to a few hundred yards.

The train slowed as it approached High Wycombe. Kincaid stood and stretched, then collected his overcoat and bag from the rack. He'd gone straight to St. Marleybone from the Yard, grabbing the emergency kit he kept in his office—clean shirt, toiletries, razor, only the necessities needed for an unexpected summons. And most were more welcome than this, a political request from the AC to aid an old school chum in a delicate situation. Kincaid grimaced. Give him an unidentified body in a field any day.

He swayed as the train lurched to a halt. Bending down to peer through the window, he scanned the station carpark for a glimpse of his escort. The unmarked panda car, its shape unmistakable even in the increasing rain, was pulled up next to the platform, its parking lights on, a gray plume of exhaust escaping from its tailpipe.

It looked like the cavalry had been called out to welcome Scotland Yard's fair-haired boy.

★   ★   ★

"Jack Makepeace. Sergeant, I should say. Thames Valley CID."
Makepeace smiled, yellowed teeth showing under the sandy bristle
of mustache. "Nice to meet you, sir." He engulfed Kincaid's hand
for an instant in a beefy paw, then took Kincaid's case and swung it
into the panda's boot. "Climb in, and we can talk as we go."

The car's interior smelled of stale cigarettes and wet wool.
Kincaid cracked his window, then shifted a bit in his seat so that
he could see his companion. A fringe of hair the same color as the
mustache, freckles extending from face into shiny scalp, a heavy
nose with the disproportionate look that comes of having been
smashed—all in all not a prepossessing face, but the pale blue eyes
were shrewd, and the voice unexpectedly soft for a man of his
bulk.

Makepeace drove competently on the rain-slick streets, snaking
his way south and west until they crossed the M40 and left the last
terraced houses behind. He glanced at Kincaid, ready to divert
some of his attention from the road.

"Tell me about it, then," Kincaid said.

"What do you know?"

"Not much, and I'd just as soon you start from scratch, if you
don't mind."

Makepeace looked at him, opened his mouth as if to ask a question, then closed it again. After a moment he said, "Okay. Daybreak
this morning the Hambleden lockkeeper, one Perry Smith, opens
the sluicegate to fill the lock for an early traveler, and a body rushes
through it into the lock. Gave him a terrible shock, as you can
imagine. He called Marlow—they sent a panda car and the
medics." He paused as he downshifted into an intersection, then
concentrated on overtaking an ancient Morris Minor that was
creeping its way up the gradient. "They fished him out, then when
it became obvious that the poor chappie was not going to spew up
the canal and open his eyes, they called us."

The windscreen wiper squeaked against dry glass and Kincaid
realized that the rain had stopped. Freshly plowed fields rose on
either side of the narrow road. The bare, chalky soil was a pale
brown, and against it the black dots of foraging rooks looked like

pepper on toast. Away to the west a cap of beech trees crowned a hill. "How'd you identify him?"

"Wallet in the poor sod's back pocket. Connor Swann, aged thirty-five, brown hair, blue eyes, height about six feet, weight around twelve stone. Lived in Henley, just a few miles upstream."

"Sounds like your lads could have handled it easily enough," said Kincaid, not bothering to conceal his annoyance. He considered the prospect of spending his Friday evening tramping around the Chiltern Hundreds, damp as a Guy Fawkes bonfire, instead of meeting Gemma for an after-work pint at the pub down Wilfred Street. "Bloke has a few drinks, goes for a stroll on the sluicegate, falls in. Bingo."

Makepeace was already shaking his head. "Ah, but that's not the whole story, Mr. Kincaid. Someone left a very nice set of prints on either side of his throat." He lifted both hands from the wheel for an instant in an eloquently graphic gesture. "It looks like he was strangled, Mr. Kincaid."

Kincaid shrugged. "A reasonable assumption, I would think. But I don't quite see why that merits Scotland Yard's intervention."

"It's not the *how*, Mr. Kincaid, but the *who*. It seems that the late Mr. Swann was the son-in-law of Sir Gerald Asherton, the conductor, and Dame Caroline Stowe, who I believe is a singer of some repute." Seeing Kincaid's blank expression, he continued, "Are you not an opera buff, Mr. Kincaid?"

"Are you?" Kincaid asked before he could clamp down his involuntary surprise, knowing he shouldn't have judged the man's cultural taste by his physical characteristics.

"I have some recordings, and I watch it on the telly, but I've never been to a performance."

The wide sloping fields had given way to heavily wooded hills, and now, as the road climbed, the trees encroached upon it.

"We're coming into the Chiltern Hills," said Makepeace. "Sir Gerald and Dame Caroline live just a bit farther on, near Fingest. The house is called 'Badger's End,' though you wouldn't think it to look at it." He negotiated a hairpin bend, and then they were running downhill again, beside a rocky stream. "We've put you up at the pub in Fingest, by the way, the Chequers. Lovely garden in the back, on a fine day. Not that you're likely to get much use of it," he added, squinting up at the darkening sky.

The trees enclosed them now. Gold and copper leaves arched tunnel-like overhead, and golden leaves padded the surface of the road. The late afternoon sky was still heavily overcast, yet by some odd trick of light the leaves seemed to take on an eerie, almost phosphorescent glow. Kincaid wondered if just such an enchanting effect had produced the ancient idea of "roads paved with gold."

"Will you be needing me?" Makepeace asked, breaking the spell. "I'd expected you to have backup."

"Gemma will be here this evening, and I'm sure I can manage until then." Seeing Makepeace's look of incomprehension, he added, "Gemma James, my sergeant."

"Rather your lot than Thames Valley." Makepeace gave something halfway between a laugh and a snort. "One of my green constables made the mistake this morning of calling Dame Caroline 'Lady Asherton.' The housekeeper took him aside and gave him a tongue- lashing he'll not soon forget. Informed him that Dame Caroline's title is hers by right and takes precedence over her title as Sir Gerald's wife."

Kincaid smiled. "I'll try to not put my foot in it. So there's a housekeeper, too?"

"A Mrs. Plumley. And the widow, Mrs. Julia Swann." After an amused sideways glance at Kincaid, he continued, "Make what you will of that one. Seems Mrs. Swann lives at Badger's End with her parents, not with her husband."

Before Kincaid could form a question, Makepeace held up his hand and said, "Watch now."

They turned left into a steep, high-banked lane, so narrow that brambles and exposed roots brushed the sides of the car. The sky had darkened perceptibly toward evening and it was dim and shadowed under the trees. "That's the Wormsley valley off to your right, though you'd hardly know it." Makepeace pointed, and through a gap in the trees Kincaid caught a glimpse of twilit fields rolling away down the valley. "It's hard to believe you're only forty miles or so west of London, isn't it, Mr. Kincaid?" he added with an air of proprietary pride.

As they reached the lane's high point, Makepeace turned left into the darkness of the beech woods. The track ran gently downhill, its thick padding of leaves silencing the car wheels. A few hundred yards on they rounded a curve and Kincaid saw the house. Its white stone shone beneath the darkness of the trees, and lamplight beamed welcomingly from its uncurtained windows. He knew immediately what Makepeace had meant about the name— Badger's End implied a certain rustic, earthy simplicity, and this house, with its smooth white walls and arched windows and doors, had an elegant, almost ecclesiastic presence.

Makepeace pulled the car up on the soft carpet of leaves, but left the engine running as he fished in his pocket. He handed Kincaid a card. "I'll be off, then. Here's the number at the local nick. I've some business to attend to, but if you'll ring up when you've finished, someone will come and collect you."

Kincaid waved as Makepeace pulled away, then stood staring at the house as the still silence of the woods settled over him. Grieving widow, distraught in-laws, an imperative for social discretion . . . not a recipe for an easy evening, or an easy case. He squared his shoulders and stepped forward.

The front door swung open and light poured out to meet him.

"I'm Caroline Stowe. It's so good of you to come."

This time the hand that took his was small and soft, and he found himself looking down into the woman's upturned face. "Duncan Kincaid. Scotland Yard." With his free hand he pulled his warrant card from his inside jacket pocket, but she ignored it, still grasping his other hand between her own.

His mind having summed up the words *Dame* and *opera* as *large*, he was momentarily taken aback. Caroline Stowe stood a fraction over five feet tall, and while her small body was softly rounded, she could by no stretch of the imagination be described as heavy.

His surprise must have been apparent, because she laughed and said, "I don't sing Wagner, Mr. Kincaid. My specialty is bel canto.

And besides, size is not relevant to strength of voice. It has to do with breath control, among other things." She released his hand. "Do come in. How rude of me to keep you standing on the threshold like some plumber's apprentice."

As she closed the front door, he looked around with interest. A lamp on a side table illuminated the hall, casting shadows on the smooth gray flagstone floor. The walls were a pale gray-green, bare except for a few large gilt-framed watercolors depicting voluptuous, bare-breasted women lounging about Romanesque ruins.

Caroline opened a door on the right and stood aside, gesturing him in with an open palm.

Directly opposite the door a coal fire burned in a grate, and above the mantel he saw himself, framed in an ornate mirror—chestnut hair unruly from the damp, eyes shadowed, their color indistinguishable from across the room. Only the top of Caroline's dark head showed beneath the level of his shoulder.

He had only an instant to gather an impression of the room. The same gray slate floor, here softened by scattered rugs; comfortable, slightly worn chintz furniture; a jumble of used tea things on a tray—all dwarfed by the baby grand piano. Its dark surface reflected the light from a small lamp, and sheet music stood open behind the keyboard. The bench was pushed back at an angle, as though someone had just stopped playing.

"Gerald, this is Superintendent Kincaid, from Scotland Yard." Caroline moved to stand beside the large rumpled-looking man rising from the sofa. "Mr. Kincaid, my husband, Sir Gerald Asherton."

"It's a pleasure to meet you," Kincaid said, feeling the response inappropriate even as he made it. But if Caroline insisted on treating his visit as a social occasion, he would play along for a bit.

"Sit down." Sir Gerald gathered a copy of the day's *Times* from the seat of an armchair and moved it to a nearby end table.

"Would you like some tea?" asked Caroline. "We've just finished, and it's no trouble to heat up the kettle again."

Kincaid sniffed the lingering odor of toast in the air and his stomach growled. From where he sat he could see the paintings he'd missed when entering the room—watercolors again, by the same artist's hand, but this time the women reclined in elegant rooms and their dresses had the sheen of watered silk. A house to tempt the appetites, he thought, and said, "No, thank you."

"Have a drink, then," Sir Gerald said. "The sun's certainly over the yardarm."

"No, I'm fine. Really." What an incongruous couple they made, still standing side by side, hovering over him as if he were a royal guest. Caroline, dressed in a peacock-blue silk blouse and dark tailored trousers, looked neat and almost childlike beside her husband's bulk.

Sir Gerald smiled at Kincaid, a great, infectious grin that showed pink gums. "Geoffrey recommended you very highly, Mr. Kincaid."

By Geoffrey he must mean Geoffrey Menzies-St. John, Kincaid's assistant commissioner, and Asherton's old schoolmate. Though the two men must be of an age, there any outward resemblance ended. But the AC, while dapper and precise enough to appear priggish, possessed a keen intelligence, and Kincaid thought that unless Sir Gerald shared that quality, the two men would not have kept up with one another over the years.

Kincaid leaned forward and took a breath. "Won't you sit down, please, both of you, and tell me what's happened."

They sat obediently, but Caroline perched straight-backed on the sofa's edge, away from the protective curve of her husband's arm. "It's Connor. Our son-in-law. They'll have told you." She looked at him, her brown eyes made darker by dilating pupils. "We can't believe it's true. Why would someone kill Connor? It doesn't make sense, Mr. Kincaid."

"We'll certainly need more evidence before we can treat this as an official murder inquiry, Dame Caroline."

"But I thought . . ." she began, then looked rather helplessly at Kincaid.

"Let's start at the beginning, shall we? Was your son-in-law well liked?" Kincaid looked at them both, including Sir Gerald in the question, but it was Caroline who answered.

23

"Of course. Everyone liked Con. You couldn't *not*."

"Had he been behaving any differently lately? Upset or unhappy for any reason?"

Shaking her head, she said, "Con was always . . . just Con. You would have to have known . . ." Her eyes filled. She balled one hand into a fist and held it to her mouth. "I feel such a bloody fool. I'm not usually given to hysterics, Mr. Kincaid. Or incoherence. It's the shock, I suppose."

Kincaid thought her definition of hysteria rather exaggerated, but said soothingly, "It's perfectly all right, Dame Caroline. When did you see Connor last?"

She sniffed and ran a knuckle under one eye. It came away smudged with black. "Lunch. He came for lunch yesterday. He often did."

"Were you here as well, Sir Gerald?" Kincaid asked, deciding that only a direct question was likely to elicit a response.

Sir Gerald sat with his head back, eyes half closed, his untidy tuft of gray beard thrusting forward. Without moving, he said, "Yes, I was here as well."

"And your daughter?"

Sir Gerald's head came up at that, but it was his wife who answered. "Julia was here, but didn't join us. She usually prefers to lunch in her studio."

Curiouser and curiouser, thought Kincaid. *The son-in-law comes to lunch but his wife refuses to eat with him.* "So you don't know when your daughter saw him last?"

Again the quick, almost conspiratorial glance between husband and wife, then Sir Gerald said, "This has all been very difficult for Julia." He smiled at Kincaid, but the fingers of his free hand picked at what looked suspiciously like moth holes in his brown woolen sweater. "I'm sure you'll understand if she's a bit . . . prickly."

"Is your daughter here? I'd like to see her, if I may. And I will want to talk to you both at more length, when I've had a chance to review the statements you've given Thames Valley."

"Of course. I'll take you." Caroline stood, and Sir Gerald followed suit. Their hesitant expressions amused Kincaid. They'd been expecting a battering, and now didn't know whether to feel relieved or disappointed. They needn't worry—they'd be glad to see the back of him soon enough.

"Sir Gerald." Kincaid stood and shook hands.

The watercolors caught his eye again as he turned toward the door. Although most of the women were fair, with delicate rose-flushed skin and lips parted to show small glistening white teeth, he realized that something about them reminded him of the woman he followed.

"This was the children's nursery," Caroline said, her breathing steady and even after the three-flight climb. "We made it into a studio for her before she left home. I suppose you might say it's been useful," she added, giving him a sideways look he couldn't interpret.

They'd reached the top of the house and the hall was unornamented, the carpeting threadbare in spots. Caroline turned to the left and stopped before a closed door. "She'll be expecting you." She smiled at Kincaid and left him.

He tapped on the door, waited, tapped again and listened, holding his breath to catch any faint sound. The echo of Caroline's footsteps had died away. From somewhere below he heard a faint cough. Hesitating, he brushed his knuckles against the door once more, then turned the knob and went in.

The woman sat on a high stool with her back to him, her head bent over something he couldn't see. When Kincaid said, "Uh, hello," she whipped around toward him and he saw that she held a paintbrush in her hand.

Julia Swann was not beautiful. Even as he formed the thought, quite deliberately and matter-of-factly, he found he couldn't stop looking at her. Taller, thinner, sharper than her mother, dressed in a white shirt with the tail out and narrow black jeans, she displayed no softly rounded curves in figure or manner. Her chin-length dark hair swung abruptly when she moved her head, punctuating her gestures.

He read his intrusion in her startled posture, felt it in the room's instantly recognizable air of privacy. "I'm sorry to bother you. I'm Duncan Kincaid, from Scotland Yard. I did knock."

"I didn't hear you. I mean, I suppose I did, but I wasn't paying attention. I often don't when I'm working." Even her voice lacked the velvety resonance of Caroline's. She slid off the stool, wiping her hands on a bit of rag. "I'm Julia Swann. But then you know all that, don't you?"

The hand she held out to him was slightly damp from contact with the cloth, but her grasp was quick and hard. He looked around for someplace to sit, saw nothing but a rather tatty and overstuffed armchair which would place him a couple of feet below the level of her stool. Instead he chose to lean against a cluttered workbench.

Although the room was fairly large—probably, he thought, the result of knocking two of the house's original bedrooms into one—the disorder extended everywhere he looked. The windows, covered with simple white rice-paper shades, provided islands of calm in the jumble, as did the high table Julia Swann had been facing when he entered the room. Its surface was bare except for a piece of white plastic splashed with bright daubs of paint, and a Masonite board propped up at a slight angle. Before she slid onto the stool again and blocked his view, he glimpsed a small sheet of white paper masking-taped to the board.

Glancing at the paintbrush still in her hand, she set it on the table behind her and pulled a packet of cigarettes from her shirt pocket. She held it toward him, and when he shook his head and said, "No, thanks," she lit one and studied him as she exhaled.

"So, Superintendent Kincaid—it is Superintendent, isn't it? Mummy seemed to be quite impressed by the title, but then that's not unusual. What can I do for you?"

"I'm sorry about your husband, Mrs. Swann." He tossed out an expected opening gambit, even though he suspected already that her response would not be conventional.

She shrugged, and he could see the movement of her shoulders under the loose fabric of her shirt. Crisply starched, buttons on the left—Kincaid wondered if it might have been her husband's.

"Call me Julia. I never got used to 'Mrs. Swann.' Always sounded to me like Con's mum." She leaned toward him and picked up a cheap porcelain ashtray bearing the words *Visit the Cheddar Gorge.* "She died last year, so that's one bit of drama we don't have to deal with."

"Did you not like your husband's mother?" Kincaid asked.

"Amateur Irish. All B'gosh and B'gorra." Then she added more affectionately, "I used to say that her accent increased proportionately to her distance from County Cork." Julia smiled for the first time. It was her father's smile, as unmistakable as a brand, and it transformed her face. "Maggie adored Con. She would have been devastated. Con's dad did a bunk when Con was a baby . . . if he ever had a dad, that is," she added, only the corners of her lips quirking up this time at some private humor.

"I had the impression from your parents that you and your husband no longer lived together."

"Not for . . ." She spread the fingers of her right hand and touched the tips with her left forefinger as her lips moved. Her fingers were long and slender, and she wore no rings. "Well, more than a year now."

Kincaid watched as she ground out her cigarette in the ashtray. "It's a rather odd arrangement, if you don't mind my saying so."

"Do you think so, Mr. Kincaid? It suited us."

"No plans to divorce?"

Julia shrugged again and crossed her knees, one slender leg swinging jerkily. "No."

He studied her, wondering just how hard he might push her. If she were grieving for her husband, she was certainly adept at hiding it. She shifted under his scrutiny and patted her shirt pocket, as if reassuring herself that her cigarettes hadn't vanished, and he thought that perhaps her armor wasn't quite impenetrable. "Do you always smoke so much?" he said, as if he had every right to ask.

She smiled and pulled the packet out, shaking loose another cigarette.

He noticed that her white shirt wasn't as immaculate as he'd thought—it had a smudge of violet paint across the breast. "Were you on friendly terms with Connor? See him often?"

"We spoke, yes, if that's what you mean, but we weren't exactly what you'd call best mates."

"Did you see him yesterday, when he came here for lunch?"

"No. I don't usually break for lunch when I'm working. Ruins my concentration." Julia stubbed out her newly lit cigarette and slid off the stool. "As you've done now. I might as well quit for the day." She gathered a handful of paintbrushes and crossed the room to an old-fashioned washstand with basin and ewer. "That's the one drawback up here," she said, over her shoulder, "no running water."

His view no longer blocked by her body, Kincaid straightened up and examined the paper taped to the drawing board. It was about the size of a page in a book, smooth-textured, and bore a faint pencil sketch of a spiky flower he didn't recognize. She had begun to lay in spots of clear, vivid color, lavender and green.

"Tufted vetch," she said, when she turned and saw him looking. "A climbing plant. Grows in hedgerows. Flowers in—"

"Julia." He interrupted the rush of words and she stopped, startled by the imperative in his voice. "Your husband died last night. His body was discovered this morning. Wasn't that enough to interrupt your concentration? Or your work schedule?"

She turned her head away, her dark hair swinging to hide her face, but when she turned back to him her eyes were dry. "You'd better understand, Mr. Kincaid. You'll hear it from others soon enough. The term 'bastard' might have been invented to describe Connor Swann.

"And I despised him."

CHAPTER

2

"A lager and lime, please." Gemma James smiled at the bartender. If Kincaid were there he would raise an eyebrow at the very least, mocking her preference. So accustomed to his teasing had she become that she actually missed it.

"A raw evening, miss." The barman set the cool glass before her, aligning it neatly in the center of a beer mat. "Have you come far?"

"Just from London. Beastly traffic getting out, though." But the sprawl of western London had finally faded behind her, and she left the M40 at Beaconsfield and followed the Thames Valley. Even in the mist she had seen some of the fine Victorian houses fronting the river, relics of the days when Londoners used the upper Thames as a playground.

At Marlow she turned north and wound up into the beech-covered hills, marveling that in a few miles she seemed to have entered a hidden world, dark and leafy and far removed from the broad, peaceful expanse of the river below.

"What are the Chiltern Hundreds?" she asked the barman. "I've heard that phrase all my life and never knew what it meant."

He set down a bottle he'd been wiping with a cloth and considered his answer. Approaching middle age, with dark, wavy, carefully groomed hair and the beginning of a belly, he seemed happy enough to pass the time chatting. The lounge was almost empty—a bit early for the regular Friday night customers, Gemma supposed—but cozy with a wood fire burning and comfortable tapestry-covered furniture. A buffet of cold pies, salads and cheeses stood at the bar's end, and she eyed it with anticipation.

Thames Valley CID had certainly been up to the mark, booking her into the pub in Fingest and giving her precise directions. When she arrived she'd found a stack of reports waiting for her in her room, and having attended to them,.she had only to enjoy her drink and wait for Kincaid.

"The Chiltern Hundreds, now," said the barman, bringing Gemma sharply back to the present, "they used to divide counties up into Hundreds, each with its own court, and three of these in Buckinghamshire came to be known as the Chiltern Hundreds because they were in the Chiltern Hills. Stoke, Burnham and Desborough, to be exact."

"Seems logical," said Gemma, impressed. "And you're very knowledgeable."

"Bit of a local history buff in my spare time. I'm Tony, by the way." He thrust a hand over the bar and Gemma shook it.

"Gemma."

"All the Hundreds are obsolete now, but the Stewardship of the Chiltern Hundreds is still a nominal office under the Chancellor of the Exchequer, the holding of which is the only reason one is allowed to resign from the House of Commons. A bit of jiggery-pokery, really, and probably the only reason the office still exists." He smiled at her, showing strong, even, white teeth. "There, I've probably told you more than you ever wanted to know. Get you a refill?"

Gemma glanced at her almost-empty glass, deciding she'd drunk as much as she ought if she wanted to keep a clear head. "Better not, thanks."

"You here on business? We don't let the rooms much this time of year. November in these hills is not exactly a drawing point for holiday-makers."

"Quite," said Gemma, remembering the fine drizzle under the darkness of the trees. Tony straightened glassware and kept an attentive eye on her at the same time, willing to talk if she wanted, but not pushing her. His self-assured friendliness made her wonder if he might be the pub's owner or manager, but in any case he was certainly a likely repository for local gossip.

"I'm here about that drowning this morning, actually. Police business."

Tony stared at her, taking in, she felt sure, the curling ginger hair drawn back with a clip, the casual barley-colored pullover and navy slacks. "You're a copper? Well, I'll be." He shook his head, his wavy hair not disturbed a whit by his incredulity. "Best-looking one I've seen, if you don't mind my saying so."

Gemma smiled, accepting the compliment in the same good humor as it was given. "Did you know him, the man that drowned?"

This time Tony tut-tutted as he shook his head. "What a shame. Oh, everyone around here knew Connor. Doubt there's a pub between here and London where he hadn't put his head in once or twice. Or a racetrack. A real Jack the Lad, that one."

"Well liked, was he?" asked Gemma, fighting her prejudice toward a man on such good terms with pints and horses. Only after she'd married Rob had she discovered that he considered flirting and gambling as inalienable rights.

"Connor was a friendly sort of bloke, always had a word and a pat on the back for you. Good for business, too. After he'd had a couple of pints he'd buy rounds for everybody in the place." Tony leaned forward against the bar, his face animated. "And what a tragedy for the family, after the other."

"What other? Whose family?" Gemma asked, wondering if she'd missed a reference to another drowning in the reports she'd read.

"Sorry." Tony smiled. "It is a bit confusing, I'm sure. Connor's wife Julia's family, the Ashertons. Been here for donkey's years. Connor was upstart Irish, second generation, I think, but all the same . . ."

"What happened to the Ashertons?" Gemma encouraged him, interested.

"I was just a couple of years out of school, back from trying it out in London." His white teeth flashed as he smiled. "Decided the big city wasn't nearly as glamorous as I'd thought. It was just about this time of year, as a matter of fact, and wet. Seemed like it had rained for months on end." Tony paused and pulled a half-pint mug from the rack, lifting it toward Gemma. "Mind if I join you?"

She shook her head, smiling. "Of course not." He was enjoying himself thoroughly now, and the longer she let him string out the story, the more detail she'd get.

He pulled a half-pint of Guinness from the tap and sipped it, then wiped the creamy foam from his upper lip before continuing. "What was his name, now? Julia's little brother. It's been twenty years, or close to it." He ran his fingers lightly over his hair, as if the admission of time passing made him conscious of his age. "Matthew, that was it. Matthew Asherton. All of twelve years old and some sort of musical prodigy, walking home from school one day with his sister, and drowned. Just like that."

The image of her own son clutched unbidden at Gemma's heart—Toby half-grown, his blond hair darkened, his face and body maturing from little-boy chubbiness, snatched away. She swallowed and said, "How terrible. For all of them, but especially Julia. First her brother and now her husband. How did the little boy drown?"

"I'm not sure anyone ever really knew. One of those freak things that happen sometimes." He shrugged and drank down half his Guinness. "Quite a hush-hush at the time. Nobody talked about it except in whispers, and it's still not mentioned to the family, I suppose."

A draft of cold air stirred Gemma's hair and swirled around her ankles as the outer door opened. She turned and watched a foursome come in and settle at a corner table, waving a familiar greeting to Tony. "Reservations in half an hour, Tony," one of the men called. "Same as usual, okay?"

"It'll be picking up a bit now," Tony remarked to Gemma as he began mixing their drinks. "Restaurant usually fills up on a Friday night—all the locals out for their weekly bit of fun, minus the kiddies." Gemma laughed, and when the air blew cool again against her back she didn't turn in anticipation.

Light fingers brushed her shoulder as Kincaid slid onto the barstool beside her. "Gemma. Propping up the bar without me, I see."

"Oh, hullo, guv." She felt the pulse jump in her throat, even though she'd been expecting him.

"And chatting up the locals, I see. Lucky bloke." He grinned at Tony. "I'll have a pint of . . . Brakspear, isn't it, that's brewed at Henley?"

"My boss," Gemma said in explanation to Tony. "Tony, this is Superintendent Duncan Kincaid."

"Nice to meet you, I'm sure." Tony gave Gemma a surprised glance as he put a hand out to Kincaid.

Gemma studied Kincaid critically. Tall and slender, brown hair slightly untidy, tie askew and tweed jacket beaded with rain—she supposed he didn't look like most people's idea of a proper Scotland Yard superintendent. And he was too young, of course. Superintendents should definitely be older and weightier.

"Tell all," Kincaid said, when he'd got his pint and Tony had busied himself serving drinks to the customers in the corner.

Gemma knew that he relied on her to digest information and spit the pertinent bits back out to him, and she rarely had to use her notes. "I've been over Thames Valley's reports." She nodded toward the rooms above their heads. "Had them waiting for me when I got in, very efficient." Closing her eyes for a moment, she marshaled her thoughts. "They had a call at seven-oh-five this morning from a Perry Smith, lockkeeper at Hambleden Lock. He'd found a body caught in his sluicegate. Thames Valley called in a rescue squad to fish the body out, and they identified him from his wallet as Connor Swann, resident of Henley-on-Thames. The lockkeeper, however, once he'd recovered from the shock a bit, recognized Connor Swann as the son-in-law of the Ashertons, who live a couple of miles up the road from Hambleden. He said the family often walked there."

"On the lock?" Kincaid asked, surprised.

"Apparently it's part of a scenic walk." Gemma frowned and picked up the thread of her story where she'd left off. "The local police surgeon was called in to examine the body. He found considerable bruising around the throat. Also, the body was very cold, but rigor had only just begun—"

"But you'd expect the cold water to retard rigor," Kincaid interrupted.

Gemma shook her head impatiently. "Usually in drowning cases rigor sets in very quickly. So he thinks it likely that the victim may have been strangled before he went in the water."

"Our police surgeon makes a bloody lot of assumptions, don't you think?" Kincaid snagged a bag of onion-flavored crisps from a display and counted out the proper coins to Tony. "We'll see what the postmortem has to say."

"Nasty things," said Gemma, eyeing the crisps distastefully.

Mouth full, Kincaid answered, "I know, but I'm starved. What about the interviews with the family?"

She finished the last of her drink before answering, taking a moment to shift mental gears. "Let's see . . . they took statements from the in-laws as well as the wife. Yesterday evening, Sir Gerald Asherton conducted an opera at the Coliseum in London. Dame Caroline Stowe was home in bed, reading. And Julia Swann, the wife, was attending a gallery opening in Henley. None of them reported having words with Connor or having any reason to think he might be worried or upset."

"Of course they didn't." Kincaid pulled a face. "And none of this means a thing without some estimate of time of death."

"You met the family, didn't you, this afternoon? What are they like?"

Kincaid made a noise that sounded suspiciously like "hummmph." "Interesting. Might be better if I let you form your own impressions, though. We'll interview them again tomorrow." He sighed and sipped his pint. "Not that I'll hold my breath waiting for a revelation. None of them can imagine why anyone would want to kill Connor Swann. So we have no motive, no suspect, and we're not even sure it's murder." Raising his glass, he made her a mock toast. "I can't wait."

A good night's sleep had imbued Kincaid with a little more enthusiasm for the case. "The lock first," he said to Gemma over breakfast in the Chequer's dining room. "I can't get much further along with this until I see it for myself. Then I want to have a look at Connor Swann's body." He gulped his coffee and squinted at her, adding, "How do you manage to look fresh and cheerful so early in the morning?" She wore a blazer the bright russet color of autumn leaves, her face glowed, and even her hair seemed to crackle with a life of its own.

"Sorry." She smiled at him, but Kincaid thought her sympathy was tinged with pity. "I can't help it. Something to do with genes, I expect. Or being brought up a baker's daughter. We rose early at my house."

"Ugh." He'd slept heavily, aided by one pint too many the night before, and it had taken him a second cup of coffee just to feel marginally alert.

"You'll get over it," Gemma said, laughing, and they finished their breakfast in companionable silence.

They drove through the quiet village of Fingest in the early morning light and took the lane leading south, toward the Thames. Leaving Gemma's Escort in the carpark a half mile from the river, they crossed the road to the pedestrian path. A chill wind blew into their faces as they started downhill, and when Kincaid's shoulder accidentally bumped against Gemma's, he felt her warmth even through his jacket.

Their path crossed the road running parallel to the river, then threaded its way between buildings and overgrown shrubbery. Not until they emerged from a fenced passage did they see the spread of the river. Leaden water reflected leaden sky, and just before them a concrete walkway zigzagged its way across the water. "Sure this is the right place?" Kincaid asked. "I don't see anything that looks like a lock."

"I can see boats on the far side, past that bank. There must be a channel."

"All right. Lead on, then." He gave a mock-gallant little bow and stepped aside.

They ventured out onto the walkway single-file, unable to walk abreast without brushing the tubular metal railing which provided some measure of safety.

Halfway out they reached the weir. Gemma stopped and Kincaid came to a halt behind her. Looking down at the torrent thundering beneath the walkway, she shivered and pulled the lapels of her jacket together. "Sometimes we forget the power of water. And the peaceful old Thames can be quite a monster, can't it?"

"River's high from the rain," Kincaid said, raising his voice over the roar. He could feel the vibration from the force of the water through the soles of his feet. Grasping the railing until the cold of the metal made his hands ache, he leaned over, watching the flood until he began to lose his equilibrium. "Bloody hell. If you intended to push someone in, this would be the place to do it." Glancing at Gemma, he saw that she looked cold and a little pinched, the dusting of freckles standing out against her pale skin. He placed a hand lightly on her shoulder. "Let's get across. It'll be warmer under the trees."

They walked quickly, heads down against the wind, eager for shelter. The walkway ran on another hundred yards or so past the weir, paralleling the bank, then turned abruptly to the left and vanished into the trees.

The respite proved brief, the belt of trees narrow, but it allowed them to catch their breaths before they came out into the open again and saw the lock before them. Yellow scene-of-crime tape had been stretched along the concrete aprons on either side of the lock, but not across the sluicegates themselves. To their right stood a sturdy red-brick house. The French-paned windows were symmetrical, one on either side of the door, but the one nearest them sported such a thatch of untrimmed green creeper that it looked like a shaggy-browed eye.

As Kincaid put a hand on the tape and bent to duck under it, a man came out the door of the house, dodging under stray twigs of creeper, and shouted at them. "Sir, you're not to go past the tape. Police orders."

Kincaid straightened up and waited, studying the man as he came toward them. Short and stocky, with gray hair bristle-cut, he wore a polo shirt bearing the Thames River Authority insignia, and carried a steaming mug in one hand. "What was the lockkeeper's name?" Kincaid said softly in Gemma's ear.

Gemma closed her eyes for a second. "Perry Smith, I think."

"One and the same, if I'm not mistaken." He pulled his warrant card from his pocket and extended it as the man reached them. "Are you Perry Smith, by any chance?"

The lockkeeper took the card with his free hand and studied it suspiciously, then scrutinized Kincaid and Gemma as if hoping they might be impostors. He nodded once, brusquely. "I've already told the police everything I know."

"This is Sergeant James," Kincaid continued in the same conversational tone, "and you're just the fellow we wanted to see."

"All I'm concerned with is keeping this lock operating properly, Superintendent, without police interference. Yesterday they made me keep the sluicegates closed while they picked about with their tweezers and little bags. Backed river traffic up for a mile," he said, and his annoyance seemed to grow. "Bloody twits, I tell you." He included Gemma in his scowl and made no apology for his language. "Didn't it occur to them what would happen, or how long it would take to clear up the mess?"

"Mr. Smith," Kincaid said soothingly, "I have no intention of interfering with your lock. I only want to ask you a few questions"—he held up a hand as Smith opened his mouth—"which I'm aware you've already answered, but I'd prefer to hear your story directly from you, not secondhand. Sometimes things get muddled along the way."

Smith's brow relaxed a fraction and he took a sip from his mug. The heavy muscles in his upper arm stood out as he raised it, straining against the sleeve-band of his knit shirt. "Muddled wouldn't be the half of it, if those jackasses yesterday set any example." Although he seemed unaware of the cold, he looked at Gemma as if seeing her properly for the first time, huddled partly in the shelter of Kincaid's body with her jacket collar held closed around her throat. "I suppose we could go inside, miss, out of the wind," he said, a bit less belligerently.

Gemma smiled gratefully at him. "Thank you. I'm afraid I didn't dress for the river."

Smith turned back to Kincaid as they moved toward the house.

"When are they going to take this bloody tape down, that's what I'd like to know."

"You'll have to ask Thames Valley. Though if the forensics team has finished, I shouldn't think it would be long." Kincaid paused as they reached the door, looking at the concrete aprons surrounding the lock and the grassy path leading upriver on the opposite side. "Doubt they will have had much luck."

The floor of the hall was covered in sisal matting and lined with well-used-looking rubber boots, the walls hung with working gear—oilskin jackets and hats, bright yellow slickers, coils of rope. Smith led them through a door on the left into a sitting room as workaday as the hall.

The room was warm, if spartan, and Kincaid saw Gemma let go of her collar and take out her notebook. Smith stood by the window, still sipping from his mug, keeping an eye on the river. "Tell us how you found the body, Mr. Smith."

"I came out just after sunup, same as always, have my first cuppa and make sure everything's shipshape for the day. Traffic starts early, some days, though not so much now as in the summer. Sure enough, upstream there was a boat waiting for me to operate the lock."

"Can't they work it themselves?" asked Gemma.

He was already shaking his head. "Oh, the mechanism's simple enough, but if you're too impatient to let the lock fill and drain properly you can make a balls-up of it."

"Then what happened?" prompted Kincaid.

"I can see you don't know much about locks," he said, looking at them with the sort of pity usually reserved for someone who hasn't learned to tie their shoelaces.

Kincaid refrained from saying that he had grown up in western Cheshire and understood locks perfectly well.

"The lock is kept empty when it's not in operation, so first I open the sluices in the head gate to fill the lock. Then when I open the head gate for the boat to enter, up pops a body." Smith sipped from his cup, then added disgustedly, "Silly woman on the boat started squealing like a pig going to slaughter, you've never heard such a racket. I came in here and dialed nine-nine-nine, just to get some relief from the noise." The corners of Smith's eyes crinkled in what might have been a smile. "Rescue people fished him out and tried to resuscitate the poor blighter, though if you ask me, anybody with a particle of sense could see he'd been dead for hours."

"When did you recognize him?" asked Gemma.

"Didn't. Not his body, anyway. But I looked at his wallet when they took it out of his pocket, and I knew the name seemed familiar. Took me a minute to place it."

Kincaid moved to the window and looked out. "Where had you heard it?"

Smith shrugged. "Pub gossip, most likely. Everyone hereabouts knows the Ashertons and their business."

"Do you think he could have fallen in from the top of the gate?" Kincaid asked.

"Railing's not high enough to keep a tall man from going over if he's drunk. Or stupid. But the concrete apron continues for a bit on the upstream side of the gate before it meets the old towpath, and there's no railing along it at all."

Kincaid remembered the private homes he'd seen upstream on this side of the river. All had immaculate lawns running down to the water, some also had small docks. "What if he went in farther upstream?"

"The current's not all that strong until you get close to the gate, so if he went in along there,"—he nodded upstream—"I'd say he'd have to have been unconscious not to have pulled himself out. Or already dead."

"What if he went in here, by the gate? Would the current have been strong enough to hold him down?"

Smith gazed out at the lock a moment before answering. "Hard to say. The current is what holds the gate closed—it's pretty fierce. But whether it could hold a struggling man down . . . unlikely, I'd say, but you can't be sure."

"One more thing, Mr. Smith," Kincaid said. "Did you see or hear anything unusual during the night?"

"I go to bed early, as I'm always up by daybreak. Nothing disturbed me."

"Would a scuffle have awakened you?"

"I've always been a sound sleeper, Superintendent. I can't very well say, now can I?"

"Sleep of the innocent?" whispered Gemma as they took their leave and Smith firmly shut his door.

Kincaid stopped and stared at the lock. "If Connor Swann were unconscious or already dead when he went in the water, how in hell did someone get him here? It would be an almost impossible carry even for a strong man."

"Boat?" ventured Gemma. "From either upstream or down. Although why someone would lift him from a boat downstream of the lock, carry him around and dump him on the upstream side, I can't imagine."

They walked slowly toward the path that would take them back across the weir, the wind at their backs. Moored boats rocked peacefully in the quiet water downstream. Ducks dived and bobbed, showing no concern with human activity that didn't involve crusts of bread. "Was he already dead? That's the question, Gemma." He looked at her, raising an eyebrow. "Fancy a visit to the morgue?"

CHAPTER

3

The smell of disinfectant always reminded Kincaid of his school infirmary, where Matron presided over the bandaging of scraped knees and wielded the power to send one home if the illness or injury proved severe enough. The inhabitants of this room, however, were beyond help from Matron's ministrations, and the disinfectant didn't quite mask the elusive tang of decay. He felt gooseflesh rise on his arms from the cold.

A quick call to Thames Valley CID had directed them to High Wycombe's General Hospital, where Connor Swann's body awaited autopsy. The hospital was old, the morgue still a place of ceramic tiles and porcelain sinks, lacking the rows of stainless-steel drawers which tucked bodies neatly away out of sight. Instead, the steel gurneys that lined the walls held humped, white-sheeted forms with toe tags peeking out.

"Who was it you wanted, now?" asked the morgue attendant, a bouncy young woman whose name tag read "Sherry" and whose demeanor seemed more suited to a nursery school.

"Connor Swann," said Kincaid, with an amused glance at Gemma.

The girl walked along the row of gurneys, flicking toe tags with her fingers as she passed. "Here he is. Number four." She tucked the sheet down to his waist with practiced precision. "And a nice clean one he is, too. Always makes it a bit easier, don't you think?" She smiled brightly at them, as if they were mentally impaired, then walked back to the swinging doors and shouted "Mickey" through the gap she made with one hand. "We'll need some help shifting him," she added, turning back to Kincaid and Gemma.

Mickey emerged a moment later, parting the doors like a bull charging from a pen. The muscles in his arms and shoulders strained the thin fabric of his T-shirt, and he wore the short sleeves rolled up, displaying an extra inch or two of bicep.

"Can you give these people a hand with number four, Mickey?" Sherry enunciated carefully, her nursery-teacher manner now mixed with a touch of exasperation. The young man merely nodded, his acne-inflamed face impassive, and pulled a pair of thin latex gloves from his back pocket. "Take all the time you want," she added to Kincaid and Gemma. "Just give me a shout when you've finished, okay? Cheerio." She whisked past them, the tail of her white lab coat flapping, and went out through the swinging doors.

They moved the few steps to the gurney and stood. In the ensuing silence Kincaid heard the soft expulsion of Gemma's breath. Connor Swann's exposed neck and shoulders were lean and well formed, his thick straight hair brown with a hint of auburn. Kincaid thought it likely that in life he had been one of those high-colored men who flushed easily in anger or excitement. His body was indeed remarkably unblemished. Some bruising showed along the left upper arm and shoulder, and when Kincaid looked closely he saw faint, dark marks on either side of the throat.

"Some bruising," Gemma said dubiously, "but not the occlusion of the face and neck you'd expect with a manual strangulation."

Kincaid bent over for a closer look at the throat. "No sign of a ligature. Look, Gemma, across the right cheekbone. Is that a bruise?"

She peered at the smudge of darker color. "Could be. Hard to tell, though. His face could easily have banged against the gate."

Connor Swann had been blessed with good bone structure, thought Kincaid, high, wide cheekbones and a strong nose and chin. Above his full lips lay a thick, neatly trimmed, reddish mustache, looking curiously alive against the gray pallor of his skin.

"A good-looking bloke, would you say, Gemma?"

"Probably attractive, yes . . . unless he was a bit too full of himself. I got the impression he was quite the ladies' man."

Kincaid wondered how Julia Swann felt about that—she hadn't impressed him as a woman willing to sit home meekly while her husband played the lad. It also occurred to him to wonder how much of his desire to see Connor had to do with assessing the physical evidence, and how much to do with his personal curiosity about the man's wife.

He turned to Mickey and raised a questioning eyebrow. "Could we have a look at the rest?"

The young man obliged wordlessly, flipping the sheet off altogether.

"He'd been on holiday, but I'd say not recently," Gemma commented as they saw the faint demarcation of a tan against belly and upper thighs. "Or maybe just summer boating on the Thames."

Deciding he might as well imitate Mickey's nonverbal style of communication, Kincaid nodded and made a rolling motion with his hand. Mickey slid both gloved hands beneath Connor Swann's body, turning him with an apparent ease betrayed only by a barely audible grunt.

Wide shoulders, faintly freckled; a thin pale band on the neck bordering the hairline, evidence of a recent haircut; a mole where the buttock began to swell from the hollow of the back—all trivial things, thought Kincaid, but all proof of Connor Swann's uniqueness. It always came, this moment in an investigation when the body became a person, someone who had perhaps liked pickle-and-cheese sandwiches, or old Benny Hill comedies.

"Had enough, guv?" Gemma said, sounding a bit more subdued than usual. "He's clean as a whistle this side."

Kincaid nodded. "Not much else to see. And nothing does us much good until we've traced his movements and got some estimate of time of death. Okay, Mickey," he added, as the expression on the young man's face indicated they might as well have been speaking in Greek. "I guess that's it. Let's look up Sherry Sunshine." Kincaid looked back as they reached the door. Mickey had already turned Connor's body and tidied the sheet as neatly as before.

They found her in a cubbyhole just to the left of the swinging doors, bent industriously over a computer keyboard, cheerful as ever. "Do you know when they've scheduled the post?" Kincaid asked.

"Um, let's see." She studied a typed schedule stuck to the wall with Sellotape. "Winnie can probably get to him late tomorrow afternoon or early the following morning."

"Winnie?" Kincaid asked, fighting the absurd vision of Pooh Bear performing an autopsy.

"Dr. Winstead." Sherry dimpled prettily. "We all call him that—he's a bit tubby."

Kincaid contemplated attending the postmortem with resignation. He had long ago got over any sort of grisly thrill at the proceedings. Now he found it merely distasteful, and the ultimate violation of human privacy sometimes struck him as unbearably sad. "You'll let me know as soon as you schedule it?"

"Quick as a wink. I'll do it myself." Sherry beamed at him.

Out of the corner of his eye Kincaid saw Gemma's expression and knew she'd rag him about buttering up the hired help. "Thanks, love," he said to Sherry, giving her his full-wattage smile. "You've been a great help." He waggled his fingers at her. "Cheerio, now."

"You're absolutely shameless," said Gemma as soon as they were through the outer doors. "That poor little duck was as susceptible as a baby."

Kincaid grinned at her. "Gets things done, though, doesn't it?"

After a few unplanned detours due to her unfamiliarity with High Wycombe's one-way system, Gemma found her way out of the town. Following Kincaid's directions, she drove southwest, back into the hidden folds of the Chiltern Hills. Her stomach grumbled a bit, but they had decided that they should interview the Ashertons again before lunch.

In her mind she ran through Kincaid's and Tony's comments

about the family, her curiosity piqued. She glanced at Kincaid, a question forming on her lips, but his unfocused gaze told her he was somewhere else entirely. He often got like that before an interview, as if it were necessary for him to turn inward before bringing that intense focus to bear.

She concentrated again on her driving, but she suddenly felt extraordinarily aware of his long legs taking up more than their share of the room in her Escort's passenger compartment, and of his silence.

After a few minutes they reached the point where she had to make an unfamiliar turning. Before she could speak, he said, "Just here. Badger's End lies about halfway along this little road." His fingertip traced a faint line on the map, between the villages of Northend and Turville Heath. "It's unmarked, a shortcut for the locals, I suppose."

Ribbons of water trickled across the pavement where a stream bed ran down through the trees and intersected the narrow road. A triangular yellow road sign warned DANGER: FLOODING, and suddenly the story Gemma had heard of Matthew Asherton's drowning seemed very immediate.

"Hard left," Kincaid said, pointing ahead, and Gemma turned the wheel. The lane they entered was high-banked, just wide enough for the Escort to pass unscathed, and on either side thick trees arched until they met and intertwined overhead. It climbed steadily, and the high banks rose until the tree roots were at eye level. On the right, Gemma caught an occasional flash through the foliage of golden fields dropping down to a valley. On the left the woods crowded, darkly impenetrable, and the light filtering through the leafy canopy over the lane seemed green and liquid.

"Sledging," Gemma said suddenly.

"What?"

"It reminds me of sledging. You know, bobsledding. Or the Olympic luge."

Kincaid laughed. "Don't accuse me of poetic fancy. Careful now, watch for a turning on the left."

They appeared to be nearing the top of the gradient when

Gemma saw a gap in the left-hand bank. She slowed and eased the car onto the leaf-padded track, following it on and slightly down-hill until she rounded a bend and came into a clearing. "Oh," she said softly, surprised. She'd expected a house built with the com-fortable flint and timber construction she'd seen in the nearby vil-lages. The sun, which had chased fitfully in and out of the cloud bank, found a gap, making dappled patterns against the white limestone walls of Badger's End.

"Like it?"

"I'm not sure." Gemma rolled down the window as she turned off the engine, and they sat for a moment, listening. Beneath the silence of the woods they heard a faint, deep hum. "It's a bit eerie. Not at all what I imagined."

"Just wait," said Kincaid as he opened the car door, "until you meet the family."

Gemma assumed that the woman who answered the door must be Dame Caroline Stowe—good quality, tailored wool slacks, blouse and navy cardigan, short, dark, well-cut hair liberally streaked with gray—everything about her spoke of conservative, middle-aged good taste. But when the woman stared at them blankly, coffee mug poised halfway to her mouth, then said, "Can I help you with something?" Gemma's certainty began to waiver.

Kincaid identified himself and Gemma, then asked for Sir Gerald and Dame Caroline.

"Oh, I'm sorry, you've just missed them. They've gone down to the undertakers for a bit. Making arrangements." She transferred the coffee mug to her left hand and held out the right to them. "I'm Vivian Plumley, by the way."

"You're the housekeeper?" Kincaid asked, and Gemma knew from the less-than-tactful query that he'd been caught off guard.

Vivian Plumley smiled. "You might say that. It doesn't offend me, at any rate."

"Good." Kincaid, Gemma saw, had recovered both aplomb and smile. "We'd like a word with you as well, if we may."

"Come back to the kitchen. I'll make some coffee." She turned

and led the way along the slate-flagged passage, then stepped back
and let them precede her through the door at its end.

The kitchen had escaped modernization. While Gemma might
sigh over photographs of gleaming space-age kitchens in maga-
zines, she knew instinctively that they provided no emotional sub-
stitute for a room like this. Nubby braided rugs softened the slate
floor, a scarred oak refectory table and ladder-backed chairs dominated the room's center, and against one wall a red-enameled Aga
radiated warmth and comfort.

"Sit down, why don't you," said Vivian Plumley, and gestured
toward the table. Gemma pulled out a chair and sat, feeling tension
she hadn't been aware of flow out of her muscles. "Elevenses?"
added Vivian, and Gemma shook her head quickly, fearing they'd lose
control of the interview entirely, seduced by the room's comfort.

Kincaid said, "No, thank you," and seated himself, taking the
chair at the table's end. Gemma took her notebook from her bag
and cradled it unobtrusively in her lap.

The drip coffeemaker worked as quickly as its expensive looks
implied. It was only a few moments before the smell of fresh coffee began to fill the room. Vivian put together a tray with mugs,
cream and sugar in silence, a woman enough at ease with herself
not to make small talk. When the coffeemaker had finished its
cycle, she filled the mugs and brought the tray to the table. "Do
help yourself. And that's real cream, I'm afraid, not dairy substi-
tute. We have a neighbor who keeps a few Jerseys."

"A treat not to be missed," said Kincaid, pouring generously
into his cup. Gemma smiled, knowing he usually drank it black.
"Are you not the housekeeper, then?" he continued easily. "Have I
put my foot in it?"

Vivian clinked her spoon around twice in her coffee cup and
sighed. "Oh, I'll tell you about myself, if you like, but it always
sounds so dreadfully Victorian. I'm actually related to Caroline,
second cousins once removed, to be exact. We're as close to the
same age as never-mind, and we were at school together." She
paused and sipped from her cup, then made a slight grimace of
discomfort. "Too hot. We drifted apart, Caro and I, once we'd fin-

ished school. We both married, her career blossomed." Vivian smiled.

"Then my husband died. An aneurysm." The palms of her hands made a slapping sound as she brushed them together. "Just like that, he was gone. I was left childless, with no job skills and not quite enough money to get by. This was thirty years ago, mind you, when not every woman grew up with the expectation of working." She looked directly at Gemma. "Quite different from your upbringing, I'm sure."

Gemma thought of her mother, who had risen in the early hours of the morning to bake every day of her married life, then worked the counter in the shop from opening till closing. The possibility of *not* working never occurred to Gemma or her sister—it had been Gemma's driving ambition for the work to be of her own choosing, not something done purely for the necessity of putting food on the table. "Yes, very different," she said, in answer to Vivian Plumley's statement. "What did you do?"

"Caro had two toddlers and a very demanding career." She shrugged. "It seemed a sensible solution. They had room, I had enough money of my own not to be totally dependent on the family, and I loved the children as if . . ."

They were your own. Gemma finished the sentence for her, and felt a rush of empathy for this woman who seemed to have made the best of what life had dealt her. She ran her fingers along the tabletop, noticing faint streaks of color embedded in the wood's grain.

Watching her, Vivian said fondly, "The children did everything at this table. They had most of their meals in the kitchen, of course. As much as their parents traveled, formal family dinners were a rare treat. School assignments, art projects—Julia did her first paintings here, when she was in grammar school."

The children this . . . the children that . . . It seemed to Gemma as if time had simply stopped with the boy's death. But Julia had been there afterward, alone. "This must all be very difficult for Julia," she said, feeling her way into the subject delicately, "after what happened to her brother."

Vivian looked away, grasping the table's edge with one hand, as if she were physically restraining herself from getting up. After a moment, she said, "We don't talk about that. But yes, I'm sure Con's death has made life more difficult than usual for Julia. It's made life difficult for all of us."

Kincaid, who had been sitting quietly, chair pushed back a bit from the table, mug cradled in his hands, leaned forward and said, "Did you like Connor, Mrs. Plumley?"

"Like him?" she said blankly, then frowned. "It never occurred to me whether or not I should like Connor. He was just . . . Connor. A force of nature." She smiled a little at her own analogy. "A very attractive man in many ways, and yet . . . I always felt a little sorry for him."

Kincaid raised an eyebrow but didn't speak, and Gemma followed his cue.

Shrugging, Vivian said, "I know it sounds a bit silly to say one felt sorry for someone as larger-than-life as Con, but Julia baffled him." The gold buttons on her cardigan caught the light as she shifted in her chair. "He could never make her respond in the way he wanted, and he hadn't any experience with that. So he sometimes behaved . . . inappropriately." A door slammed in the front of the house and she cocked her head, listening. Half-rising from her chair, she said, "They're back. Let me tell—"

"One more thing, please, Mrs. Plumley," Kincaid said. "Did you see Connor on Thursday?"

She sank down again, but perched on the edge of her seat with the tentative posture of one who doesn't intend staying long. "Of course I saw him. I prepared lunch—just cold salads and cheese—and we all ate together in the dining room."

"All except Julia?"

"Yes, but she often works through luncheon. I took a plate up to her myself."

"Did Connor seem his usual self?" Kincaid asked, his tone conversational, but Gemma knew from his still concentration that he was intent on her answer.

Vivian relaxed as she thought, leaning back in her chair again and absently tracing the raised flower pattern on her mug with her fingers. "Con was always teasing and joking, but perhaps it seemed a bit forced. I don't know." She looked up at Kincaid, frowning. "Quite possibly I'm distorting things after the fact. I'm not sure I trust my own judgment."

Kincaid nodded. "I appreciate your candor. Did he mention any plans for later in the day? It's important that we trace his movements."

"I remember him glancing at his watch and saying something about a meeting, but he didn't say where or with whom. That was toward the end of the meal, and as soon as everyone had finished I came in here to do the washing up, then went to my room for a lie-down. You might ask Caro or Gerald if he said something more to them."

"Thank you. I'll do that," Kincaid said with such courtesy that Gemma felt sure it would never occur to Vivian Plumley that she'd just told him how to do his job. "It's strictly a formality, of course, but I must ask you about your movements on Thursday night," he added almost apologetically.

"An alibi? You're asking me for an alibi for Connor's death?" Vivian asked, sounding more surprised than offended.

"We don't yet know exactly when Connor died. And it's more a matter of building known factors—the more we know about the movements of everyone connected with Connor, the easier it becomes to see gaps. Logic holes." He made a circular gesture with his hands.

"All right." She smiled, appeased. "That's easy enough. Caro and I had an early supper in front of the fire in the sitting room. We often do when Gerald's away."

"And after that?"

"We sat before the fire, reading, watching the telly, talking a little. I made some cocoa around ten o'clock, and when we'd finished it I went up to bed." She added with a touch of irony, "I remember thinking it had been a particularly peaceful and pleasant evening."

"Nothing else?" Kincaid asked, straightening up in his chair and pushing away his empty mug.

"No," Vivian said, but then paused and stared into space for a moment. "I do remember something, but it's quite silly." When Kincaid nodded encouragement, she continued. "Just after I'd fallen asleep I thought I heard the doorbell, but when I sat up and listened, the house was perfectly quiet. I must have been dreaming. Gerald and Julia both have their own keys, of course, so there was no need to wait up for them."

"Did you hear either of them come in?"

"I thought I heard Gerald around midnight, but I wasn't properly awake, and the next thing I knew it was daybreak and the rooks were making a god-awful racket in the beeches outside my window."

"Couldn't it have been Julia?" Kincaid asked.

She thought for a moment, her brow furrowed. "I suppose it could, but if it's not terribly late, Julia usually looks in on me before she goes up."

"And she didn't that evening?"

When Vivian shook her head, Kincaid smiled at her and said, "Thank you, Mrs. Plumley. You've been very helpful."

This time, before rising, Vivian Plumley looked at him and said, "Shall I tell them you're here?"

Sir Gerald Asherton stood with his back to the sitting room fire, hands clasped behind him. He made a perfect picture of a nineteenth-century country squire, thought Gemma, with his feet spread apart in a relaxed posture and his bulk encased in rather hairy tweeds. He even sported suede elbow patches on his jacket. The only things needed to complete the tableau were a pipe and a pair of hunting hounds sprawled at his feet.

"So sorry to have kept you waiting." He came toward them, pumped their hands and gestured them toward the sofa.

Gemma found the courtesy rather disarming, and suspected it was meant to be.

"Thank you, Sir Gerald," Kincaid said, returning it in kind. "And Dame Caroline?"

"Gone for a bit of a lie-down. Found the business at the undertakers rather upsetting, I'm afraid." Sir Gerald sat in the armchair opposite them, crossed one foot over his knee and adjusted his trouser leg. An expanse of Argyle sock in autumnal orange and brown appeared between shoe and trouser cuff.

"If you don't mind my saying so, Sir Gerald," Kincaid smiled as he spoke, "it seems a little odd that your daughter didn't take care of the arrangements herself. Connor was, after all, her husband."

"Just so," answered Sir Gerald with a touch of asperity. "Sometimes these things are best left to those not quite so close to the matter. And funeral directors are notorious for preying on the emotions of the newly bereaved." Gemma felt a stab of pity at the reminder that this burly, confident man spoke from the worst possible personal experience.

Kincaid shrugged and let the matter drop. "I need to ask you about your movements on Thursday night, sir." At Sir Gerald's raised eyebrow, he added, "Just a formality, you understand."

"No reason why I shouldn't oblige you, Mr. Kincaid. It's a matter of public record. I was at the Coliseum, conducting a performance of *Pelleas and Melisande*." He favored them with his large smile, showing healthily pink gums. "Extremely visible. No one could have impersonated me, I assure you."

Gemma imagined him facing an orchestra, and felt sure he dominated the hall as easily as he dominated this small room. From where she sat she could see a photograph of him atop the piano, along with several others in similar silver frames. She stood up unobtrusively and went to examine them. The nearest showed Sir Gerald in a tuxedo, baton in hand, looking as comfortable as he did in his country tweeds. In another he had his arm around a small dark-haired woman who laughed up at the camera with a voluptuous prettiness.

The photograph of the children had been pushed to the back, as if no one cared to look at it often. The boy stood slightly in the foreground, solid and fair, with an impish gap-toothed grin. The girl was a few inches taller, dark-haired like her mother, her thin face gravely set. This was Julia, of course. Julia and Matthew.

"And after?" she heard Kincaid say, and she turned back to the conversation, rather embarrassed by her lapse of attention.

52

Sir Gerald shrugged. "It takes a while to wind down after a performance. I stayed in my dressing room for a bit, but I'm afraid I didn't take notice of the time. Then I drove straight home, which must have put me here sometime after midnight."

"Must have?" Kincaid asked, his voice tinged with skepticism.

Sir Gerald held out his right arm, baring a hairy wrist for their inspection. "Don't wear a watch, Mr. Kincaid. Never found it comfortable. And a nuisance taking it off for every rehearsal or performance. Always lost the bloody things. And the car clock never worked properly."

"You didn't stop at all?"

Shaking his head, Sir Gerald answered with the finality of one used to having his word taken as law. "I did not."

"Did you speak to anyone when you came in?" Gemma asked, feeling it was time she put an oar in.

"The house was quiet. Caro was asleep and I didn't wake her. I can only assume the same for Vivian. So you see, young lady, if it's an alibi you're after," he paused and twinkled at Gemma, "I suppose I haven't one."

"What about your daughter, sir? Was she asleep as well?"

"I'm afraid I can't say. I don't remember seeing Julia's car in the drive, but I suppose someone could have given her a lift home."

Kincaid stood. "Thank you, Sir Gerald. We will need to talk to Dame Caroline again, at her convenience, but just now we'd like to see Julia."

"I believe you know your way, Mr. Kincaid."

"Good God, I feel like I've been dropped right in the bloody middle of a drawing room comedy." Gemma turned her head to look at Kincaid as she preceded him up the stairs. "All manners and no substance. What are they playing at in this house?" As they reached the first landing, she stopped and turned to face him. "And you'd think these women were made of glass, the way Sir Gerald and Mrs. Plumley coddle them. 'Mustn't upset Caroline . . . mustn't upset Julia,'" she hissed at him, remembering a bit belatedly to lower her voice.

Kincaid merely raised an eyebrow in that imperturbable manner she found so infuriating. "I'm not sure I'd consider Julia Swann a good candidate for coddling." He started up the next flight, and Gemma followed the rest of the way without comment.

The door swung open as soon as Kincaid's knuckles brushed it. "Bless you, Plummy. I'm star—" Julia Swann's smile vanished abruptly as she took in their identity. "Oh. Superintendent Kincaid. Back so soon?"

"Like a bad penny," Kincaid answered, giving her his best smile.

Julia Swann merely stuck the paintbrush she'd held in her hand over her ear and stepped back enough to allow them to enter. Studying her, Gemma compared the woman to the thin, serious child in the photo downstairs. That Julia was certainly visible in this one, but the gawkiness had been transmuted into sleek style, and the innocence in the child's gaze had been lost long ago.

The shades were drawn up, and a pale, watery light illuminated the room. The center worktable, bare except for palette and white paper neatly masking-taped to a board, relieved the studio's general disorder. "Plummy usually brings me up a sandwich about this time," Julia said, as she shut the door and returned to the table. She leaned against it, gracefully balancing her weight, but Gemma had the distinct impression that the support she drew from it was more than physical.

A finished painting of a flower lay on the table. Gemma moved toward it almost instinctively, hand outstretched. "Oh, it's lovely," she said softly, stopping just short of touching the paper. Spare and sure in design, the painting had an almost oriental flavor, and the intense greens and purples of the plant glowed against the matte-white paper.

"Bread and butter," said Julia, but she smiled, making an obvious effort to be civil. "I've a whole series commissioned for a line of cards. Upscale National Trust, you know the sort of thing. And I'm behind schedule." Julia rubbed at her face, leaving a smudge of paint on her forehead, and Gemma suddenly saw the weariness that her smart haircut and trendy black turtleneck and leggings couldn't quite camouflage.

Gemma traced the rough edge of the watercolor paper with a finger. "I suppose I thought the paintings downstairs must be yours, but these are quite different."

"The Flints? I should hope so." Some of the abruptness returned to Julia's manner. She shook a cigarette from a pack on a side table and lit it with a hard strike of a match.

"I wondered about them as well," Kincaid said. "Something struck me as familiar."

"You probably saw some of his paintings in books you read as a child. William Flint wasn't as well known as Arthur Rackham, but he did some marvelous illustrations." Julia leaned against the worktable and narrowed her eyes against the smoke rising from her cigarette. "Then came the breastscapes."

"Breastscapes?" Kincaid repeated, amused.

"They are technically quite brilliant, if you don't mind the banal, and they certainly kept him comfortably in his old age."

"And you disapprove?" Kincaid's voice held a hint of mockery.

Julia touched the surface of her own painting as if testing its worth, then shrugged. "I suppose it is rather hypocritical of me. These keep me fed, and they supported Connor in the lifestyle to which he'd become accustomed."

To Gemma's surprise, Kincaid didn't nibble at the proffered bait, but instead asked, "If you dislike Flint's watercolors, why do they hang in almost every room in the house?"

"They're not mine, if that's what you're thinking. A few years ago Mummy and Daddy got bitten by the collector's bug. Flints were all the rage and they jumped on the bandwagon. Perhaps they thought I'd be pleased." Julia gave them a brittle little smile. "After all, as far as they're concerned, one watercolor looks pretty much like another."

Kincaid returned her smile, and a look of understanding passed between them, as if they'd shared a joke. Julia laughed, her dark hair swinging with the movement of her head, and Gemma felt suddenly excluded. "Exactly what lifestyle did your husband need to support, Mrs. Swann?" she asked, rather too quickly, and she heard an unintended note of accusation in her voice.

Propping herself up on her work stool, Julia swung one black-booted foot as she ground the stub of her half-smoked cigarette into an ashtray. "You name it. I sometimes thought Con felt honor-bound to live up to an image he created—whiskey, women and an eye for the horses, everything you'd expect from your stereotypical Irish rogue. I wasn't always sure he enjoyed it as much as he liked you to think."

"Were there any women in particular?" Kincaid asked, his tone so lightly conversational he might have been inquiring about the weather.

She regarded him quizzically. "There was always a woman, Mr. Kincaid. The particulars didn't concern me."

Kincaid merely smiled, as if refusing to be shocked by her cynicism. "Connor stayed on in the flat you shared in Henley?"

Julia nodded, sliding off the stool to pull another cigarette from the crumpled packet. She lit it and leaned back against the table, folding her arms against her chest. The paintbrush still positioned over her ear gave her an air of slightly rakish industry, as if she might be a Fleet Street journalist relaxing for a brief moment in the newsroom.

"You were in Henley on Thursday evening, I believe?" Kincaid continued. "A gallery opening?"

"Very clever of you, Mr. Kincaid." Julia flashed him a smile. "Trevor Simons. Thameside."

"But you didn't see your husband?"

"I did not. We move in rather different circles, as you might have guessed," said Julia, the sarcasm less veiled this time.

Gemma glanced at Kincaid's face, anticipating an escalating response, but he only answered lazily, "So I might."

Julia ground out her cigarette, barely smoked this time, and Gemma could see a release of tension in the set of her mouth and shoulders. "Now if you don't mind, I really must get back to work." She included Gemma this time in the smile that was so like her father's, only sharper around the edges. "Perhaps you could—"

"Julia."

It was an old interrogation technique, the sudden and imperative use of the suspect's name, a breaking down of barriers, an invasion of personal space. Still, the familiarity in Kincaid's voice shocked Gemma. It was as if he knew this woman down to her bones and could sweep every shred of her artifice away with a casual flick of a finger.

Julia remained frozen in mid-sentence, her eyes locked on Kincaid's face. They might have been alone in the room.

"You were only a few hundred yards from Connor's flat. You could have stepped out for a smoke by the river, bumped into him, arranged to meet him later."

A second passed, then another, and Gemma heard the rustle as Julia shifted her body against the worktable. Then Julia said slowly, "I could have. But I didn't. It was my show, you see—my fifteen minutes in the limelight—and I never left the gallery at all."

"And afterward?"

"Oh, Trev can vouch for me well enough, I think. I slept with him."

CHAPTER

4

"Division of labor," Kincaid told Gemma as they stopped for a quick lunch at the pub in Fingest. "You see if you can confirm Sir Gerald's alibi—that'll allow you a night or two at home with Toby—and I'll tackle Henley. I want to go over Connor Swann's flat myself, and I want to have a word with—what did Julia say his name was? Simons, that was it—Trevor Simons, at his gallery. I'd like to know a bit more about Julia's movements that night," he added, and Gemma gave him a look he couldn't interpret.

They finished their sandwiches under Tony's watchful eye, then Gemma ran upstairs to pack her bag. Kincaid waited in the graveled carpark, jingling the change in his pockets and drawing furrows in the gravel with his toe. The Ashertons were very plausible, but the more he thought about it, the more difficult it became to make sense of what they had told him. They seemed to have been on close terms with a son-in-law their daughter barely tolerated, and yet they also seemed to go to great lengths to avoid confrontation with Julia. He made a *J* in the gravel with his shoe, then carefully raked it over again. How had Julia Swann really felt about her husband? In his mind he saw her again, her thin face composed and her dark eyes fixed on his, and he found he didn't quite buy the tough persona she wore so successfully.

Gemma came out with her case, turning back for a moment to wave good-bye to Tony. The sun sparked from her hair, and it was only then that Kincaid realized it had ventured out from the clouds that had hidden it through the morning.

"Ready, guv?" asked Gemma as she stowed her things in the boot and slid behind the wheel of her Escort. Kincaid put his speculations aside and got in beside her. She seemed to him refreshingly uncomplicated, and he offered up a silent thanks, as he often did, for her competent cheerfulness.

Leaving the hills behind, they took the wide road to Henley. They had a glimpse of the river beneath the Henley Bridge, then it vanished behind them as the one-way system shunted them into the center of town. "Can you get back to the pub all right, guv?" Gemma asked as she pulled up to let Kincaid out in Henley's marketplace.

"I'll ask the local lads for a lift. I could pull rank and requisition a car, of course," he added, grinning at her, "but just now I think I'd rather not be bothered with parking the bloody thing."

He stepped out of the car and gave the door a parting thump with his hand, as if he were slapping a horse on its way. Gemma let up on the brake, but before nosing back into the traffic she rolled down the Escort's driver's-side window and called to him, "Mind how you go."

Turning back, he waved jauntily to her, then watched the car disappear down Hart Street. The sudden note of concern in her voice struck him as odd. It was she who was driving back to London, while he merely intended an unannounced interview and a recce of Connor Swann's flat. He shrugged and smiled—he'd quite grown to like her occasional solicitousness.

Henley Police Station lay just across the street, but after a moment's hesitation he turned and instead climbed the steps to the Town Hall. A cardboard sign taped to the wall informed him that Tourist Information could be found downstairs, and as he descended, he wrinkled his nose at the standard public building accoutrements—cracked lino and the sour smell of urine.

Fifty pence bought him a street map of the town, and he unfolded it as he walked thankfully back out into the sun. He saw that his way lay down Hart Street and along the river, so tucking the map in his jacket and his hands in his pockets, he strolled down the hill. The square tower of the church seemed to float against the softly colored hills beyond the river, and it drew him on like a lodestone. "St. Mary the Virgin," he said aloud as he reached it, thinking that for an Anglican Church the syllables rolled off the tongue with a very Catholic resonance. He wondered where they meant to bury Connor Swann. Irish Catholic, Irish Protestant? Could it possibly matter? He didn't yet know enough about him to hazard a guess.

Crossing the busy street, he stood for a moment on the Henley Bridge. The Thames spread peacefully before him, so different from the thunder of water through Hambleden Weir. The river course wound north for a bit after Henley, curved to the east before it reached Hambleden, then meandered northeast before turning south toward Windsor. Could Connor have gone in the river here, in Henley, and drifted downstream to Hambleden Lock? He thought it highly unlikely, but made himself a mental note to check with Thames Valley.

He took a last look at the red-and-white Pimm's umbrellas beckoning temptingly from the terrace of the Angel pub, but he had other fish to fry.

A few hundred yards beyond the pub he found the address. Next door to the tearoom a discreet sign announced THE GALLERY, THAMESIDE, and a single painting in an ornate gilded frame adorned the shop window. The door chimed electronically as Kincaid pushed it open, then clicked softly behind him, shutting out the hum of sound from the riverside.

The silence settled around him. Even his footsteps were muffled by a thickly padded Berber carpet covering the floor. No one seemed to be about. A door stood open in back of the shop, revealing a small walled garden, and beyond that another door.

Kincaid looked round the room with interest. The paintings, spaced generously around the walls, seemed to be mostly late nineteenth- and early twentieth-century watercolors, and most were river landscapes.

In the room's center a pedestal held a sleek bronze of a crouching cat. Kincaid ran his hand over the cool metal and thought of Sid. He had made arrangements with his neighbor, Major Keith, to look after the cat when he was away from home. Although the major professed to dislike cats, he looked after Sid with the same gruff tenderness he had shown to the cat's former owner. Kincaid thought that for the major, as well as himself, the cat formed a living link to the friend they had lost.

Near the garden door stood a desk, its cluttered surface a contrast to the spare neatness he saw everywhere else. Kincaid glanced quickly at the untidy papers, then moved into the second small room which lay a step down from the first.

He caught his breath. The painting on the opposite wall was a long narrow rectangle, perhaps a yard wide and a foot high, and it was lit by a lamp mounted just above it. The girl's body almost filled the frame. Dressed in shirt and jeans, she lay on her back in a meadow, eyes closed, hat tilted back on her auburn hair, and beside her on the grass a basket of ripe apples spilled over onto an open book.

A simple-enough composition, almost photographic in its clarity and detail, but it possessed a warmth and depth impossible to capture with a camera. You could feel the sun on the girl's upturned face, feel her contentment and pleasure in the day.

Other paintings by the same artist's hand were hung nearby, portraits and landscapes filled with the same vivid colors and intense light. As Kincaid looked at them he felt a sense of longing, as if such beauty and perfection existed forever just out of his reach, unless he, like Alice, could step through the frame and into the artist's world.

He had bent forward to peer at the illegibly scrawled signature when behind him a voice said, "Lovely, aren't they?"

Startled, Kincaid straightened and turned. The man stood in the back doorway, his body in shadow as the sun lit the garden behind him. As he stepped into the room, Kincaid saw him more clearly—tall, thin and neat-featured, with a shock of graying hair and glasses that gave him an accountantlike air at odds with the casual pullover and trousers he wore.

The door chimed as Kincaid started to speak. A young man came in, his face white against the dead-black of his clothes and dyed hair, a large and battered leather portfolio tucked under his arm. His getup would have been laughable if not for the look of supplication on his face. Kincaid nodded to Trevor Simons, for so he assumed the man who had come in from the garden to be, and said, "Go ahead. I'm in no hurry."

Rather to Kincaid's surprise, Simons looked carefully at the drawings. After a few moments he shook his head and tucked them back into the portfolio, but Kincaid heard him give the boy the name of another gallery he might try. "The trouble is," he said to Kincaid as the door chimed shut, "he can't paint. It's a bloody shame. They stopped teaching drawing and painting in the art colleges back in the sixties. Graphic artists—that's what they all want to be—only no one tells them there aren't any jobs. So they come out of art college like this wee chappie," he nodded toward the street, "hawking their wares from gallery to gallery like itinerant peddlers. You saw it—fairly competent airbrushed crap, without a spark of originality. If he's lucky he'll find a job frying up chips or driving a delivery van."

"You were courteous enough," said Kincaid.

"Well, you have to have some sympathy, haven't you? It's not their fault they're ignorant, both in technique and in the realities of life." He waved a hand dismissively. "I've nattered on long enough. What can I do for you?"

Kincaid gestured toward the watercolors in the second room, "These—"

"Ah, she's an exception," Simons said, smiling. "In many ways. Self-taught, for one, which was probably her salvation, and very successful at it, for another. Not with these," he added quickly, "although I think she will be, but with the work she does on commission. Stays booked two years in advance. It's very difficult for an artist who is successful commercially to find the time to do really creative work, so this show meant a lot to her."

Realizing the answer even as he asked and feeling an utter fool, Kincaid said, "The artist—who is she?"

Trevor Simons looked puzzled. "Julia Swann. I thought you knew."

"But . . ." Kincaid tried to reconcile the flawless but rather emotionally severe perfection of Julia's flowers with these vibrantly alive paintings. He could see similarities now in technique and execution, but the outcome was astonishingly different. Making an attempt to collect himself, he said, "Look. I think perhaps I ought to go out and come in again, I've made such a muddle of things. My name's Duncan Kincaid," he extended his warrant card in its folder, "and I came to talk to you about Julia Swann."

Trevor Simons looked from the warrant card to Kincaid and back again, then said rather blankly, "It looks like a library permit. I always wondered, you know, when you see them on the telly." He shook his head, frowning. "I don't understand. I know Con's death has been a dreadful shock for everyone, but I thought it was an accident. Why Scotland Yard? And why me?"

"Thames Valley has treated it as a suspicious death from the beginning, and asked for our assistance at Sir Gerald Asherton's request."

Kincaid had delivered this with no intonation, but Simons raised an eyebrow and said, "Ah."

"Indeed," Kincaid answered, and when their eyes met it occurred to him that he might be friends with this man under other circumstances.

"And me?" Simons asked again. "Surely you can't think Julia had anything to do with Con's death?"

"Were you with Julia all Thursday evening?" Kincaid said, pushing a bit more aggressively, although the note of incredulity in Simons's voice had struck him as genuine.

Unruffled, Simons leaned against his desk and folded his arms. "More or less. It was a bit of a free-for-all in here." He nodded, indicating the two small rooms. "People were jammed in here like sardines. I suppose Julia might have popped out to the loo or for a smoke and I wouldn't have noticed, but not much longer than that."

"What time did you close the gallery?"

"Tenish. They'd eaten and drunk everything in sight, and left a wake of litter behind like pillaging Huns. We had to push the last happy stragglers out the door."

LEAVE THE GRAVE GREEN

"We?"

"Julia helped me tidy up."

"And after that?"

Trevor Simons looked away for the first time. He studied the river for a moment, then turned back to Kincaid with a reluctant expression. "I'm sure you've seen Julia already. Did she tell you she spent the night? I can't imagine her being silly enough to protect my honor." Simons paused, but before Kincaid could speak he went on. "Well, it's true enough. She was here in the flat with me until just before daybreak. A small attempt at discretion, creeping out with the dawn," he added with a humorless smile.

"She didn't leave you at any time before that?"

"I think I would have noticed if she had," Simons answered, this time with a genuine flash of amusement, then he quickly sobered and added, "Look, Mr. Kincaid, I don't make a habit of doing this sort of thing. I'm married and I've two teenage daughters. I don't want my family hurt. I know," he continued hurriedly, as if Kincaid might interrupt him, "I should have considered the consequences beforehand, but one doesn't, does one?"

"I wouldn't know," Kincaid answered in bland policemanese, all the while thinking, *Does one not, or does one consider the consequences and choose to act anyway?* The image of his ex-wife came to him, her straight flaxen hair falling across her shuttered face. *Had Vic considered the consequences?*

"You don't live here, then?" he asked, breaking the train of thought abruptly. He gestured toward the door across the garden.

"No. In Sonning, a bit farther upriver. The flat was included in the property when I bought the gallery, and I use it mainly as a studio. Sometimes I stay over when I'm painting, or when I've an opening on."

"You paint?" asked Kincaid, a little surprised.

Simons's smile was rueful. "Am I a practical man, Mr. Kincaid? Or merely a compromised one? You tell me." The question seemed to be hypothetical only, for he continued, "I knew when I left art school I wasn't quite good enough, didn't have that unique combination of talent and luck. So I used a little family money and bought this gallery. I found it a bit ironic that Julia's opening also marked the anniversary of my twenty-fifth year here."

Kincaid wasn't inclined to let him off the hook, although he suspected his curiosity was more personal than professional. "You didn't answer my question."

"Yes, I paint, and I feel insulted if I'm referred to as a 'local artist' rather than an 'artist who paints locally.' It's a fine distinction, you understand," he added mockingly. "Silly, isn't it?"

"What sort of things do you paint?" Kincaid asked, scanning the paintings on the walls of the small room.

Simons followed his gaze and smiled. "Sometimes I do hang my own work, but I haven't any up just now. I've had to make room for Julia's paintings, and frankly I've other things that sell better than mine, although I do paint Thames landscapes. I use oils—I'm not good enough yet to paint in watercolor, but one day I will be."

"Is what Julia does that difficult, then?" Kincaid allowed himself to study Julia's lamplit painting, and discovered that he had been deliberately resisting doing so. It drew him, as she did, in a way that felt both familiar and perilous. "I always thought that one just made a choice, watercolors or oils, depending on what one liked."

"Watercolor is much more difficult," Simons said patiently. "In oil you can make any number of mistakes and just as easily cover them up, the more the merrier. Watercolor requires a confidence, perhaps even a certain amount of ruthlessness. You must get it right the first time."

Kincaid looked at Julia's paintings with new respect. "You said she was self-taught? Why not art college, with her talent?"

Simons shrugged. "I suppose her family didn't take her seriously. Musicians do tend to be rather one-dimensional, even more so than visual artists. Nothing else exists for them. They eat, sleep and breathe music, and I imagine that to Sir Gerald and Dame Caroline, Julia's paintings were just amusing dabs of color on paper." He stepped down into the lower room and walked over to the large painting, staring at it. "Whatever the reason, it allowed her to develop in her own way, with no taint of graphic mediocrity."

"You have a special relationship," Kincaid said, watching the way

Trevor Simons's slender body blocked the painting in an almost protective posture. "You admire her—do you also resent her?"

After a moment Simons answered, his back still to Kincaid. "Perhaps. Can we help but envy those touched by the gods, however briefly?" He turned and the brown eyes behind the spectacles regarded Kincaid candidly. "Yet I have a good life."

"Then why have you risked it?" Kincaid said softly. "Your wife, family . . . perhaps even your business?"

"I never intended it." Simons gave a self-mocking bark of laughter. "Famous last words—I never meant to do it. It was just . . . Julia."

"What else didn't you intend, Trevor? Just how far did your loss of judgment take you?"

"You think *I* might have killed Connor?" His eyebrows shot up above the line of his spectacles and he laughed again. "I can't lay claim to sins of that magnitude, Mr. Kincaid. And why would I want to get rid of the poor bloke? Julia had already chewed him up and spat out the partially digested remains."

Kincaid grinned. "Very descriptively put. And will she do the same to you?"

"Oh, I expect so. I've never been able to delude myself sufficiently to think otherwise."

Pushing aside an untidy stack of papers, Kincaid sat on the edge of Simons's desk and stretched out his legs. "Did you know Connor Swann well?"

Simons put his hands in his pockets and shifted his weight in the manner of a man suddenly territorially displaced. "Only to speak to, really. Before they separated he came in with Julia occasionally."

"Was he jealous of you, do you think?"

"Con? Jealous? That would be the pot calling the kettle black! I never understood why Julia put up with him as long as she did."

A passerby stopped and peered at the painting in the window, as had several others since Kincaid had come into the gallery. Beyond her the light had shifted, and the shadows of the willows lay longer on the pavement. "They don't come in," Kincaid said as he watched her move toward the tea shop and pass from his view.

"No. Not often." Simons gestured at the paintings lining the walls. "The prices are a bit steep for impulse buying. Most of my customers are regulars, collectors. Though sometimes one of those window-shoppers will wander in and fall in love with a painting, then go home and save up pennies out of the house-keeping or the beer money until they have enough to buy it." He smiled. "Those are the best, the ones that know nothing about art and buy out of love. It's a genuine response."

Kincaid looked at the illuminated painting of the girl in the meadow, her eyes gently closed, her faintly freckled face tilted to the sun, and acknowledged his own experience. "Yes, I can see that."

He stood and regarded Trevor Simons, who, whatever his sins, seemed a perceptive and decent man. "A word of advice, Mr. Simons, which I probably shouldn't give. An investigation like this moves out in ripples—the longer it takes the wider the circle becomes. If I were you I'd do some damage control—tell your wife about Julia if you can. Before we do."

Kincaid sat at the table nearest the window in the tea shop. The tin pot had leaked as he poured, and his cup sat in a wet ring on the speckled plastic tabletop. At the next table he recognized the woman who had stopped at the gallery window a few minutes before—middle-aged, heavyset, her graying hair tightly crimped. Although the air in the shop was warm enough to form faint steamy smudges on the windowpanes, she still wore a waterproof jacket over her bulky cardigan. Perhaps she feared it might rain unexpectedly inside? When she looked up, he smiled at her, but she looked away, her face frozen in an expression of faint disapproval.

Gazing idly at the river again, he fingered the key in his trouser pocket. Gemma had acquired Connor's key, address and a description of the property from Thames Valley along with the initial reports. Until a year ago Julia and Connor had lived together in the flat he thought must be just along the terrace, near the willow-covered islands he could see from the window. Julia might have stopped in here often for a morning coffee or a cup of afternoon tea. He imagined her suddenly, sitting across the booth from him in a black sweater, smoking jerkily, frowning in concentration. In his mind she rose and went out into the street. She stood before the gallery for a moment, as if hesitating, then he heard the door chime as she opened it and went in.

Shaking his head, Kincaid downed the remains of his tea in one gulp. He slid from the booth and presented his soggy bill to the girl behind the counter, then followed Julia's phantom out into the lengthening shadows.

He walked toward the river meadows, gazing alternately at the placid river on his left and the blocks of flats on his right. It surprised him that these riverside addresses weren't more elegant. One of the larger buildings was neo-Georgian, another Tudoresque, and both were just a trifle seedy, like dowagers out in soiled housecoats. The shrubbery grew rankly in the gardens, brightened only by the dark red dried heads of sedum and the occasional pale blue of Michaelmas daisies. But it was November after all, Kincaid thought charitably, looking at the quiet river. Even the kiosk advertising river trips and boats for hire was shuttered and locked.

The road narrowed and the large blocks of flats gave way to lower buildings and an occasional detached house. Here the river seemed less separate from the land, and when he reached the high black wrought-iron fence he recognized it from the scrawled description in his pocket. He grasped two of the spiked bars in his hands and peered through them. A commemorative ceramic plaque set into the wall of the nearest building informed him that the flats were quite recently developed, so perhaps Julia and Connor had been among the first tenants. They were built to look like boathouses, in a soft-red brick with an abundance of white-trimmed windows, white deck railings and white peaked gables adorned with gingerbread. Kincaid thought them a bit overdone, but pleasantly so, for they harmonized with both the natural landscape and the surrounding buildings. Like Prince Charles, he found most contemporary architecture to be a blight upon the landscape.

Dodging an array of parked boats and trailers, Kincaid walked along the fence until he found a gate. The flats were staggered behind a well-tended garden, and none was quite identical to the next. He found the house easily, one of the three-tiered variety, raised above the ground on stiltlike supports. Feeling suddenly as if he were trespassing, he fitted the key in the lock, but no one called out to him from the adjacent decks.

He had expected black and white.

Illogically, he supposed, considering the intensity of color Julia used in her paintings. This was a softer palette, almost Mediterranean, with pale yellow walls and terra-cotta floors. Casually provincial furniture filled the sitting room and a fringed Moroccan rug softened the tile floor. On a tiled platform against one wall stood an enameled wood-burning stove. A small painted table in front of the sofa held a chess set. Had Connor played, Kincaid wondered, or had it been merely for show?

A sport jacket lay crumpled over the back of a chair, an untidy pile of newspapers spilled from sofa to floor and a pair of boat shoes peeked from beneath the coffee table. The male clutter seemed incongruous, an intrusion on an essentially feminine room. Kincaid ran his forefinger across a tabletop, then brushed off the resulting gray fuzz against his trouser leg. Connor Swann had not been much of a housekeeper.

Kincaid wandered into the adjoining kitchen. It had no windows, but opened to the sitting room with its view of the river. Unlike the sitting room, however, it looked immaculate. Cans of olive oil and colored-glass bottles of vinegar stood out like bright flags against the oak cabinets and yellow countertops, and a shelf near the cooktop held an array of well-thumbed cookbooks. *Julia Child*, read Kincaid, *The Art of Cooking. The Italian Kitchen. La Cucina Fresca*. There were more, some with lavish color photographs that made him hungry just looking. Glass jars filled with pasta lined another open shelf.

Kincaid opened the fridge and found it well stocked with condiments, cheeses, eggs and milk. The freezer held a few neatly wrapped and labeled packages of meat and chicken, a loaf of French bread, and some plastic containers of something Kincaid guessed might be homemade soup stock. A pad beneath the telephone held the beginnings of a grocery list: *aubergines, tomato paste, red-leaf lettuce, pears*.

The descriptions Kincaid had heard of Connor Swann had not led him to expect an accomplished and enthusiastic cook, but this man had obviously not resorted to zapping frozen dinners in the microwave.

The first floor held a master bedroom and bath done in the same soft yellows as the ground floor, and a small room which apparently served as an office or study. Kincaid continued up the stairs to the top floor.

It had been Julia's studio. The wide windows let in a flood of late afternoon light, and over the willow-tops he could see the winding Thames. A bare table stood in the center of the room, and an old desk pushed against one wall held some partially used sketch pads and a wooden box filled with odds and ends of paint tubes. Curiously, Kincaid rummaged through them. He hadn't known that professional watercolors came in tubes. *Windsor Red. Scarlet Lake. Ultramarine Blue*. The names ran through his mind like poetry, but the tubes left the fine dust of neglect on his fingertips. The room itself felt empty and unused.

He slowly retraced his steps, stopping once more at the door to the bedroom. The bed was hastily made, and a pair of trousers lay thrown over a chair, belt dangling.

The sense of a life interrupted hung palpably in the air. Connor Swann had meant to shop for groceries, prepare dinner, put out the newspapers, brush his teeth, slide under the warmth of the blue-and-yellow quilt on the bed. Kincaid knew that unless he came to an understanding of who Connor Swann had been, he had little hope of discovering who had killed him, and he realized that all his knowledge and perceptions of him were filtered through Julia and her family.

This was Julia's house. Every room bore her imprint, and except for the kitchen, Connor seemed to have only drifted across its surface. Why had Julia left it, like a commander who held all the advantages retreating from the citadel?

Kincaid turned from the bedroom and went into the study. The room contained nothing but a desk and chair facing the window, and a wing-backed chair with a reading lamp. Sitting in the straight-backed chair, he turned on the green-shaded desk lamp and began picking desultorily through the clutter.

A leather-bound appointment book came first to hand. Starting with January, Kincaid flipped slowly through it. The names of the racetracks jumped out first—Epsom, Cheltenham, Newmarket . . . They rotated regularly through the months. Some had times written beside them, others sharp exclamation points. A good day?

Kincaid went back to the beginning, starting over more carefully. In between races he began to see the pattern of Connor's social life. Dates for lunch, dinner, drinks, often accompanied by a name, a time and the words *Red Lion. Bloody hell*, thought Kincaid, *the man had kept up an exhausting social schedule.* And to make it worse, pubs and hotels called the Red Lion were as common as sheep in Yorkshire. He supposed the logical place to start would be the plush old hotel here in Henley, next to the church.

Golf dates appeared often, as well as the notation *Meet with J.*, followed by a dash and varying names, some cryptic, some, like Tyler Pipe and Carpetland, obviously businesses. It looked as though these weren't all social engagements, but rather business appointments, entertaining clients of some sort. Kincaid had assumed that Connor lived off the Asherton income, and nothing in the Thames Valley reports had led him to think otherwise, but perhaps that hadn't been the case. He closed the book and began shuffling through the papers on the desktop, then had a thought and opened the diary again. *Lunch at B.E.* appeared every Thursday, regular as clockwork.

The stack on the desktop resolved itself into ordinary household bills, betting slips, a set of racing-form books, a corporate report from a firm in Reading, and an auction catalogue. Kincaid shrugged and continued his inventory. Paperclips, paper knife, a mug emblazoned with HENLEY ART FEST, which held a handful of promotional pens.

He found Connor's checkbook in the left-hand drawer. A

quick look through the register revealed the expected monthly payments, as well as regular deposits labeled *Blackwell, Gillock and Frye*. A firm of solicitors? wondered Kincaid? An interesting pattern began to form—he returned to the beginning of the register, double-checking. The first check written after every deposit was made out to a K. Hicks, and the amounts, although not the same, were always sizable.

Lost as he was in speculation, it took a moment for the soft click from downstairs to penetrate Kincaid's consciousness. He looked up. Dusk had fallen as he worked. Through the window the outline of the willows showed charcoal against a violet sky.

The sounds were more definitive this time—a louder click, followed by a creak. Kincaid slid from the chair and moved quietly out into the hall. He listened for a moment, then went quickly down the stairs, keeping his feet carefully to the outside of the treads. When he reached the last step, the light came on in the sitting room. He listened again, then stepped around the corner.

She stood by the front door, one hand still on the light switch. The glow from the table lamps revealed tight jeans, a fuzzy pink sweater in a weave so loose it revealed the line of her bra, impossibly high heels, blond hair permed into Medusa-like ropes. He could see the quick rise and fall of her chest beneath the sweater.

"Hullo," he said, trying on a smile.

She took one gulping breath before she shrieked. "Who the bloody hell are you?"

CHAPTER
5

Disoriented, Gemma reached out and touched the other side of the double bed, patted it. Empty. Opening her eyes, she saw the faint gray light brightening the wrong side of the room.

She came fully awake. New flat. No husband. Of course. Sitting up against the pillows, she pushed the tangle of hair away from her face. It had been months since she dreamed of Rob, and she had thought that particular ghost well laid to rest.

The hot water had just begun to gurgle through the radiator pipes as the automatic timer switched on the central heating. For a panicked moment she wondered why the alarm hadn't gone off, then relaxed in relief. It was Sunday. She closed her eyes and snuggled down into the pillows, feeling that luxurious laziness that comes with waking early and knowing one doesn't have to get up.

Sleep, however, refused to be coaxed back. The thought of the interview she'd managed to schedule later in the morning at the Coliseum niggled at her consciousness until finally, with a yawn, she swung her feet from under the duvet. The opera had seemed the logical place to start checking out Gerald Asherton's story, and she found herself looking forward to her day with a tingle of pleasure.

When her toes touched the floor they curled involuntarily from the cold, and she fumbled for her slippers as she shrugged into her dressing gown. At least she could take advantage of the time before Toby awakened to have a quiet cup of coffee and organize her thoughts for the day.

A few minutes later the flat was warming nicely and she sat at the black-slatted table in front of the garden windows, cradling a hot mug in her hands and questioning her sanity.

She had sold her house in Leyton—three bedrooms, semidetached with garden, a symbol in brick and pebbledust of Rob's unrealistic plans for their marriage—and instead of buying the sensible flat in Wanstead she'd had in mind, she'd leased . . . this. She gazed round the room, bemused.

Her estate agent had begged, "Just have a quick look, Gemma, that's all I ask. I know it's not what you're looking for, but you simply must see it." And so she had come, and seen, and signed on the dotted line, finding herself the surprised tenant of the converted garage behind a square detached Victorian house in a tree-lined street in Islington. The house itself was unexpected, standing as it did between two of Islington's most elegant Georgian terraces, but it occupied its space with the confidence of good breeding.

The garage was separate from the house, and lower than the garden, so that the hip-high windows which lined one entire wall of the flat were actually ground level on the outside. The owners, a psychiatrist who worked from a shed in the garden, and his Dutch wife, had done up the garage in what the agent described as "Japanese minimalist" decor.

Gemma almost laughed aloud, thinking of it. An exercise in "minimalist living" would be a fitting description of what it had become for her. The flat was basically one large room, furnished with a futon and a few other sleek, contemporary pieces. Cubbyholes along the wall opposite the bed contained kitchen and water closet, and a storage room with a small window had become Toby's bedroom. The arrangement didn't allow much privacy, but privacy with a small child was a negligible quality anyway, and Gemma couldn't imagine sharing her bed with anyone in the foreseeable future.

Gemma's furniture and most of their belongings had been stored in the back of her parents' bakery in Leyton High Street. Her mum had shaken her faded red curls and tut-tutted. "What were you thinking of, love?"

A quiet, tree-lined street with a park at its end. A green, walled garden, filled with interesting nooks and crannies for a little boy to hide in. A secret place, filled with possibilities. But Gemma had merely said, "I like it, Mum. And it's nearer the Yard," doubting her mother would understand.

She felt stripped clean, pared down to essentials, serene in the room's black-and-gray simplicity.

Or at least she had until this morning. She frowned, wondering again what had made her feel so unsettled, and the image of twelve-year-old Matthew Asherton came unbidden to her mind.

She rose, put two slices of brown bread in the toaster that stood on the tabletop and went to kiss Toby awake.

Having deposited Toby at her mum's, Gemma took the tube to Charing Cross. As the train pulled away, the rush of wind down the tunnel whipped her skirt around her knees and she hugged the lapels of her jacket together. She left the station and entered the pedestrian mall behind St. Martin-in-the-Fields, and rounding the church into St. Martin's Lane she found the outside no better. A gust of north wind funneled down the street, flinging grit and scraps of paper and leaving tiny whirlwinds in its wake.

She rubbed her eyes with her knuckles and blinked several times to clear them, then looked about her. Before her on the corner stood the Chandos Pub, and just beyond it a black-on-white vertical sign said LONDON COLISEUM. Blue and white banners emblazoned with the letters ENO surrounded it and drew her eyes upward. Against the blue-washed canvas of the sky, the ornate white cupola stood out sharply. Near the top of the dome, white letters spelled out ENGLISH NATIONAL OPERA rather sedately, and Gemma thought they must be lit at night.

Something tugged at her memory and she realized she'd been here before. She and Rob had been to a play at the Albury Theatre up the street, and afterward had stopped for a drink at the Chandos. It had been a warm night and they'd taken their drinks outside, escaping the smoky crush in the bar. Gemma remembered sipping her Pimm's and watching the operagoers spill out onto the pavement, their faces animated, hands moving with quick gestures as they dissected the performance. "It might be fun," she'd said rather wistfully to Rob.

He had smiled in his condescending way and said, light voice mocking, "Old cows in silly costumes screeching their lungs out? Don't be stupid, Gem."

Gemma smiled now, thinking of the photo she'd seen of Caroline Stowe. Rob would've fallen over himself if he'd come face-to-face with her. Old cow, indeed. He'd never know what he had missed.

She pushed through the lobby doors, feeling a small surge of excitement at her own entrance into this glamorous fairy-tale world. "Alison Douglas," she said to the heavy gray-haired woman at the reception desk. "The orchestra manager's assistant. I've an appointment with her."

"You'll have to go round the back, then, ducks," the woman answered in less than rarified accents. She made a looping motion with her finger. " Round the block, next the loading bay."

Feeling somewhat chastened, Gemma left the plush-and-gilt warmth of the lobby and circled the block in the indicated direction. She found herself in an alleylike street lined with pub and restaurant delivery entrances. With its concrete steps and peeling paint, the stage entrance to the London Coliseum was distinguished only by the increasingly familiar ENO logo near the door. Gemma climbed up and stepped inside, looking around curiously at the small lino-floored reception area.

To her left a porter sat inside a glass-windowed kiosk; just ahead another door barred the way into what must be the inner sanctum. She announced herself to the porter and he smiled as he handed her a sign-in sheet on a clipboard. He was young, with a freckled face and brown hair that looked suspiciously as if it were growing out from a Mohawk cut. Gemma looked more closely, saw the tiny puncture in his earlobe which should have held an earring. He'd made a valiant effort to clean up for the job, no doubt.

"I'll just give Miss Alison a ring," he said as he handed her a sticky badge to wear. "She'll be right down for you." He picked up the phone and murmured something incomprehensible into it.

Gemma wondered if he'd been on duty after last Thursday evening's performance. His friendly grin augured well for an interview, but she had better wait until she wouldn't be interrupted.

Church bells began to ring close by. "St. Martin's?" she asked.

He nodded, checking the clock on the wall behind him. "Eleven o'clock on the dot. You can set your watch by it."

Was there a congregation for eleven o'clock services, Gemma wondered, or did the church cater solely to tourists?

Remembering how surprised she'd been when Alison Douglas had agreed to see her this morning, she asked the porter, "Business as usual here, even on a Sunday morning?"

He displayed the grin. "Sunday matinee. One of our biggest draws, especially when it's something as popular as *Traviata*."

Puzzled, Gemma tugged her notebook from her purse and flipped quickly through it. "*Pelleas and Melisande*. I thought you were doing *Pelleas and Melisande*."

"Thursdays and Saturdays. Productions—"

The inner door opened and he paused as a young woman came through, then continued to Gemma, "You'll see." He winked at her. "Alison'll make sure you do."

"I'm Alison Douglas." Her cool hand clasped Gemma's firmly. "Don't mind Danny. What can I do for you?"

Gemma took in the short light brown hair, black sweater and skirt, platform shoes, which didn't quite raise her to Gemma's height, but Alison Douglas's most notable characteristic was an air of taking herself quite seriously.

"Is there somewhere we could talk? Your office, perhaps?"

Alison hesitated, then opened the inner door, indicating by a jerk of her head that Gemma should precede her through it. "You'd better come along in, then. Look," she added, "we've a performance in just under three hours and I've things I absolutely must do. If you don't mind following along behind me we can talk as we go."

"All right," Gemma agreed, doubting she'd get a better offer.

They had entered a subterranean maze of dark green corridors. Already lost, Gemma followed hard on Alison Douglas's heels as they twisted and turned, went up, down and around. Occasionally, she looked down at the dirty green carpet beneath her feet, wondering if she recognized the pattern of that particular stain. Could she follow them like Hansel and Gretel's bread crumbs? The smells of damp and disinfectant made her want to sneeze.

Alison turned back to speak to her, stopped suddenly and smiled. Gemma felt sure her bewilderment had been entirely visible, and thought for once she ought to be grateful her every emotion registered on her face.

"Back-of-house," Alison said, her brusque manner softening for the first time. "That's what all the unglamorous bits are called. It's quite a shock if one's never been backstage, isn't it? But this is the heart of the theater. Without this"—she gestured expansively around her—"nothing happens out front."

"The show doesn't go on?"

"Exactly."

Gemma suspected that the key to loosening Alison Douglas's tongue was her work. "Miss Douglas, I'm not sure I understand what you do."

Alison moved forward again as she spoke. "My boss—Michael Blake—and I are responsible for all the administrative details of the running of the orchestra. We—" Glancing at Gemma's face, she hesitated, seeming to search for a less complicated explanation. "We make sure everything and everyone are where they should be when they should be. It can be quite a demanding business. And Michael's away for a few days just now."

"Do you deal directly with the conductors?" Gemma asked, taking advantage of the opening, slight as it was, but the corridor turned again and Alison pushed aside the faded plush curtain which barred their way. She stepped back to allow Gemma to pass through first.

Gemma stopped and stared, her mouth open in surprise. Beside her, Alison said softly, "It is rather amazing, isn't it? I begin to take it for granted until I see it through someone else's eyes.

This is the largest theater in the West End, and it has the largest backstage area of any theater in London. That's what allows us to put on several productions simultaneously."

The cavernous space bustled with activity. Pieces of scenery belonging to more than one production stood side by side in surreal juxtaposition. "Oh," Gemma said, watching a huge section of stone wall roll easily across the floor, guided by two men in coveralls. "So that's what Danny meant. Thursdays and Saturdays Sir Gerald conducts *Pelleas and Melisande*—Fridays and Sundays someone else is doing . . . what did he say?"

"*La Traviata*. Look." Alison pointed across the stage. "There's Violetta's ballroom, where she and Alfredo sing their first duet. And there"—she gestured toward the section of stone wall, now slotted neatly into a recess—"that's part of King Arkel's castle, from *Pelleas*." She looked at Gemma, studied her watch, looked once again at Gemma and said, "There are a few things I simply must see to. Have a look around here, why don't you, while I get things in hand. After that I'll try to manage a quarter-hour in the canteen with you." She was already moving away from Gemma as she finished, the soles of her platform shoes clicking on the wooden floor.

Gemma walked to the lip of the stage and looked out. Before her the tiers of the auditorium rose in baroque splendor, blue velvet accented with gilt. The chandeliers hung from the dome high above her like frosted moons. She imagined all the empty seats filled, and the expectant eyes upon her, waiting for her to open her mouth and sing. Cold crept up her spine and she shivered. Caroline Stowe might look delicate, but to stand on a stage like this and face the crowd required a kind of strength Gemma didn't possess.

She looked down into the pit and smiled. At least Sir Gerald had some protection, and could turn his back on the audience.

A thread of music came from somewhere, women's voices carrying a haunting, lilting melody. Gemma turned and walked toward the back of the stage, straining to hear, but the banging and thumping going on around her masked even the sound's direction. She didn't notice Alison Douglas's return until the woman spoke. "Did you see the pit? We jam one hundred nineteen players into that space, if you can imagine that, elbow to—"

Gemma touched her arm. "That music—what is it?"

"What—?" Alison listened for a moment, puzzled, then smiled. "Oh, that. That's from *Lakme*, Mallika's duet with Lakme in the high priest's garden. One of the girls in *Traviata* is singing Mallika next month at Covent Garden. I suppose she's swotting by listening to a recording." She glanced at her watch, then added, "We can get that cup of tea now, if you like."

The music faded. As Gemma followed Alison back into the maze of corridors she felt an odd sadness, as if she'd been touched by something beautiful and fleeting. "That opera," she said to Alison's back, "does it have a happy ending?"

Alison looked back over her shoulder, her expression amused. "Of course not. Lakme sacrifices herself to protect her lover, in the end."

The canteen smelled of frying chips. Gemma sat across the table from Alison Douglas, drinking tea strong enough to put fur on her tongue and trying to find a comfortable position for her backside in the molded plastic chair. Around them men and women dressed in perfectly ordinary clothes drank tea and ate sandwiches, but when Gemma caught snippets of conversation it contained such obscure musical and technical terms that it might as well have been a foreign language. She pulled her notebook from her handbag and took another sip of tea, grimacing at the tannin's bite. "Miss Douglas," she said as she saw Alison touch the face of her wristwatch with her fingertips, "I appreciate your time. I'll not take up any more than necessary."

"I'm not sure I understand how I can help you. I mean, I know about Sir Gerald's son-in-law. It's an awful thing to happen, isn't it?" Her forehead creased as she frowned, and she looked suddenly very young and unsure, like a child encountering tragedy for the first time. "But I can't see what it has to do with me."

Gemma flipped open her notebook and uncapped her pen, then laid both casually beside her teacup. "Do you work closely with Sir Gerald?"

"No more so than with any of the conductors"—Alison paused and smiled—"but I enjoy it more. He's such a dear. Never gets in a tizzy, like some of them."

Hesitating to admit she didn't understand how the system worked, Gemma temporized with, "Does he conduct often?"

"More than anyone except our music director." Alison leaned over the table toward Gemma and lowered her voice. "Did you know that he was offered the position, but declined it? This was all years ago, way before my time, of course. He said he wanted to have more freedom to work with other orchestras, but I think it had something to do with his family. He and Dame Caroline started with the company back at Sadler's Wells—he would have been the obvious choice."

"Does Dame Caroline still sing with the company? I would have thought . . . I mean, she has a grown daughter . . . "

Alison laughed. "What you mean is that she's surely past it, right?" She leaned forward again, her animated face revealing how much she enjoyed teaching the uninitiated. "Most sopranos are in their thirties before they really hit their stride. It takes years of work and training to develop a voice, and if they sing too much, too soon, they can do irreparable damage. Many are at the peak of their careers well into their fifties, and a few exceptional singers continue beyond that. Although I must admit, sometimes they look a bit ridiculous playing the ingenue parts when they get really long in the tooth." She grinned at Gemma, then continued more seriously. "Not that I think that would have happened to Caroline Stowe. I can't imagine her looking ridiculous at any age."

"You said 'would have happened.' I don't—"

"She retired. Twenty years ago, when their son died. She never sang publicly again." Alison had lowered her voice, and although her expression was suitably concerned, she told the story with the relish people usually reserve for someone else's misfortune. "And she was brilliant. Caroline Stowe might have been one of the most renowned sopranos of our time." Sounding genuinely regretful, Alison shook her head.

Gemma took a last sip of tea and pushed her cup away as she

thought about what she'd heard. "Why the title, then, if she stopped singing?"

"She's one of the best vocal coaches in the country, if not the world. A lot of the most promising singers in the business have been taught, and are still being taught, by Caroline Stowe. And she's done a tremendous amount for the company." Alison gave a wry smile, adding, "She's a very influential lady."

"So I understand," said Gemma, reflecting that it was Dame Caroline's influence, and Sir Gerald's, that had dragged the Yard into this investigation in the first place. Seeing Alison straighten up in her chair, Gemma asked, "Do you know what time Sir Gerald left the theater on Thursday evening?"

Alison thought for a moment, wrinkling her forehead. "I really don't know. I spoke to him in his dressing room just after the performance, around eleven o'clock, but I didn't stay more than five minutes. Had to meet someone," she added with a dimple and a lowering of her lashes. "You'll have to ask Danny. He was on duty that night."

"Did Sir Gerald seem upset in any way? Anything different about his routine that night?"

"No, not that I can think—" Alison stopped, hand poised over her teacup. "Wait. There was something. Tommy was with him. Of course, they've known each other practically forever," she added quickly, "but we don't often see Tommy here after a performance, at least not in the conductor's dressing room."

Feeling the sense of the interview fast escaping her, Gemma said distinctly, "Who exactly is Tommy?"

Alison smiled. "I forgot you wouldn't know. Tommy is Tommy Godwin, our Wardrobe Manager. And it's not that he considers one of his visits akin to a divine blessing, like some costume designers I could name"—she paused and rolled her eyes—"but if he's here at the theater he's usually busy with Running Wardrobe."

"Is he here today?"

"Not that I know of. But I expect you can catch him tomorrow at LB House." This time Gemma's bewilderment must have been evident, because before she could form a question, Alison continued. "That's Lilian Baylis House, in West Hampstead, where we have our Making Wardrobe. Here." She reached for Gemma's notebook. "I'll write down the address and phone number for you."

A thought occurred to Gemma as she watched Alison write in a looping, schoolgirl hand. "Did you ever meet Sir Gerald's son-in-law, Connor Swann?"

Alison Douglas flushed. "Once or twice. He came to ENO functions sometimes." She returned the pen and notebook, then ran her fingers around the neck of her black sweater.

Gemma cocked her head while she considered the woman across the table—attractive, about her own age, and single, if her unadorned left hand and the date she'd alluded to were anything to go by. "Shall I take it he tried to chat you up?"

"He didn't mean anything by it," Alison said, a little apologetically. "You know, you can tell."

"All flash and no substance?"

Alison shrugged. "I'd say he just liked women . . . he made you feel special." She looked up, and for the first time Gemma noticed that her eyes were a light, clear brown. "We've all talked about it, of course. You know what the gossip mill's like. But this is the first time I've really let myself think . . ." She swallowed once, then added slowly. "He was a lovely man. I'm sorry he's dead."

The canteen tables were emptying rapidly. Alison looked up and grimaced, then bustled Gemma back into the dark green tunnels. Murmuring an apology, she left Gemma once again in Danny the porter's domain.

"'Ullo, miss," said Danny, ever cheerful. "You get what you came for?"

"Not quite." Gemma smiled at him. "But you may be able to help me." She pulled her warrant card from her handbag and held the open case where he could see it clearly.

"Crikey!" His eyes widened and he looked her up and down. "You don't look like a copper."

"Don't get cheeky with me, mate," she said, grinning. Resting her elbows on the counter-sill, she leaned forward earnestly. "Can you tell me what time Sir Gerald signed out last Thursday evening, Danny?"

"Ooh, alibis, is it?" The glee on Danny's face made him look like an illustration right out of an Enid Blyton novel.

"Routine inquiries just now," Gemma said, managing to keep a straight face. "We need to know the movements of everyone who might have had contact with Connor Swann the day he died."

Danny lifted a binder from the top of a stack and opened it at the back, flipping through the last few pages. "Here." He pointed, holding the page up where Gemma could see. "Midnight on the dot. That's what I remembered, but I thought you'd want—what is it, corroboration?"

Sir Gerald's signature suited him, thought Gemma, a comfortable but strong scrawl. "Did he usually stay so long after a performance, Danny?"

"Sometimes." He glanced at the sheet again. "But he was last out that night. I remember because I wanted to lock up—had a bird waiting in the wings, you might say." He winked at Gemma. "There was something, though," he said more hesitantly. "That night . . . Sir Gerald . . . well, he was half-cocked, like."

Gemma couldn't keep the surprise from her voice. "Sir Gerald was drunk?"

Danny ducked his head in embarrassment. "I didn't really like to say, miss. Sir Gerald always has a kind word for everybody. Not like some."

"Has this happened before?"

Danny shook his head. "Not so as I can remember. And I've been here over a year now."

Gemma quickly entered Danny's statement in her notebook, then closed it and returned it to her bag. "Thanks, Danny. You've been a great help."

He passed over the sign-in sheet for her initial, his grin considerably subdued.

"Cheerio, then," she said as she turned toward the door.

Danny called out to her before she could open it. "There's one other thing, miss. You know the son-in-law, the one what snuffed it?" He held up his ledger and pointed to an entry near Sir Gerald's. "He was here that day as well."

CHAPTER
6

Eggs, bacon, sausage, tomatoes, mushrooms—and could that possibly be kidneys? Kincaid pushed the questionable items a little to one side with the tip of his fork. Kidneys in steak-and-kidney pie he could manage, but kidneys at breakfast were a bit much. Otherwise the Chequers had done itself proud. Surveying his breakfast laid out on the white tablecloth, complete with china teapot and a vase of pink and yellow snapdragons, he began to think he should feel grateful for Sir Gerald Asherton's influence. His accommodations when out of town on a case were seldom up to these standards.

As he'd slept late, the more righteous early risers had long since finished their breakfasts and he had the dining room to himself. He gazed out through the leaded windows at the damp and windy morning as he ate, enjoying his unaccustomed leisure. Leaves drifted and swirled, their golds and russets a bright contrast against the still-green grass of the churchyard. The congregation began to arrive for the morning service, and soon the verges of the lanes surrounding the church were lined with cars parked end to end.

Wondering lazily why a church in a village as small as Fingest would draw such a crowd, he was suddenly struck by the desire to see for himself. He pushed a last bite of toast and marmalade into his mouth. Still chewing, he ran upstairs, grabbed a tie from his room and hastily knotted it on his way back down.

He slipped into the last pew just as the church bells began to ring. The notices tacked up in the vestibule answered his question quickly enough—this was the parish church, of course, not just the village church, and he must have been living too long in the city not to have realized it. It was also most likely the Ashertons' church. He wondered who knew them and if some of those gathered had come out of curiosity, hoping to see the family.

None of the Ashertons were in evidence, however, and as the peaceful order of the service settled over him, he found his mind drawn back to the previous evening's revelations.

It had taken him a few minutes to calm her down enough to get her name—Sharon Doyle—and even then she'd taken his warrant card and examined it with the intensity of the marginally literate.

"I've come for me things," she said, shoving the card back at him as if it might burn her fingers. "I've a right to 'em. I don't care what anybody says."

Kincaid backed up until he reached the sofa, then sat down on its edge. "Who would say you didn't?" he asked easily.

Sharon Doyle folded her arms, pushing her breasts up against the thin weave of her sweater. "Her."

"Her?" Kincaid repeated, resigned to an exercise in patience.

"You know. Her. The wife. *Julia*," she mimicked in an accent considerably more precise than her own. Hostility seemed to be triumphing over fright, but although she moved nearer him, she still stood with her feet planted firmly apart.

"You have a key," he said, making it a statement rather than a question.

"Con gave it to me."

Kincaid looked at the softly rounded face, young beneath the makeup and bravado. Gently, he said, "How did you find out Connor was dead?"

She stared at him, her lips pressed together. After a moment her hands dropped to her sides and her body sagged like a rag doll that had lost its stuffing. "Down the pub," she answered so quietly that he read her lips as much as heard her.

"You'd better sit down."

Folding into the chair across from him as if unaware of her body, she said, "Last night. I'd gone round to the George. He hadn't rung me up when he said, so I thought 'I'm bloody well not going to sit home on my own.' Some bloke'd buy me a drink, chat me up—serve Con bloody well right." Her voice wavered at the last and she swallowed, then wet her lips with the pink tip of her tongue. "The regulars were all talking about it. I thought they were havin' me on, at first." She fell silent and looked away from him.

"But they convinced you?"

Sharon nodded. "Local lad came in, he's a constable. They said, 'Ask Jimmy. He'll tell you.'"

"Did you?" Kincaid prompted after another moment's silence, wondering what he might do to loosen her tongue. She sat huddled in her chair, arms folded again across her breasts, and as he studied her he thought he saw a faint blue tinge around her lips. Remembering a drinks trolley he'd seen near the wood-stove as he explored the room, he stood and went over to it. He chose two sherry glasses from the glassware on the top shelf, filling them liberally from a bottle of sherry he found beneath.

On closer inspection he discovered that the stove was laid ready for a fire, so he lit it with a match from the box on the tiled hearth and waited until the flames began to flicker brightly. "This will take the chill off," he said as he returned and offered the drink to Sharon. She looked up at him dully and lifted her hand, but the glass tipped as she took it, spilling pale gold liquid over the rim. When he wrapped her unresponsive fingers around the stem, he found them icy to the touch. "You're freezing," he said, chiding her. "Here, take my jacket." He slipped off his tweed sport coat and draped it over her shoulders, then circled the room until he found the thermostat for the central heating. The room's glass-and-tile Mediterranean look made for a pleasant effect, he decided, but it wasn't too well suited for the English climate.

"Good girl." He sat down again and lifted his own glass. She'd drunk some of hers, and he thought he saw a faint flush of color on her cheeks. "That's better. Cheers," he added, sipping his sherry,

91

then said, "You've had a rough time, I think, since last night. Did you ask the constable, then, about Connor?"

She drank again, then wiped her hand across her lips. "He said, 'Why you want to know, then?' and gave me this fishy-eyed look, so I knew it was true."

"Did you tell him why you wanted to know?"

Sharon shook her head and the blond curls bounced with the movement. "Said I just knew him, that's all. Then they started a slanging match about whose round it was, and I slipped out the door by the loo."

Her survival instincts had functioned well, even in shock, Kincaid thought, a good indication that she'd had plenty of experience looking out for herself. "What did you do then?" he asked. "Did you come here?"

After a long moment she nodded. "Stood about outside for hours, bloody well freezing it was, too. I still thought, you know, maybe . . ." She put the fingers of both hands over her mouth quickly, but he'd seen her lip tremble.

"You had a key," he said gently. "Why didn't you come in and wait?"

"Didn't know who might come in here, did I? Might tell me I hadn't any right."

"But today you got up your courage."

"Needed my things, didn't I?" she said, but she looked away, and Kincaid fancied there was more to it than that.

"Why else did you come, Sharon?"

"You wouldn't understand."

"Try me."

She met his eyes and seemed to see in them some possibility of empathy, for after a moment she said, "I'm nobody now, do you see? I thought I'd never have another chance just to be here, like . . . we had some good times here, Con and me. I wanted to remember."

"Didn't you think Con might have left you the flat?" Kincaid asked.

Looking down into her glass, she swirled the few remaining drops of sherry. "Couldn't," she said so quietly that he had to lean forward to hear.

"Why couldn't he?"

"Not his."

The drink didn't seem to have done much in the way of lubricating her tongue, Kincaid thought. Getting anything out of her was worse than pulling teeth. "Whose is it, then?"

"Hers."

"Connor was living in Julia's flat?" He found the idea very odd indeed. Why hadn't she booted him out and stayed herself, rather than going back home to her parents? It sounded much too amicable an arrangement for a couple who had supposedly not been speaking to one another.

Of course, he added to himself as he considered the girl sitting across from him, it might not have been true. Perhaps Connor had needed a handy excuse. "Is that why Connor didn't have you move in with him?"

His jacket slipped from Sharon's shoulders as she shrugged, reexposing the pale swell of her breasts through the weave of the pink fuzzy sweater. "He said it wasn't right, it being Julia's house and all."

Kincaid hadn't imagined Connor Swann being a great one for moral scruples, but then Connor was proving to be full of surprises. Glancing at the open-plan kitchen, he asked, "Do you cook?"

Sharon looked at him as if he had a slate loose. "Course I can cook. What do you take me for?"

"No, I mean, who did the cooking here, you or Connor?"

She thrust her lower lip out in a pout. "'E wouldn't let me touch a thing in there, like it was a bloody church or something. Said fry-ups were nasty, and he'd not have anything boiled in his kitchen but eggs and water for the pasta." Still absently holding her glass, she stood and wandered over to the dining table. She traced a finger across its surface. "'E cooked for me, though. No bloke ever did that. Nobody ever cooked anything for me but me mum and me gran, come to think of it." Looking up, she stared at Kincaid as if seeing him for the first time. "You married?"

He shook his head. "I was once, a long time ago."

"What happened?"

"She left. Met someone else." He said the words flatly, with an ease born of years of practice, yet it still amazed him that such simple sentences could contain such betrayal.

Sharon considered that, then nodded. "Con made me supper—'dinner,' I mean—he'd always remind me to say 'dinner.' Candlelight, best dishes. He'd make me sit while he brought me things—'Try this, Shar, try that, Shar.' Funny things, too." She smiled at Kincaid. "Sometimes I felt like a kid playing dress-up. Would you do things like that for a girl?"

"I've been known to. But I'm afraid I'm not up to Con's standards—my cooking runs more to omelets and cheese-on-toast." He didn't add that he'd never been inclined to play Pygmalion.

The brief animation that had lit Sharon's face faded. She came slowly back to her chair, empty glass trailing from her fingertips. In a still little voice she said, "It won't happen to me again."

"Don't be silly," he scolded, hearing the false heartiness in his voice.

"Not like with Con, it won't." Looking directly at Kincaid, she said, "I know I'm not what blokes like him go for—always said it was too good to be true. A fairy tale." She rubbed the sides of her face with her fingers, as if her jaws ached from unshed tears. "There's not been anything in the papers. Do you know about the . . . arrangements?"

"No one in the family's rung you?"

"Rung me?" she said, some of her earlier aggression returning. "Who the hell do you think would've rung me?" She sniffed, then added, mincing the names, "Julia? Dame Caroline?"

Kincaid gave the question serious consideration. Julia seemed determined to ignore the fact that her husband had existed, much less died. And Caroline? He could imagine her performing a distasteful, but necessary, duty. "Perhaps, yes. If they had known about you. I take it they didn't?"

Dropping her gaze to her lap, she said a little sullenly, "How should I know what Con told them—I only know what he told me." She pushed the hair from her face with chubby fingers, and Kincaid noticed that the nail on her index finger was broken to the quick. When she spoke again the defiance had gone from her voice. "He said he'd take care of us—little Hayley and me."

"Hayley?" Kincaid said blankly.

"My little girl. She's four. Had her birthday last week." Sharon smiled for the first time.

This was a twist he hadn't expected. "Is she Con's daughter, too?"

She shook her head vehemently. "Her dad buggered off soon as he knew I was going to have her. Rotten swine. Not heard a word from him since."

"But Con knew about her?"

"Course he did. What do you take me for, a bloody tart?"

"Of course not," Kincaid said soothingly, and, eyeing her empty glass, unobtrusively fetched the bottle. "Did Con get on with little Hayley, then?" he asked, dividing the last of the sherry between them.

When she didn't answer, he thought perhaps he'd gone over the mark with the sherry, but after a moment she said, "Sometimes I wondered . . . if it was really her he wanted, not me. Look." Digging in her handbag, she pulled out a worn leather wallet. "That's Hayley. She's lovely, isn't she?"

It was a cheap studio portrait, but even the artificial pose and tatty props couldn't spoil the little girl's beauty. As naturally blond as her mother might have been as a child, she had dimples and an angelic, heart-shaped face. "Is she as good as she looks?" Kincaid asked, raising an eyebrow.

Sharon laughed. "No, but you'd never think it to look at her, would you? Con called her his little angel. He'd tease her, call her names in this silly Irish voice. 'Me little darlin','" she said in a credible Irish accent. "You know, things like that." For the first time her eyes filled with tears. She sniffed and wiped the back of her hand across her nose. "Julia didn't want any kids. That's why he wanted the divorce, but Julia wouldn't give it to him."

"Julia wouldn't divorce Connor?" Kincaid asked, thinking that although no one had actually said, that wasn't the impression he'd had from Julia or her family.

"When the two years were up he was going to divorce her— that's how long it takes, you know, to obtain a divorce without the other party's consent." She said the last bit so precisely Kincaid thought she must have memorized it, perhaps repeating something Connor had said in order to comfort herself.

"And you were going to wait for him? Another year, was it?"

"Why shouldn't I have done?" she said, her voice rising. "Con never gave me reason to think he wouldn't do what he said."

Why indeed? thought Kincaid. *What better prospect had she?* He looked at her, sitting back a little in her chair now, with her lower lip pushed out belligerently and both hands clasped around the stem of the sherry glass. Had she loved Connor Swann, or had she merely seen him as an attractive meal ticket? And how had such an unlikely union taken place? He certainly doubted that they had moved in the same social circles. "Sharon," he said carefully, "tell me, how did you and Connor meet?"

"In the park," she said, nodding toward the river. "Just there, in the Meadows. You can see it from the road. In the spring, it was. I was pushing Hayley in the swings and she fell out, skinned her knee. Con came over and talked to her, and before you knew it she'd stopped her bawling and was laughing at him." She smiled, remembering. "Him and his Irish blarney. He brought us back here to look after her knee." When Kincaid raised an eyebrow at that, she hurried on. "I know what you're thinking. At first I was afraid he might be . . . well, you know, a bit funny. But it wasn't like that at all."

Sharon looked relaxed now, and warm, sitting with her feet in their preposterous shoes stretched out in front of her, sherry glass cradled in her lap. "What was it like?" Kincaid asked softly.

She took her time answering, studying her glass, the fan of her darkly mascaraed lashes casting shadows on her cheeks. "Funny. What with his job and all, it seemed like Con knew everybody. Always lunches and dinners and drinks and golfing. Busy, you know, important." She raised her eyes to Kincaid's. "I think he was lonely. In between all those engagements, there wasn't anything."

Kincaid thought about the desk diary he'd seen upstairs, with its endless round of appointments. "Sharon, what was Con's job?"

"'E was in advertising." Wrinkling her brow, she said, "Blakely, Gill . . . I can never remember. In Reading, it was."

That certainly made sense of the diary. Remembering the deposit stubs, he recited, "Blackwell, Gillock and Frye."

"That's it." Pleased at his cleverness, she beamed at him.

Kincaid ran back through the checkbook register in his mind. If Connor had helped Sharon out financially, he had done it on a cash basis—there had been no checks made out in her name. Unless he had passed the money through someone else. Casually, he asked, "Do you happen to know someone called Hicks?"

"That Kenneth!" she said furiously, sitting up and sloshing what remained of her drink. "Thought you were him, didn't I, when I first came in and heard you upstairs. Thought he'd come for what he could get, like a bloody vulture."

Was that why she'd been so frightened? "Who is he, Sharon? What connection did he have with Con?"

A little apologetically, she said, "Con liked the horses, see? That Kenneth, he worked for a bookie, ran Con's bets for him. 'E was always hanging about, treated me like I was dirt."

If that were the case, Connor Swann had not played the ponies lightly. "Do you know what bookmaker Kenneth Hicks worked for?"

She shrugged. "Somebody here in the town. Like I said, he was always hanging about."

Remembering all the Red Lion notations in the diary, Kincaid wondered if that had been their regular meeting place. "Did Con go to the Red Lion Hotel often? The one next to the chur—?"

Already shaking her head, she interrupted, "All tarted up for the tourists, that one. A posh whore, Con called it, where you couldn't get a decent pint."

The girl was a natural mimic, with a good memory for dialogue. When she quoted Con, Kincaid could hear the cadence of his voice, even the faint hint of Irish accent.

"No," she continued, "it was the Red Lion in Wargrave he liked. A real pub, with good food at a decent price." She smiled, showing a faint dimple like her daughter's. "The food was the thing, you know—Con wouldn't go anywhere he didn't like the food." Putting her glass to her lips and turning it end up, she drained the last few drops. "'E even took me there, a few times, but mostly he liked to stay at home."

Kincaid shook his head at the contradictions. The man had lived a boozing, betting life-in-the-fast-lane, by all accounts, but had preferred to stay at home with his mistress and her child. Connor had also, according to his diary, had lunch with his in-laws every single Thursday for the past year.

Kincaid thought back to the aftermath of his own marriage. Although Vic had left him, her parents had somehow managed to cast him as the villain of the piece, and he had never heard from them again, not so much as a card at Christmas or on his birthday. "Do you know what Con did on Thursdays, Sharon?" he asked.

"Why should I? Same as any other day, far as I know," she added, frowning.

So she hadn't known about the regular lunch with the in-laws. What else had Connor conveniently not told her? "What about last Thursday, Sharon, the day he died? Were you with him?"

"No. 'E went to London, but I don't think he'd meant to, before-hand. When I'd given Hayley her supper, I came over and he'd just come in. All wound up he was, too, couldn't sit still with it."

"Did he say where he'd been?"

Slowly, she shook her head. "Said he had to go out again for a bit. 'To see a man about a dog,' he said, but that was just his way of being silly."

"And he didn't tell you where he was going?"

"No. Told me not to get my knickers in a twist, that he'd be back." Slipping off her high-heeled sandals, she tucked her feet up in the armchair and rubbed at her toes with sudden concentration. She looked up, her eyes magnified by a film of moisture. "But I couldn't stay, 'cause it were Gran's bridge night and I had to see to Hayley. I couldn't . . ." Wrapping her arms around her calves, she buried her face against her knees. "I didn't . . ." she whispered, her voice muffled by the fabric of her jeans ". . . wouldn't even give him a kiss when he left."

So she had been pouting, her feelings hurt, and had childishly snubbed him, thought Kincaid. A small failing, an exhibition of ordinary lovers' behavior, to be laughed about later in bed, but this time there could be no making up. Of such tiny things are made lifetimes of guilt, and what she sought from him was absolution. Well, he would give whatever was in his power to bestow. "Sharon. Look at me." Slipping forward in his chair, he reached out and patted her clasped hands. "You couldn't know. We're none of us perfect enough to live every minute as if it might be our last. Con loved you, and he knew you loved him. That's all that matters."

Her shoulders moved convulsively. He sat back quietly, watching her, until he saw her body relax and begin a barely perceptible rocking, then he said, "Con didn't say anything else about where he was going or who he meant to see?"

She shook her head without lifting it. "I've thought and thought. Every word he said, every word I said. There's nothing."

"And you didn't see him again that night?"

"I said I didn't, didn't I?" she said, raising her face from her knees. Weeping had blotched her fair skin, but she sniffed and ran her knuckles under her eyes unselfconsciously. "What do you want to know all this stuff for, anyway?"

At first her need to talk, to release some of her grief, had been greater than anything else, but now Kincaid saw her natural wariness begin to reassert itself. "Had Con been drinking?" he asked.

Sharon sat back in her chair, looking puzzled. "I don't think so—at least he didn't seem like it, but sometimes you couldn't tell, at first."

"Had a good head, did he?"

She shrugged. "Con liked his pint, but he wasn't ever mean with it, like some."

"Sharon, what do you think happened to Con?"

"Silly bugger went for a walk along the lock, fell in and drowned! What do you mean 'What happened to him?' How the bloody hell should I know what happened to him?" She was almost shouting, and bright spots of color appeared on her cheekbones.

Kincaid knew he'd received the tail end of the anger she couldn't vent on Connor—anger at Connor for dying, for leaving her. "It's difficult for a grown man to fall in and drown, unless he's had a heart attack or is falling-down drunk. We won't be able to rule those possibilities out until after the autopsy, but I think we'll find that Connor was in good health and at least relatively sober." As he spoke her eyes widened and she shrank back in her chair, as if she might escape his voice, but he continued relentlessly. "His throat was bruised. I think someone choked him until he lost consciousness and then very conveniently shoved him in the river. Who would have done that to him, Sharon? Do you know?"

"The bitch," she said on a breath, her face blanched paper-white beneath her makeup.

"What—"

She stood up, propelled by her anger. Staggering, she lost her balance and fell to her knees before Kincaid. "That bitch!"

A fine spray of spittle reached his face. He smelled the sherry on her breath. "Who, Sharon?"

"She did everything she could to ruin him and now she's killed him."

"Who, Sharon? Who are you talking about?"

"Her, of course. Julia."

The woman sitting beside Kincaid nudged him. The congregation was rising, lifting and opening hymnals. He'd heard only snippets of the sermon, delivered in a soft and scholarly voice by the balding vicar. Standing quickly, he scrabbled for a hymnal and peeked at his neighbor's to find the page.

He sang absently, his mind still replaying his interview with Connor Swann's mistress. In spite of Sharon's accusations, he just didn't think that Julia Swann had the physical strength necessary to choke her husband and shove him into the canal. Nor had she had the time, unless Trevor Simons was willing to lie to protect her. None of it made sense. He wondered how Gemma was getting on in London, if she had found out anything useful in her visit to the opera.

The service came to a close. Although the congregants greeted one another and chatted cheerfully as they filed out, nowhere did he hear Connor or the Ashertons mentioned. They glanced curiously and a little shyly at Kincaid, but no one spoke to him. He followed the crowd out into the churchyard, but instead of returning to the hotel, he turned his collar up, stuck his hands in his pockets and wandered among the headstones. Distantly, he heard the sounds of car doors slamming and engines starting, but the wind hummed against his ears. Leaves rustled in the thick grass like small brown mice.

He found what he had been halfway looking for behind the church tower, beneath a spreading oak.

"The family," said a voice behind him, "seems to have been more than ordinarily blessed and cursed."

Startled, Kincaid turned. Contemplating the headstone, the vicar stood with his hands clasped loosely before him and his feet spread slightly apart. The wind whipped his vestments against his legs and blew the strands of thinning, gray hair across his bony skull.

The inscription said simply: MATTHEW ASHERTON, BELOVED SON OF GERALD AND CAROLINE, BROTHER OF JULIA. "Did you know him?" Kincaid asked.

The vicar nodded. "In many ways an ordinary boy, transformed into something beyond himself by the mere act of opening his mouth." He looked up from the headstone and Kincaid saw that his eyes were a fine, clear gray. "Oh yes, I knew him. He sang in my choir. I taught him his catechism, as well."

"And Julia? Did you know Julia, too?"

Studying Kincaid, the vicar said, "I noticed you earlier, a new face in the congregation, a stranger wandering purposefully about among the headstones, but you did not seem to me to be a mere sensation seeker. Are you a friend of the family?"

In answer Kincaid removed his warrant card from his pocket and opened the case. "Duncan Kincaid. I'm looking into the death of Connor Swann," he said, but even as he spoke he wondered if that were now the entire truth.

The vicar closed his eyes for a moment, as if conducting a private communication, then opened them and blinked before fixing Kincaid with his penetrating stare. "Come across the way, why don't you, for a cup of tea. We can talk, out of this damnable wind."

*　　　　*　　　　*

"Brilliance is a difficult enough burden for an adult to bear, much less a child. I don't know how Matthew Asherton would have turned out, if he had lived to fulfill his promise."

They sat in the vicar's study, drinking tea from mismatched mugs. He had introduced himself as William Mead, and as he switched on the electric kettle and gathered mugs and sugar onto a tray, he told Kincaid that his wife had died the previous year. "Cancer, poor dear," he'd said, lifting the tray and indicating that Kincaid should follow him. "She was sure I'd never be able to manage on my own, but somehow you muddle through. Although," he added as he opened the study door, "I must admit that housekeeping was never my strong suit."

His study bore him out, but it was a comfortable sort of disorder. The books looked as if they might have leaped off the shelves, spreading out onto every available surface like a friendly, invading army, and the bits of wall space not covered by books contained maps.

Setting his mug on the small space the vicar had cleared for him on a side table, Kincaid went to examine an ancient-looking specimen which was carefully preserved behind glass.

"Saxton's map of the Chilterns, 1574. This is one of the few that show the Chilterns as a whole." The vicar coughed a little behind his hand, then added, out of what Kincaid thought must be a lifetime's habit of honesty, "It's only a copy, of course, but I enjoy it nonetheless. It's my hobby—the landscape history of the Chilterns.

"I'm afraid," he continued with an air of confession, "that it takes up a good deal more of my time and interest than it should, but when one has written a sermon once a week for close on half a century, the novelty pales. And these days, even in a rural parish like this one, for the most part our work is saving bodies, rather than souls. I can't remember when I've had someone come to me with a question of faith." He sipped his tea and gave Kincaid a rather rueful smile.

Kincaid, wondering if he looked as though he needed saving,

smiled back and returned to his chair. "You must know the area well, then."

"Every footpath, every field, or close enough." Mead stretched out his legs, exhibiting the trainers he had slipped into upon returning to the house. "My feet must be nearly as well traveled as Paul's on the road to Damascus. This is an ancient countryside, Mr. Kincaid—ancient in the sense the term is used in landscape history, as opposed to planned countryside. Although these hills are part of the calcareous backbone that underlies much of southern England, they're much more heavily wooded than most chalk downlands—this, and the layer of clay with flints in the soil, kept the area from extensive agricultural development."

Kincaid cradled his warm mug in both hands and positioned his feet near the glowing bars of the electric fire, prepared to listen to whatever dissertation the vicar might offer. "So that's why so many of the houses here are built from flints," he said, remembering how incongruous the pale smooth limestone walls of Badger's End had seemed, glowing in the dusk. "I'd noticed, of course, but hadn't carried the thought any further."

"Indeed. You will also have noticed the pattern of fields and hedgerows in the valleys. Many can be traced back to pre-Roman times. It is the 'Immanuel's Land' of John Bunyan's *Pilgrim's Progress*, '. . . a most pleasant mountainous country, beautiful with woods, vineyards, fruits of all sorts; flowers also with springs and fountains; very delectable to behold.'

"My point, Mr, Kincaid," continued the vicar, twinkling at him, "lest you grow impatient with me, is that although this is a lovely countryside, a veritable Eden, if you will, it is also a place where change occurs slowly and things are not easily forgotten. There has been a dwelling of some sort at Badger's End since medieval times, at the least. The facade of the present house is Victorian, though you wouldn't think it to look at it, but some of the less visible parts of the house go back much further."

"And the Ashertons?" Kincaid asked, intrigued.

"The family has been there for generations, and their lives are very much intertwined with the fabric of the valley. No one who lives here will forget the November that Matthew Asherton drowned—communal memory, you might say. And now this." He shook his head, his expression reflecting a genuine compassion unmarred by any guilty pleasure in another's misfortune.

"Tell me what you remember about that November."

"The rain." The vicar sipped his tea, then pulled a crumpled, white handkerchief from his breast pocket and gently patted his lips. "I began to think quite seriously about the story of Noah, but spirits sank as the water rose and I remember doubting my parishioners would find a sermon on the subject very uplifting. You're not familiar with the geography of the area, are you, Mr. Kincaid?"

Kincaid assumed the question to be rhetorical, as the vicar had gone to his desk and begun rooting among the papers even as he spoke, but he answered anyway. "No, Vicar, I can't say that I am."

The object of the search proved to be a tattered Ordnance Survey map, which the vicar unearthed with obvious delight from beneath a pile of books. Opening it carefully, he spread it before Kincaid. "The Chiltern Hills are a legacy of the last Ice Age. They lie across the land at a horizontal angle, from the northeast to the southwest, do you see?" He traced a darker green oblong with his fingertip. "The north side is the escarpment, the southern the dip-slope, with valleys running down it like fingers. Some of these valleys bear rivers—the Lea, the Bulbourne, the Chess, the Wye, and others—all tributaries of the Thames. In others the springs and surface-flow only break out when the water table reaches the surface—during the winter or other times of particularly heavy rain." Sighing, he gave the map a gentle tap with a forefinger before folding it again. "Hence their name—winterbournes. It's quite pretty, isn't it? Very descriptive. But they can be treacherous in flood, and that, I'm afraid, was the downfall of poor young Matthew."

"What exactly happened?" asked Kincaid. "I've only really heard the story secondhand."

"The only one who will ever know *exactly* what happened is Julia, as she was with him," said the vicar, with an attention to detail worthy of a policeman. "But I'll do my best to piece it together. The children were walking home from school and took a familiar shortcut through the woods. The rain had given us a brief respite, for the first time in days. Matthew, indulging in some horseplay along the bank of the stream, fell in and was caught by the current. Julia tried to reach him, going dangerously far into the water herself, and, failing, ran home for help. It was too late, of course. I think it quite likely that the boy had stopped breathing before Julia left him."

"Did Julia tell you the story herself?"

Mead nodded as he sipped his tea, then set his cup down and continued. "In bits and snatches, rather less than coherently, I'm afraid. You see, she was quite ill afterward, what with the shock and the chill. No one thought to see to her until hours later, and she'd been soaked to the skin. Even that was Mrs. Plumley's doing—the parents were entirely too distraught to remember her at all.

"She developed pneumonia. It was touch and go for a bit." Shaking his head, he held his hands out toward the electric fire, as if the memory had made him cold. "I visited her every day, taking it in turn with Mrs. Plumley to sit with her during the worst of it."

"What about her parents?" asked Kincaid, feeling the stirrings of outrage.

Distress creased the vicar's gentle face. "The grief in that house was as thick as the water that drowned Matthew, Mr. Kincaid. They had no room in their minds or hearts for anything else."

"Not even their daughter?"

Very quietly, almost to himself, Mead said, "I think they couldn't bear to look at her, knowing that she was alive and he was not." He met Kincaid's eyes, adding more briskly, "There now, I've said more than I should. It's been a long time since I've thought of it, and Connor's death has brought it all back."

"There's more you're not telling me." Kincaid sat forward in his chair, not willing to let the matter drop.

"It's not my place to pass judgment, Mr. Kincaid. It was a difficult time for everyone concerned."

Kincaid translated that as meaning that Mead thought the Ashertons had behaved abominably, but wouldn't allow himself to say so. "Sir Gerald and Dame Caroline are certainly solicitous of their daughter now."

"As I said, Mr. Kincaid, it was all a very long time ago. I'm only sorry that Julia has had another such loss."

A movement at the window caught Kincaid's eye. The wind had raised a dervish of leaves on the vicar's lawn. It spun for a moment, then collapsed. A few leaves drifted toward the window, lightly tapping the panes. "You said you knew Matthew, but you must have come to know Julia quite well, actually."

The vicar swirled the dregs of his tea in his mug. "I'm not sure anyone knows Julia well. She was always a quiet child, watching and listening where Matthew would plunge into things. It made the rare response from her all the sweeter, and when she took an interest in something it seemed genuine, not merely the latest enthusiasm."

"And later?"

"She did talk to me, of course, during her illness, but it was a hodgepodge, childish delirium. And when she recovered she became quite withdrawn. The only time I had a glimpse of the child I knew was at her wedding. She had that glow that almost all brides have, and it softened the edges." His tone affectionate, the vicar's smile invited Kincaid's understanding.

"I can almost imagine that," Kincaid said, thinking of the smile he'd seen when Julia had opened the door to them, thinking it was Plummy. "You said you married them, Vicar? But I thought—"

"Connor was Catholic, yes, but he didn't practice, and Julia preferred to be married here at St. Barts." He nodded at the church, its distinctive double tower just visible across the lane. "I counseled Connor as well as Julia before the wedding, and I must say I had my doubts, even then."

"Why was that?" Kincaid had developed a considerable regard for the vicar's perceptions.

"In some odd way he reminded me of Matthew, or of Matthew as he might have been had he grown up. I don't know if I can explain it . . . he was perhaps a bit too glib for my liking—with such outward charm it's sometimes difficult to tell what runs beneath the surface. An ill-fated match, in any event."

"Apparently," Kincaid agreed wryly. "Although I'm a bit confused as to who wouldn't divorce whom. Julia certainly seems to have grown to dislike Connor." He paused, weighing his words. "Do you think she could have killed him, Vicar? Is she capable of it?"

"We all carry the seeds of violence, Mr. Kincaid. What has always fascinated me is the balance of the equation—what factor is it that allows one person to tip over the edge, and another not?" Mead's eyes held knowledge accumulated over a lifetime of observing the best and worst of human character, and it occurred to Kincaid once again that their callings were not dissimilar. The vicar blinked and continued, "But to answer your question, no, I do not think Julia capable of killing anyone, no matter what the circumstances."

"Why do you say 'anyone,' Vicar?" Kincaid asked, puzzled.

"Only because there were rumors at the time of Matthew's death, and you are bound to hear them if you poke long enough under rocks. Open accusations might have been refutable, but not the faceless whispers in the dark."

"What did they say, the whisperers?" Kincaid said, knowing the answer even as he spoke.

Mead sighed. "Only what you might expect, human nature being what it is, as well as being fueled by her sometimes obvious jealousy of her brother. They insinuated that she didn't try to save him . . . that she might even have pushed him."

"She was jealous of him, then?"

The vicar sat up a bit in his chair and for the first time sounded a bit irascible. "Of course she was jealous! As any normal child would have been, given the circumstances." His gray eyes held Kincaid's. "But she also loved him, and would never willingly have allowed harm to come to him. Julia did as much to save her brother as anyone could expect of a frightened thirteen-year-old, probably more." He stood up and began collecting the tea things on the tray. "I don't possess the temerity to call a tragedy like that an act of God. And accidents, Mr. Kincaid, are often unanswerable."

Placing his mug carefully on the tray, Kincaid said, "Thank you, Vicar. You've been very kind."

Mead stood, tray balanced in his hands, gazing out the window at the churchyard. "I don't profess to understand the workings of fate. Sometimes it's best not to, in my business," he added, the twinkle surfacing again, "but I've always wondered. The children usually took the bus home from school, but they were late that day and had to walk instead. What kept them?"

CHAPTER

7

Kincaid reshuffled the files on his desk and ran a hand through his hair until it stood up like a cockscomb. The late Sunday afternoon lull at the Yard usually provided the perfect time to catch up on paperwork, but today concentration eluded him. He stretched and glanced at his watch—past teatime, and the sudden hollow sensation in his stomach reminded him he'd missed lunch altogether. Tossing the reports he'd managed to finish into the out tray, he stood up and grabbed his jacket from the peg.

He'd go home, look after Sid, repack his bag, perhaps grab a Chinese take-away. Ordinarily the prospect would have contented him, but today it didn't ease the restlessness that had dogged him since he left the vicarage and caught the train back to London. The image of Julia rose again in his mind. Her face was younger, softer, but pale against the darkness of her fever-matted hair, and she tossed in her white-sheeted bed, uncomforted.

He wondered just how much political clout the Ashertons wielded, and how carefully he need tread.

It was not until he'd exited the Yard garage into Caxton Street that he thought of phoning Gemma again. He'd rung periodically during the afternoon without reaching her, although she must have been finished with her interview at the ENO hours ago. He eyed the cellular phone but didn't pick it up, and as he rounded St. James Park he found himself heading toward Islington rather than Hampstead. It had been weeks since Gemma moved into the new flat, and her rather embarrassed delight when she spoke of it intrigued him. He'd just pop by on the off-chance he'd catch her at home.

When he remembered how carefully she had avoided inviting him to her house in Leyton, he pushed it to the back of his mind.

He pulled up in front of the address Gemma had given, studying the house before him. A detached Victorian built of smooth honey-colored stone, it was one of a hodgepodge of houses lying rather incongruously between two of Islington's Georgian crescents. Its two bow-fronted windows caught the late afternoon sun, and an iron fence surrounded the well-tended garden. From the front steps two large black dogs of indeterminate breed regarded him alertly, ready to protest if he should cross the bounds of the gate. Remembering Gemma's description, he left the car in the nearest space and walked around the corner, following the garden wall.

The garage doors were painted a cheerful daffodil yellow, as was the smaller door to their left. Above it a discreet, black number *2* satisfied him that he had indeed found the right place. He knocked, and when no one answered, he sat down on the step leading up to the garden, eased his back into a comfortable position against the bars of the narrow gate and prepared to wait.

He heard her car before he saw it. "You'll get a ticket, parking on the double-yellows," he said as she opened the door.

"Not when it's my own garage I'm blocking. What are you doing here, guv?"

She unbuckled Toby's seat belt and he clambered across her, shouting with excitement.

"Nice to be appreciated," Kincaid said, slapping Toby's palm, then lifting him up and tousling the straight, fair hair. "Your engine's developing a bit of a knock," he continued to Gemma as she locked the Escort.

She grimaced. "Don't remind me. Not just yet, anyway." They stood awkwardly for a moment, Gemma clutching a bouquet of pink roses to her chest, and as the silence lengthened he grew ever more uncomfortable.

Why had he thought he could breach her carefully maintained barriers without consequence? His invasion seemed to stand between them, tangible as stone. He said, "I'm sorry. I'll not come in. It's just that I couldn't reach you, and I thought we should connect." Feeling more apologetic by the second, he added, "I could take you and Toby for something to eat."

"Don't be daft." She dug in her handbag for her keys. "Do come in, please." Smiling at him, she unlocked the door and stood back. Toby darted between them with a whoop. "This is it," she said as she entered behind him.

Her clothes hung on an open rack beside the door. Brushing against a dress, he smelled for an instant the floral scent of the perfume she usually wore. He took his time, looking around with pleasure, considering. The simplicity surprised him, yet in some way it did not. "It suits you," he said finally. "I like it."

Gemma moved as if released, crossing the room to the tiny closet of a kitchen, filling a vase with water for the roses. "So do I. So does Toby, I think," she said, nodding at her son, who was busily yanking out drawers from the bank beneath the garden windows. "But I've had a particularly severe thrashing from my mum this afternoon. She doesn't think it a suitable place for a child."

"On the contrary," he said, wandering about the room on a closer tour of inspection. "There's something rather childlike about it, like a playhouse. Or a ship's cabin, where everything has its place."

Gemma laughed. "I told her my granddad would have loved it. He was in the navy." She placed the roses on the small coffee table, the splash of pink the single accent in the black and gray room.

"Red would have been the obvious choice," he said, smiling.

"Too boring." Two pairs of cotton knickers, a bit faded and frayed about the elastic, hung suspended in front of the radiator. Flushing, Gemma snatched them down and tucked them away in a drawer beside the bed. She lit lamps and closed the blinds, shutting out the twilit garden. "I'll just get changed."

"Let me take you out." He still felt he needed to make amends. "If you don't already have plans," he added, giving her an easy out. "Or we'll have a quick drink and catch up, and I'll be on my way."

She stood for a moment, jacket in one hand and hanger in the other, looking around the room as if assessing the possibilities. "No. There's a Europa just around the corner. We'll pick up a few things and cook." She hung the jacket up decisively, then pulled jeans and a sweater from a chest beneath the rack.

"Here?" he asked, eyeing the kitchen dubiously.

"Coward. All it takes is a bit of practice. You'll see."

"It does have its limitations," Gemma admitted as they pulled chairs up to the half-moon table. "But you learn to adapt. And it's not as though I have time to do much fancy cooking." She looked pointedly at Kincaid as she filled his wineglass.

"Copper's life. You'll get no sympathy from me," he said with a grin, but in truth he admired her determination. With its long, unpredictable hours and heavy caseload, CID was a tough proposition for a single mother, and he thought Gemma managed remarkably well. It didn't do to let his compassion show, however, as she bristled at anything she could construe as special treatment.

"Cheers." He lifted his glass. "I'll drink to your adaptability anytime." They'd cooked pasta on the gas ring and served it with ready-made sauce, a green salad, a loaf of freshly baked French bread and a bottle of fairly respectable red wine—not bad fare from a kitchen the size of a broom closet.

"Oh, wait. I almost forgot." Gemma slipped out of her chair and rummaged in her handbag, retrieving a cassette tape. She popped the tape into the player on the shelf above the bed and brought the case to Kincaid. "It's Caroline Stowe, singing Violetta in *Traviata*. It's the last recording she made."

Kincaid listened to the gentle, almost melancholy strains of the overture. As they shopped, he had told Gemma about his encounter with Sharon Doyle and his visits with Trevor Simons and the vicar, and Gemma had related her interviews at the Coliseum. She'd given her usual attention to detail, but there had been an added element in her recital, an interest which stretched beyond the bounds of the case.

"This is the drinking song," she said as the music changed. "Alfredo sings about his carefree life, before he meets Violetta." Toby banged his cup enthusiastically on the table in time to the rollicking music. "Listen, now," Gemma said softly. "That's Violetta."

The voice was darker, richer than he'd expected, and even in the first few phrases he could hear its emotional power. He looked at Gemma's rapt face. "You're fascinated by all this, aren't you?"

Gemma sipped her wine, then said slowly, "I suppose I am. I never would have thought it. But there's something . . ." She looked away from him and busied herself cutting Toby's pasta into smaller pieces.

"I don't think I've ever seen you at a loss for words, Gemma," Kincaid said, a little amused. "You're more likely to be guilty of the opposite sin. What is it?"

She looked up at him, pushing a stray copper hair from her cheek. "I don't know. I can't explain it," she said, but her hand went to her chest in a gesture more eloquent than words.

"Did you buy this today?" he asked, tapping the cassette case. A younger Caroline Stowe looked back at him, her delicate beauty accented by the nineteenth-century costume she wore.

"At the ENO shop."

He grinned at her. "You're converted, aren't you? A proselyte. I'll tell you what—you interview Caroline Stowe tomorrow. We still need a more detailed account of her movements on Thursday evening. And you can satisfy your curiosity."

"What about the autopsy?" she asked, wiping Toby's hands with a cloth. "I'd expected to go with you." She patted Toby on the bottom as she scooted him out of his chair with a whispered, "Jammy time, love."

Watching her, Kincaid said, "I'll manage it myself this time. You stay in town until you manage to see Tommy Godwin, then drive to Badger's End and tackle Dame Caroline."

She opened her mouth to protest, but closed it again after a moment and returned to collecting salad on her fork. Attending autopsies was a particular point of honor with her, and Kincaid felt surprised she hadn't offered more of an objection.

"I've put Thames Valley onto tracing Kenneth Hicks," he said, pouring a little more wine into his glass.

"The bookie's runner? Why would he want to get rid of his source of cash? They'll never collect anything from Connor Swann now."

Kincaid shrugged. "Maybe they wanted to make an example of him, start a few rumors among the big gamblers—this is what's in store if you don't pay up, mate."

Gemma finished her pasta and pushed her plate away, then picked up another piece of bread and buttered it in an absent-minded way. "But he did pay up, regularly. A bookie's dream, I should think."

"They could have had an argument over a payment. Maybe Connor found Kenneth was skimming off the top, threatened to tell the boss."

"We don't know that he was." Gemma stood up and began clearing their dishes. "We don't know much of anything, for that matter." Setting down the stack of plates again, she ticked off on her fingers, "We need to map out Connor's day. We know he had lunch at Badger's End, and that he was meeting someone, but we don't know who. Why did he go to London? Who did he see at the Coliseum? Where did he go that night, after he came back from London? Who did he see then?"

Kincaid grinned at her. "Well, that at least gives us someplace to start," he said, viewing a return of her usual combativeness with relief.

After Gemma had put Toby to bed, he tried to help with the washing up, but the kitchen would not hold more than one at a time. "Sardines?" Kincaid suggested as he squeezed in behind her to put away the bread. The top of her head fit just under his chin, and he was suddenly aware of the curves of her body, aware of how easy it would be to put his hands on her shoulders and hold her against him. Her hair tickled his nose and he stepped back to sneeze.

Gemma turned and gave him a look he couldn't read, then said brightly, "Try the chair, why don't you, while I finish up."

Eyeing the curving chrome-and-black leather article dubiously, Kincaid said, "Are you sure it's not an instrument of torture? Or a sculpture?" But when he lowered himself gingerly into it, he found it enormously comfortable.

His expression must have given him away, because Gemma laughed and said, "You didn't trust me."

She pulled a dining chair near him and they chatted amiably, finishing their wine. He felt at peace, free of the restless tension that had disturbed him earlier, reluctant to maneuver himself out of the chair and go home. But when he saw her smother a yawn, he said, "Early start for both of us. I'd better be off." She didn't demur.

It was only as he drove home that he realized he hadn't told her of Sharon Doyle's accusations that Julia Swann had killed her husband. Hysteria, he thought, shrugging. Not worth recounting.

A small voice reminded him that neither had he told her of Julia's illness after her brother's death, and his only excuse for this omission was that telling the vicar's story smacked of betrayal in a way he couldn't explain.

Backstage at the Coliseum should have prepared Gemma for Lilian Baylis House, but Alison's description had misled her. "A big, old house, a bit difficult to get to. Used to be a recording studio for Decca Records." From that Gemma envisioned a genteel place, set back in a large garden, populated by ghosts of rock stars.

"Bit difficult to get to" had proved to be more than an understatement. Not even her well-thumbed *London A to Z* prevented her from arriving a half-hour late for her appointment with Tommy Godwin, flustered, her hair escaping from its clip and her breath coming hard after a three-block sprint from the only available parking space. She felt the beginnings of a blister where her new shoe rubbed her heel.

The dark blue sign with its white ENO legend identified the

house easily enough, which was just as well, as it bore no resemblance whatsoever to Gemma's fantasy. A square, heavy house with soot-darkened red brick, it stood sandwiched between a dry cleaners and an auto-parts shop in a busy shopping street just off the Finchley Road.

Squelching the thought that she might not have become so hopelessly muddled if she'd had her mind on her driving instead of Kincaid's visit the previous evening, she tucked a stray hair into place and pulled open the door.

A man leaned against the doorjamb of the receptionist's cubicle, chatting with a young woman in jeans. "Ah," he said, straightening up and holding a hand out to Gemma, "I see we won't have to send your colleagues out searching for you, after all, Sergeant. It is Sergeant James, is it not?" He looked down the considerable length of his nose at her, as if assuring himself he hadn't made a mistake. "Had a bit of trouble getting here, I'd say, from the look of you." As the young woman handed Gemma a clipboard similar to the one Danny had used at the Coliseum, he looked at her and shook his head. "You really should have warned her, Sheila. Not even London's finest can be expected to navigate the wilds north of the Finchley Road without a snag."

"It was rather dreadful," Gemma said with feeling. "I knew where you were, but I couldn't get here from there, if you see what I mean. I'm still not quite sure how I did."

"No doubt you'd like to powder your nose," he said, "before you have your wicked way with me. I'm Tommy Godwin, by the way."

"So I'd gathered," retorted Gemma, escaping gratefully to the loo. Once safely behind the closed door, she surveyed her reflection in the fly-specked mirror with dismay. Her navy suit, Marks and Sparks best, might as well have been jumble sale beside Tommy Godwin's casual elegance. Everything about the man, from the nubby silk of his sport jacket to the warm shine of his leather slip-on shoes, spoke of taste, and of the money spent to indulge it. Even his tall, thin frame lent itself to the act, and his fair, graying hair was sleekly and expensively barbered. A swipe of lipstick and a comb provided little defense, but Gemma did the best she could, then squared her shoulders and went out to regain charge of her interview.

She found him in the same relaxed posture as before. "Well then, Sergeant, feeling better?"

"Much, thank you. Is there somewhere we could have a word?"

"We might steal five uninterrupted minutes in my office. Up the stairs, if you don't mind." He propelled her forward with a light hand upon her back, and Gemma felt she'd once again been out-maneuvered. "This is officially the buying office, the costume coordinator's domain," he continued, ushering her through a door at the top of the stairs, "but we all use it. As you might guess."

Every available inch of the small room seemed to be covered—papers and costume sketches spilled from the worktables onto the floor, bolts of fabric leaned together in corners like old drunkards propping one another up and shelves on the walls held rows of large black books.

"Bibles," said Godwin, following her gaze. Gemma's face must have registered her surprise, because he smiled and added, "That's what they're called, really. Look." He ran his finger along the bindings, then pulled one down and opened it on the worktable. "Kurt Weill's *Street Scene*. Every production in rep has its own bible, and as long as that production is performed the bible is adhered to in the smallest possible detail."

Gemma watched, fascinated, as he slowly turned the pages. The detailed descriptions of sets and costumes were accompanied by brightly colored sketches, and each costume boasted carefully matched fabric swatches as well. She touched the bit of red satin glued next to a full-skirted dress. "But I thought . . . well, that every time you put on an opera it was different, new."

"Oh no, my dear. Productions sometimes stay in rep as long as ten or fifteen years, and are often leased out to other companies. This production, for instance"—he tapped the page—"is a few years old, but if it should be done next year in Milan, or Santa Fe, their Wardrobe will be responsible for securing this exact fabric, down to the dye lot, if possible." Gently closing the book, he sat on the edge of a drafting stool and crossed his long legs, displaying the perfection of his trouser crease. "There are some up-and-coming directors who insist that a show they've originated mustn't be done without them, no matter where it's performed. Upstarts, the lot of them."

Making an effort to resist the fascination of the brightly colored pages, Gemma gently closed the book. "Mr. Godwin, I understand you attended last Thursday evening's performance at the Coliseum."

"Back to business, is it, Sergeant?" He drew his brows together in mock disappointment. "Well, if you must, you must. Yes, I popped in for a bit. It's a new production, and I like to keep an eye on things, make sure one of the principals doesn't need a nip here or a tuck there."

"Do you usually drop in on Sir Gerald Asherton after the performance as well?"

"Ah, I see you've done your homework, Sergeant." Godwin smiled at her, looking as delighted as if he were personally responsible for her cleverness. "Gerald was in particularly fine form that night—I thought it only fitting to tell him so."

Growing increasingly irritated by Tommy Godwin's manner, Gemma said, "Sir, I'm here because of the death of Sir Gerald's son-in-law, as you very well know. I understand that you've known the family for years, and under the circumstances I think your attitude is a little cavalier, don't you?"

For an instant he looked at her sharply, his thin face still, then the bright smile fell back into place. "I'm sure I deserve to be taken to task for not expressing the proper regret, Sergeant," he said, clicking his tongue against his teeth. "I've known Gerald and Caroline since we were all in nappies." Pausing, he raised an eyebrow at Gemma's look of disbelief. "Well, at least in Julia's case it's quite literally true. I was the lowest of the lowly in those days, junior assistant to the women's costume cutter. Now it takes three years of design school to qualify for that job, but in those days most of us blundered into it. My mother was a dressmaker—I knew a sewing machine inside and out by the time I was ten."

If that were the case he'd certainly done a good job of acquiring his upper-middle-class veneer, thought Gemma. Her surprise must have shown, because he smiled at her and added, "I had a talent for copying as well, Sergeant, that I've put to good use.

"Junior assistant cutters don't fit the principals' costumes, but sometimes they are allowed to fit the lesser luminaries, the has-beens and the rising stars. Caro was a fledgling in those days, still too young to have mastered control of that marvelous natural talent, but ripe with potential. Gerald spotted her in the chorus and made her his protégée. He's thirteen years her elder—did you know that, Sergeant?" Godwin tilted his head and examined her critically, as if making sure he had his pupil's attention. "He had a reputation to consider, and oh, my, tongues did wag when he married her."

"But I thought—"

"Oh, no one remembers that now, of course. It was all a very long time ago, my dear, and their titles weren't even a twinkle in the Queen's eye."

The hint of weariness in his voice aroused her curiosity. "Is that how you met Caroline, fitting her costumes?"

"You're very astute, Sergeant. Caro had married Gerald by that time, and produced Julia. She'd sometimes bring Julia to fittings, to be fussed and cooed over, but even then Julia showed little evidence of being suitably impressed."

"Impressed by what, Mr. Godwin? I'm not sure I follow you."

"Music in general, my dear, and in particular the whole tatty, overblown world of opera." Sliding from the stool, he walked to the window and stood, hands in his pockets, looking down into the street. "It's like a bug, a virus, and I think some people have a predisposition for catching it. Perhaps it's genetic." He turned and looked at her. "What do you think, Sergeant?"

Gemma fingered the costume sketches lying loose on the table, thinking of the chill that had gripped her as she heard *Traviata*'s finale for the first time. "This . . . predisposition has nothing to do with upbringing?"

"Certainly not in my case. Although my mother had a fondness for dance bands during the war." Hands still in his pockets, he did

119

a graceful little box-step, then gave Gemma a sideways glance. "I always imagined I was conceived after a night spent swinging to Glen Miller or Benny Goodman," he added with a mocking half-smile. "As for Caroline and Gerald, I don't think it ever occurred to them that Julia wouldn't speak their language."

"And Matthew?"

"Ah, well, Matty was a different story all together." He turned away again as he spoke, then fell silent, gazing out the window.

Why, wondered Gemma, did she meet this stone wall every time she brought up Matthew Asherton? She remembered Vivian Plumley's words: "We don't talk about that," and it seemed to her that twenty years should have provided more solace.

"Nothing was ever the same after Caro left the company," Godwin said softly. He turned to Gemma. "Isn't that what they always say, Sergeant, the best times of one's life are only recognized in retrospect?"

"I wouldn't know, sir. It seems a bit cynical to me."

"Ah, but you've contradicted yourself, Sergeant. I can see you do have an opinion."

"Mr. Godwin," Gemma said sharply, "my opinion is not in question here. What did you and Sir Gerald talk about last Thursday night?"

"Just the usual pleasantries. To be honest, I don't remember. I can't have been there more than five or ten minutes." He came back to the stool and leaned against the edge of its seat. "Do take the weight off, Sergeant. You'll go back to your station and accuse me of dreadful manners."

Gemma kept firmly to her position, back against the worktable. She was finding this interview difficult enough without conducting the rest of it on a level with Tommy Godwin's elegant belt buckle. "I'm fine, sir. Did Sir Gerald seem upset or behave in an unusual way?"

Glancing down his long nose, he said with mild sarcasm, "As in dancing about with a lampshade on his head? Really, Sergeant, he seemed quite the ordinary fellow. Still a bit charged up from the performance, but that's only to be expected."

"Had he been drinking?"

"We had a drink. But it's Gerald's custom to keep a bottle of good single-malt whiskey in his dressing room for visitors, and I can't say I've ever seen him any the worse for it. Thursday night was no exception."

"And you left the theater after your drink with Sir Gerald, Mr. Godwin?"

"Not straight away, no. I did have a quick word with one of the girls in Running Wardrobe." The coins in his pocket jingled softly as he shifted position.

"How long a word, sir? Five minutes? Ten minutes? Do you remember what time you signed out with Danny?"

"Actually, Sergeant, I didn't." He ducked his head as sheepishly as an errant schoolboy. "Sign out, that is. Because I hadn't signed in, and that's quite frowned upon."

"You hadn't signed in? But I thought it was required of everyone."

"In theory it is. But it's not a high-security prison, my dear. I must admit I wasn't feeling entirely sociable when I arrived on Thursday evening. The performance had already started when I came in through the lobby, so I just gave one of the ushers a wink and stood in the back." He smiled at Gemma. "I've spent too much of my working life on my feet, I suppose, to feel comfortable staying in one position for very long." As if to demonstrate, he left the drafting stool and came to stand near Gemma. Lifting a swatch of tartan satin from the table, he hefted it, then ran his fingers over its surface. "This ought to do nicely for *Lucia*—"

"Mr. Godwin. Tommy." Gemma's use of his first name caught his attention, and for an instant she saw again the stillness beneath his surface prattle. "What did you do when the performance finished?"

"I've told you, I went straight to Gerald's—" He stopped as Gemma shook her head. "Oh, I see what you mean. How did I get to Gerald's dressing room? It's quite simple if you know your way around the warren, Sergeant. There's a door in the auditorium that leads to the stage, but it's unmarked, of course, and I doubt anyone in the audience would ever notice it."

"And you left the same way? After you spoke to Sir Gerald

and"—"Gemma paused and flipped back through her notes—"the girl in Running Wardrobe."

"Got it in one, my dear."

"I'm surprised you found the lobby doors still unlocked."

"There are always a few stragglers, and the ushers have to tidy up."

"And I don't suppose you remember what time this was, or that anyone saw you leave," Gemma said with an edge of sarcasm.

Rather contritely, Tommy Godwin said, "I'm afraid not, Sergeant. But then one doesn't think about having to account for oneself, does one?"

Determined to break through his air of polished innocence, she pushed him a little more aggressively. "What did you do when you left the theater, Tommy?"

He propped one hip on the edge of the worktable and folded his arms. "Went home to my flat in Highgate, what else, dear Sergeant?"

"Alone?"

"I live alone, except for my cat, but I'm sure she'll vouch for me. Her name is Salome, by the way, and I must say it suits—"

"What time did you arrive home? Do you by any chance remember that?"

"I do, actually." He paused and smiled at her, as if anticipating praise. "I have a grandfather clock and I remember it chiming not long after I came in, so it must have been before midnight."

Stalemate. He couldn't prove his statements, but without further evidence she had no way to disprove them. Gemma stared at him, wondering what lay beneath his very plausible exterior. "I'll need your address, Mr. Godwin, as well as the name of the person you spoke to after you saw Sir Gerald." She tore a page from her notebook and watched as he wrote the information in a neat left-handed script. Running back through the interview in her mind, she realized what had been nagging her, and how deftly Tommy Godwin had sidestepped.

"Just how well did you know Connor Swann, Mr. Godwin? You never said."

He carefully capped her pen and returned it, then began folding the paper into neat squares. "I met him occasionally over the years, of course. He wasn't exactly my cup of tea, I must say. It baffled me that Gerald and Caro continued to put up with him when even Julia wouldn't, but then perhaps they knew something about him that I didn't." He raised an eyebrow and gave Gemma a half-smile. "But then one's judgment of character is always fallible, don't you find, Sergeant?"

CHAPTER

8

The High Wycombe roundabout reminded Kincaid of a toy he'd had as a child, a set of interlocking plastic gears that had revolved merrily when one turned a central crank. But in this case five mini-roundabouts surrounded a large one, humans encased in steel boxes did the revolving, and no one in the Monday morning crush was the least bit merry. He saw an opening in the oncoming traffic and shot into it, only to be rewarded by a one-fingered salute from an impatient lorry driver. "Same to you, mate," Kincaid muttered under his breath as he escaped gratefully from the last of the mini-roundabouts.

A holdup on the M40 had delayed him, and he arrived at High Wycombe's General Hospital a half-hour late for the postmortem. Kincaid tapped on the door of the autopsy room and opened it just enough to put his head in. A small man in green surgical scrubs stood facing the stainless-steel table, his back to Kincaid. "Dr. Winstead, I presume?" Kincaid asked. "Sorry I'm late." He entered the room and let the door swing shut behind him.

Winstead tapped the foot switch on his recorder as he turned. "Superintendent Kincaid?" He edged the microphone away from his mouth with the back of his wrist. "Sorry I can't shake," he added, holding up his gloved hands in demonstration. "You've missed most of the fun, I'm afraid. Started a bit early, trying to catch up on the backlog. Should have had your fellow done Saturday, yesterday at the latest, but we had a council housing fire. Spent the weekend identifying remains."

Tubby, with a mop of curly, graying hair and boot-button black eyes, Winstead lived up to his sobriquet. Kincaid found himself thinking that his vision of Pooh Bear with scalpel in hand hadn't been too far off the mark. And like many forensic pathologists Kincaid had come across, Winstead seemed unfailingly jolly. "Find anything interesting?" Kincaid inquired, just as glad that Winstead's body blocked part of his view of the steel table. Although he'd grown accustomed to the gaping Y-incision and peeled-forward scalp, he never enjoyed the sight.

"Nothing to jump for joy over, I'm afraid." He turned his back on Kincaid, his gloved hands again busy. "One or two things to finish up, then we could nip over to my office, if you like."

Kincaid stood watching, the cold air from the vents blowing in torrents down the back of his neck. At least there wasn't much smell to contend with, cold water and refrigeration having done a good bit toward retarding the body's natural processes. Although he could look at almost anything, he still had to fight the gag response triggered by the odor of a ripe corpse.

A young woman in scrubs came in, saying, "Ready for me, Winnie?"

"I'll just leave the tidying up to my assistant," Winstead said over his shoulder to Kincaid. "She likes to do the pretty work. Don't you, Heather darling?" he added, smiling at her. "Gives her a sense of job satisfaction." He peeled off his gloves, tossed them in a rubbish bin and scrubbed his hands at the sink.

Heather rolled her eyes indulgently. "He's just jealous," she said sotto voce to Kincaid, "because I'm neater than he is." She slipped on a pair of gloves and continued. "This chap's mum would be proud of him by the time I'm finished, isn't that so, Winnie?"

At least Connor Swann's adoring mum had been spared admiring Heather's handiwork, thought Kincaid. He wondered if Julia would defy convention to the extent of avoiding the mortuary and the funeral.

As Winstead ushered Kincaid from the room he said, "She's right, I'm afraid. I get the job done, but she's a perfectionist, and her hand is much finer than mine." He led Kincaid down several halls, stopping on the way to retrieve two coffees from a vending machine. "Black?" he asked, pushing buttons with familiarity.

Kincaid accepted the paper cup and sipped, finding the liquid just as dreadful as its counterpart at the Yard. He followed Winstead into his office and stopped, examining the human skull which adorned the doctor's desk. Attached to the facial surface by pins were small cylinders of rubber, each of varying height with a black number inked on its tip. "Voodoo or art, Doctor?"

"A facial reconstruction technique, lent to me by an anthropologist chum. A guess as to sex and race is made by measuring certain characteristics of the skull, then the skin depth markers are placed according to information from statistical tables. Clay is added to a thickness that conforms to the markers, and Bob's your uncle, you have a human face again. It's quite effective, actually, even if this stage does look like something from *Nightmare on Elm Street*. Heather is interested in forensic sculpture, and with her hands I don't doubt she'd be good at it."

Before Winstead wandered too far on the subject of the lovely Heather's attributes, Kincaid thought he had better redirect him. "Tell me, Doctor," he said as they settled into worn leather chairs, "did Connor Swann drown?"

Winstead knitted his brows, an exercise which made him look comical rather than fierce, and seemed to bring himself back to the body in question. "That's a pretty problem, Superintendent, as I'm sure you very well know. Drowning is impossible to prove by autopsy. It is, in fact, a diagnosis of exclusion."

"But surely you can tell if he had water in his lungs—"

"Do hold on, Superintendent, let me finish. Water in the lungs is not necessarily significant. And I didn't say I couldn't tell you anything, only that it couldn't be proved." Winstead paused and drank from his cup, then made a face. "I'm an eternal optimist, I suppose— I always expect this stuff to be better than it is. Anyway, where was I?" He smiled benignly and took another sip of his coffee.

Kincaid decided Winstead was teasing him deliberately, and that the less he fussed the faster he'd hear the results. "You were about to tell me what you *couldn't* prove."

"Gunshot wounds, stabbing, blunt trauma—all fairly straightforward, cause of death easily determined. A case like this, however, is a puzzle, and I like puzzles." Winstead uttered this with such relish that Kincaid half-expected him to rub his hands together in anticipatory glee. "There are two things which contradict drowning," he continued, holding up the requisite fingers. "No foreign material present in the lungs. No sand, no nice slimy river-bottom weeds. If one inhales great gulps of water in the act of drowning, one usually takes in a few undesirable objects as well." He folded down one finger and waggled the remainder at Kincaid. "Secondly, rigor mortis was quite delayed. The temperature of the water would account for some degree of retardation, of course, but in an ordinary, garden-variety drowning the person struggles violently, depleting the ATP in their muscles, and this depletion speeds up the onset of rigor considerably."

"But what if there was a struggle before he went in the water? His throat was bruised—he might have been unconscious. Or dead."

"There are several indications that he died quite a few hours before his body was discovered," Winstead admitted. "The stomach contents were only partially digested, so unless your Mr. Swann ate a very late supper indeed, I'd guess he was dead by midnight, or as close to it as makes no difference. When the analysis of the stomach contents comes back from the lab you may be able to pinpoint that last meal."

"And the bruising—"

Winstead held up a hand, palm out like a traffic warden. "There is another possibility, Superintendent, that would account for Mr. Swann having been alive when he went in the water. Dry drowning. The throat closes at first contact with the water, constricting the airway. No water gets into the lungs. But, as the laryngospasm relaxes after death, it is impossible to prove. It would explain, however, the lack of foreign matter in the lungs."

"What causes a dry drowning, then?" Kincaid asked, willing himself again to be patient and let the doctor have his bit of fun.

"That's one of nature's little mysteries. Shock would probably be your best catchall explanation, if you must have one." Winstead paused and drank from his cup, then looked surprised that it hadn't miraculously improved in the interval since his last tasting. "Now, about this throat business you're so keen on. I'm afraid that's inconclusive as well. There was some external bruising—I understand you visited the morgue?" When Kincaid nodded, he continued, "You'll have seen it, then—but there was no corresponding internal damage, no crushing of the hyoid processes. Nor did we find any occlusion of the face or neck."

"No spots in the eyes?"

Winstead beamed at him. "Exactly. No petechiae. Of course, it's possible that either by accident or design, someone put enough pressure on his carotid arteries to render him unconscious, then shoved him in the river."

"Could a woman exert that much pressure?"

"Oh, a woman would be quite capable physically, I should think. But I would have expected more than just bruising—fingernail marks, abrasions—and there were none. He was clean as a whistle. And I doubt very much if a woman could have rendered him unconscious without her hands suffering some trauma from the struggle."

Kincaid digested this for a moment. "So what you're telling me is" —he touched the tip of one index finger to the other—"that *a:* you don't know how Connor Swann died, and if you can't give me *cause of death*, I have to assume that *b* follows: you won't hazard a guess as to *manner of death.*"

"Most drownings are accidental, and almost always alcohol-related. We won't know his blood alcohol until the report comes back from the lab, but I'd be willing to bet it was quite high. However"—up came the traffic warden hand again as Kincaid opened his mouth to speak—"if you want my off-the-record opinion . . ." Winstead sipped from his coffee again, although Kincaid had long since abandoned his, finding an inconspicuous spot for the cup among the litter on Winstead's desk. "Most accidental drownings are also fairly straightforward. Bloke goes out fishing with his friends, they all have a few too many, bloke falls in and his friends are too pissed to pull him out. Corroborating stories from several witnesses—end of case. But in this instance," the intelligent boot-button eyes fixed on Kincaid, "I'd say there are a good deal too many unanswered questions. No indications of suicide?"

Kincaid shook his head. "None."

"Then I'd say there's not much doubt he was helped into that river in one way or another, but I'd also say you're going to have a hell of a time proving it." Winstead smiled as if he'd just delivered a welcome pronouncement.

"What about time of death?"

"Sometime between when he was last seen and when he was found." Winstead chortled at his own humor. "Seriously, Superintendent, if you want my intuitive stab at it, I'd say between nineish and midnight, or perhaps nine and one o'clock."

"Thank you, I think." Kincaid stood up and held out a hand. "You've been . . . um, extremely helpful."

"Glad to be of service." Winstead shook Kincaid's hand and smiled, the Pooh Bear resemblance more pronounced than ever. "We'll get the report to you as soon as the lab work comes back. Can you find your way to the front? Cheerio, then."

As Kincaid left the office he glanced back. The skull seemed to be superimposed upon Winstead's chubby form, and as Winstead waved Kincaid could have sworn the skull grinned a little more widely.

Kincaid left the hospital feeling little further forward than before. Although now more certain of the fact, he still had no concrete proof that Connor had been murdered. Nor had he a plausible motive, or any real suspects.

Hesitating when he reached his car, he glanced at his watch. Once Gemma had managed to track down Tommy Godwin, she would be on her way to interview Dame Caroline, and as long as she was looking into the Asherton end of things, he had better concentrate on Connor. Connor was the key—until he knew more about Connor nothing else would fall into place.

It was time he did a little prying into the part of Connor's life that did not seem to be connected to the Ashertons. Using his phone, he ascertained the address of Gillock, Blackwell, Gillock and Frye, then took the road south to Maidenhead and Reading.

*   *   *

He never came to Reading without thinking of Vic. She had grown up here, gone to school here, and as he'd entered the city from the north, he made a quick detour down the street where her parents had lived. The suburb boasted comfortable semidetached houses and well-tended gardens, with an occasional garden gnome peeking tastefully from behind a hedge. He had found the neighborhood dreadful then, and he discovered that time had done nothing to soften his opinion.

Easing the car to a halt, he let the engine idle while he studied the house. So unaltered did it appear that he wondered if it had been held in some sort of stasis while time eddied around it, and he had changed and aged. He saw it as he'd seen it the first time Vic took him home to meet her parents, down to the determined shine on the brass letterbox. They had looked upon him with well-bred disapproval, dismayed that their beautiful and scholarly daughter should have taken up with a policeman, and with a stab of discomfort he remembered that he had felt faintly ashamed of his less-than-conventional family. His parents had always cared more for books and ideas than the acquisition of middleclass possessions, and his childhood in their rambling house in the Cheshire countryside had been far removed from this tidy, ordered world.

He slipped the Midget into first gear and eased out the clutch, listening to the engine's familiar sputtering response. Perhaps Vic had chosen someone more suitable for the second go-round. He, at least, was well out of it. With that thought came a sense of release and the welcome realization that he did, actually, finally, mean it.

The snarl of Reading traffic hadn't improved since his last visit, and as he sat drumming his fingers on the steering wheel in the queue for city-center parking, he remembered how much he had always disliked the place. It combined the worst of modern architecture with bad city planning, and the results were enough to make anyone's blood pressure rise.

Once he'd parked the car he found the modern block of offices which housed the advertising agency without too much difficulty. A pretty receptionist greeted him with a smile as he entered the third-floor suite. "Can I help you, sir?" she asked, and her voice held a hint of curiosity.

He knew she must be trying to catalogue him—not a familiar client or supplier, no briefcase or samples to mark him as a commercial traveler—and he couldn't resist teasing her a bit. Her short bobbed dark hair and heart-shaped face gave her an appealing innocence. "Nice office," he said, looking slowly around the reception area. Modular furniture, dramatic lighting, art-deco advertising prints carefully framed and placed—it added up, he thought, to clever use of limited funds.

"Yes, sir. Is there someone you wanted to see?" she asked a little more forcefully, her smile fading.

He removed his warrant card and handed her the open folder. "Superintendent Duncan Kincaid, Scotland Yard. I'd like to speak to someone about Connor Swann."

"Oh." She looked from his face to the card and back again, then her brown eyes filled with tears. "Isn't it just awful? We only heard this morning."

"Really? Who notified you?" he asked, casually retrieving his card.

She sniffed. "His father-in-law, Sir Gerald Asherton. He rang John—that's Mr. Frye—"

A door opened in the hallway behind her desk and a man came out, shrugging into a sport jacket. "Melissa, love, I'm off to the—" His hand up to tighten his tie, he stopped as he saw Kincaid.

"Here's Mr. Frye now," she said to Kincaid, then added to her boss, "A man from Scotland Yard, here about Connor, John."

"Scotland Yard? Connor?" Frye repeated, and his momentary bewilderment gave Kincaid a chance to study him. He judged him to be about his own age, but short, dark, and already acquiring that extra layer of padding that comes with desk-bound affluence.

Kincaid introduced himself, and Frye recovered enough to shake hands. "What can I do for you, Superintendent? I mean, from what Sir Gerald said, I didn't expect . . ."

Smiling disarmingly, Kincaid said, "I just have a few routine questions about Mr. Swann and his work."

Frye seemed to relax a bit. "Well, look, I was just going round to the pub for some lunch, and I've got a client meeting as soon as I get back. Could we talk and grab a bite at the same time?"

"Suits me." Kincaid realized that he was ravenously hungry, a not unexpected side effect of attending an autopsy, but the prospect of the culinary delights to be found in a Reading pub didn't fill him with anticipation.

As they walked the block to the pub, Kincaid glanced at his companion. Three-piece suit in charcoal gray, expensively cut, but the waistcoat strained its buttons; midday beard shadow; hair slicked back in the latest yuppie fashion; and as Kincaid matched his stride to the shorter man's, he caught the scent of musky after-shave. He thought Connor had given the same attention to his appearance—and advertising was, after all, a business of image.

They made desultory chitchat until they reached their destination, and as they entered the White Hart, Kincaid's spirits lifted considerably. Plain and clean, the pub had an extensive lunch menu chalked on a board and was filled with escapees from other offices, all busily eating and talking. He chose the plaice, with chips and salad, his stomach rumbling. Turning to Frye, he asked, "What are you drinking?"

"Lemonade." Frye grimaced apologetically. "I'm slimming, I'm afraid. I love beer, but it goes straight to my middle." He patted his waistcoat.

Kincaid bought him a lemonade and ordered a pint for himself, not feeling the least bit of guilt at giving his companion cause for envy. Carrying their drinks, they threaded their way to a small table near the window. "Tell me about Connor Swann," he said as they settled into their seats. "How long had he worked for you?"

"A little over a year. Gordon and I needed someone to do the selling, you see. We're neither of us really good at it, and we'd acquired enough clients that we thought we could justify—"

"Gordon's your partner?" Kincaid interrupted. "I thought there were three of you." He sipped his pint and wiped a bit of foam from his lip with his tongue.

"I'm sorry. I'd better start at the beginning, hadn't I?" Frye looked longingly at Kincaid's celery, sighed and went on. "I'm *Frye*, of course, Gordon is *Gillock*, and there isn't a *Blackwell*. When we went out on our own three years ago, we thought Gillock and Frye sounded like a fishmongers'." Frye smiled a little sheepishly. "The Blackwell was just to add a bit of class. Anyway, I function as creative director and Gordon does the media buying and oversees production, so we were stretched pretty thin. When we heard through a friend that Connor might be interested in an account executive's position, we thought it was just the ticket."

The barmaid appeared at their table with laden plates. Tall and blond, she might have been a Valkyrie in jeans and sweater. She bestowed a ravishing smile upon them along with their lunches and made her way back through the crowd. "That's Marian," Frye said. "We call her the Ice Maiden. Everyone's madly in love with her and she enjoys it immensely."

"Does the adjective refer to her looks or her disposition?" Kincaid looked at Frye's plate of cold salad and tucked happily into his steaming fish and chips.

"I'm not allowed fried things, either," Frye said, eyeing Kincaid's food wistfully. "Marian's disposition is sunny enough, but she's not generous with her favors. Even Connor struck out."

"Did he chat her up?"

"Does the sun rise every morning?" Frye asked sarcastically, pushing a sprig of watercress into the corner of his mouth with his little finger. "Of course Con chatted her up. It was as natural to him as breathing—" He stopped, looking stricken. "Oh Christ, that was tasteless. I'm sorry. It's just that I haven't quite taken it in yet."

Kincaid squeezed a little more lemon on his excellent fish and asked, "Did you like him? Personally, I mean."

Frye looked thoughtful. "Well yes, I suppose I did. But it's not that simple. We were quite chuffed to have him at first, as I said. Of course, we wondered why he would have left one of the best firms in London for us, but he said he'd been having domestic problems, wanted to be a bit closer to home, get out of the London rat race, that sort of thing." He took another bite of salad and chewed deliberately.

Kincaid wondered if Frye's sorrowful expression reflected his opinion of his lunch or his feelings about Connor. "And?" he prompted gently.

"I suppose it was naive of us to have believed it. But Con could be very charming. Not just with women—men liked him, too. That was part of what made him a good salesman."

"He was good at his job?"

"Oh yes, very. When he put his mind to it. But that was the problem. He was so full of enthusiasm at first—plans and ideas for everything—that I think Gordon and I were rather swept away." Frye paused. "Looking back on it, I can see that there was a kind of frantic quality to it, but I didn't realize it at the time."

"Back up just a bit," Kincaid said, his forkful of chips halted in midair. "You said you were naive to have believed Connor's reasons for coming to work for you—did you find they weren't true?"

"Let's say he left a good deal out," Frye answered ruefully. "A few months later we began hearing trickles through the grapevine about what had really happened." He drew his brows together in a frown. "Didn't his wife tell you? You have spoken to the wife?"

"Tell me what?" Kincaid avoided the question, trying to fit the vivid image of Julia in his mind into that neutral possessive. *The wife.*

Frye scraped ham salad and shredded carrot into a neat pile in the center of his plate. "Con's firm in London handled the ENO account. That's how he met her—at some reception or other. I suppose she must have attended with her family. So when she left him and he had a . . ." Looking rather embarrassed, Frye studied his plate and pushed his food around with his fork. "I guess you'd call it an emotional breakdown. Apparently he went quite bonkers—broke down crying in front of clients, that sort of thing. The firm kept it all very hush-hush—I suppose they felt they couldn't risk offending the Ashertons by publicly turning him out on his ear."

They had all been very discreet, Kincaid thought. Had compassion entered into it at all? "The firm gave him a recommendation when he came to you?"

"We wouldn't have taken him on, otherwise," Frye answered matter-of-factly.

"When did things begin to go wrong?"

An expression of guilt replaced the embarrassment on Frye's face. "It's not that Con was a total washout—I didn't mean to give you that impression."

"I'm sure you didn't," Kincaid said soothingly, hoping to forestall Frye's *let's not speak ill of the dead* qualifications.

"It was a gradual thing. He missed appointments with clients— always with a good excuse, mind you, but after a few times even good excuses begin to wear thin. He promised things we couldn't deliver—" He shook his head in remembered dismay. "That's a creative director's nightmare. And all those new accounts he was going to bring in, all those connections he had . . ."

"Didn't materialize?"

Frye shook his head regretfully. "'Fraid not."

Kincaid pushed away his empty plate. "Why did you keep him on, Mr. Frye? It certainly sounds as if he became more of a liability than an asset."

"Call me John, why don't you," Frye said. Leaning forward confidentially, he continued, "The funny thing is, a few months ago Gordon and I had just about screwed ourselves up to give him the sack, but then things started to improve. Nothing earth-shaking, but he seemed to become a bit more dependable, a bit more interested."

"Any idea what prompted the change?" Kincaid asked, thinking of Sharon and little Hayley.

Frye shrugged. "Not a clue."

"Did you know he had a girlfriend?"

"Girlfriends, you mean. Plural," Frye said with emphasis. With the resigned air of the much-married, he added, "Once my wife met him a few times, it was more than my life was worth to have a pint with him after work. She was sure he'd lead me into temptation." He smiled. "Fortunately, or unfortunately, depending on your point of view, I never had Connor's knack with women."

The lunchtime crowd had thinned. Relieved from the crush at the bar, Marian came to collect their empty plates. "Anything else, lads? A sweet? There's some smashing gâteau left—"

"Don't torment me, please." Frye put his hands over his face with a moan.

Marian scooped up Kincaid's plate and gave him a most un-icy wink. Smothering a chuckle, he thought that Frye's wife needn't have worried about Connor's influence—her husband's weaknesses obviously lay in other directions. That train of thought reminded him of a particular weakness they hadn't addressed. "Were you aware of Connor's gambling debts?"

"Debts?" Frye asked, draining the last drop of lemonade from his glass. "I knew he liked a bit of racing, but I never knew it was that serious."

"Ever hear of a chap called Kenneth Hicks?"

Frye wrinkled his brow for a moment, then shook his head. "Can't say that I have."

Kincaid pushed his chair back, then stopped as another question occurred to him. "John, did you ever meet Connor's wife, Julia?"

Frye's reaction surprised him. After a moment of rather sheepish throat-clearing, he finally looked Kincaid in the eye. "Well, um, I wouldn't say I exactly met her."

Kincaid raised an eyebrow. "How can you 'not exactly' meet someone?"

"I saw her. That is, I went to see her, and I did." At Kincaid's even more doubtful expression he colored and said, "Oh hell, I feel an idiot, a right prat. I was curious about her, after all I'd heard, so when I saw the notice in the paper of her show in Henley . . ."

"You went to the opening?"

"My wife was away at her mum's for the night, and I thought, well, why not, there's no harm in it."

"Why should there have been?" Kincaid asked, puzzled.

"I want to paint," Frye said simply. "That's why I studied art in the first place. My wife thinks it's frivolous of me—two kids to support and all that—"

"—and artists are bad influences?" Kincaid finished for him.

"Something like that." He smiled ruefully. "She does get a bit carried away sometimes. Thinks I'd bugger off and leave them to starve, I suppose, if someone waggled a paintbrush under my nose."

"What happened at the opening, then? Did you meet Julia?"

Frye gazed dreamily past Kincaid's shoulder. "She's quite strik-ing, isn't she? And her paintings . . . well, if I could paint like that, I wouldn't spend my life doing print layouts for White's Plumbing Supply and Carpetland." He gave a self-deprecating gri-mace. "But I can't." Focusing again on Kincaid, he added, "I didn't meet her, but not from lack of trying. I'd drunk my cheap cham-pagne—not without a good bit of it knocked down my shirt-front by careless elbows—and had almost made my way through the mob to her when she slipped out the front door."

"Did you follow her?"

"Eventually I elbowed my way to the door, thinking I'd at least pay my respects on my way out."

"And?" Kincaid prompted impatiently.

"She was nowhere in sight."

CHAPTER 9

The trees arched overhead, their branches interlocking like twined fingers, squeezing tighter and tighter—Gemma blew a wisp of hair from her face and said, "Silly goose." The words seemed to bounce back at her, then it was quiet again inside the car except for an occasional squeaking as the twigs and rootlets protruding from the banks brushed against the windows. The sound reminded her of fingernails on chalkboard. London and Tommy Godwin's urbane civility seemed a world away, and for a moment she wished she'd insisted on attending the autopsy with Kincaid. He had left a message for her at the Yard, summing up the rather inconclusive results.

She shifted down into second gear as the gradient grew steeper. Kincaid had been with her when she'd driven this way the first time, his presence forestalling any lurking claustrophobia. It was all quite silly, really, she chided herself. It was just a narrow road, after all, and some of her discomfort could surely be put down to her London-bred distrust of the country.

Nevertheless, she spied the turning for Badger's End with some relief, and soon bumped to a stop in the clearing before the house. She got out of the car and stood for a moment. Even in the chill air, the damp scent of leaf mold reached her nose, rich as autumn distilled.

In the stillness she heard the same curious, high-pitched humming sound she and Kincaid had noticed before. She looked up, searching for power lines, but saw only more leaves and a patch of uniformly gray sky. Perhaps it was some sort of generator or transformer, or—she smiled, her temper improving by the moment—UFOs. She'd try that one on the guv.

Her lips still curved in the hint of a smile as she rang the bell. Vivian Plumley opened the door, as she had before, but this time she smiled as she recognized Gemma. "Sergeant. Please come in."

"I'd like a word with Dame Caroline, Mrs. Plumley," Gemma responded as she stepped into the flagged hall. "Is she in?"

"She is, but she's teaching just now."

Gemma heard the piano begin, then a soprano voice singing a quick, lilting line. Words she couldn't distinguish interrupted the singing, then a second voice repeated the line. Darker and more complex than the first voice, it possessed an indefinable uniqueness. Even through the closed sitting room door, Gemma recognized it instantly. "That's Dame Caroline."

Vivian Plumley regarded her with interest. "You have a good ear, my dear. Where have you heard her?"

"On a tape," Gemma said shortly, suddenly reluctant to confess her interest.

Vivian glanced at her watch. "Come and have a cuppa. She should be finished shortly."

"What are they singing?" Gemma asked as she followed Vivian down the hall.

"Rossini. One of Rosina's arias from *The Barber of Seville*. In Italian, thank goodness." She smiled over her shoulder at Gemma as she pushed open the door into the kitchen. "Although in this household that's not the most politically correct thing to say."

"Because of the ENO's policy?"

"Exactly. Sir Gerald is quite firm in agreeing with their position. I think Caro has always preferred singing an opera in its original language, but she doesn't express her opinion too forcefully." Vivian smiled again, affectionately. The disagreement was obviously a long-standing family tradition.

"Something smells heavenly," Gemma said, taking a deep breath. After her previous visit, the kitchen seemed as comforting and familiar as home. The red Aga radiated heat like a cast-iron heart, and on its surface two brown loaves rested on a cooling rack.

"Bread's just out of the oven," Vivian said as she assembled mugs and a stoneware teapot on a tray. On the Aga a copper tea-kettle stood gently steaming.

"You don't use an electric kettle?" Gemma asked curiously.

"I'm a dinosaur, I suppose. I've never cared for gadgets. Turning her attention fully on Gemma, Vivian added, "You will have some hot bread, won't you? It's getting on for teatime."

"I had some lunch before I left London," Gemma said, remembering the cold and greasy sausage roll hastily snatched from the Yard canteen after her interview at LB House. "But yes, I'd love some, thanks." She went nearer as Vivian poured boiling water into the pot and began slicing the bread. "Whole meal?"

"Yes. Do you like it?" Vivian looked pleased. "It's my trade-mark, I'm afraid, and my therapy. It's hand kneaded twice, and takes three risings, but it puffs up in the oven like a dream." She gave Gemma a humorous glance. "And it's hard to stay frustrated with life when you've done that much pounding."

As they seated themselves at the scarred oak table, Gemma confided, "I grew up in a bakery. My parents have a small shop in Leyton. Most everything's done by machine, of course, but Mum could usually be persuaded to let us get our hands in the dough."

"It sounds a good upbringing," Vivian said approvingly as she poured tea into Gemma's mug.

A flowery cloud of steam enveloped Gemma's face. "Earl Grey?"

"You do like it, I hope? I should have asked. It's a habit—that's what I always have in the afternoons."

"Yes, thank you," Gemma answered demurely, thinking that if she were to make a practice of taking afternoon tea in houses like this, she had bloody well better learn to like it.

She ate her bread and butter in appreciative silence, wiping the last crumbs from the plate with her fingertip. "Mrs. Plumley—"

"Everyone calls me Plummy," Vivian said in invitation. "The children started it when they were tots, and it stuck. I've rather grown to like it."

"All right, then. Plummy." Gemma thought the name suited her. Even dressed as she was today, in a brightly colored running suit and coordinating turtleneck, Vivian Plumley had about her an aura of old-fashioned comfort. Noticing that the other woman still wore her wedding ring, Gemma half-consciously rubbed the bare finger on her left hand.

They sat quietly, drinking their tea, and in the relaxed, almost sleepy atmosphere, Gemma found that a question came as easily as if she had been talking to friend. "Didn't you find it odd that Connor stayed on such close terms with the family after he and Julia separated? Especially with no children involved . . ."

"But he knew them first, you see, Caro and Gerald. He'd met them through his job, and cultivated them quite actively. I remember thinking at the time that he seemed quite smitten with Caro, but then she's always collected admirers the way other people collect butterflies."

Although Plummy had uttered this without the least hint of censure, Gemma had a sudden vision of a struggling moth pinned ruthlessly to a board. "Ugh," she said, wrinkling her nose in distaste. "I could never stand the thought."

"What?" asked Plummy. "Oh, butterflies, you mean. Well, perhaps it was an unkind comparison, but men always seem to flutter so helplessly around her. They think she needs looking after, but the truth of it is that she's quite capable of looking after herself. Personally, I can't imagine it." She smiled at Gemma. "I don't think I've ever inspired that desire in anyone."

Gemma thought of Rob's automatic assumption that she would provide for his every need, both physical and emotional. It had never occurred to him that she might have a few of her own. She said. "I never thought of it quite like that, but men haven't fallen over themselves trying to look after me, either." Sipping her tea, she continued, "About Dame Caroline—you said you were at school together. Did she always want to sing?"

Plummy laughed. "Caro was front and center from the day she was born. At school she sang the leading part in every program. Most of the other girls quite despised her, but she never seemed to notice. She might as well have worn blinkers—she knew what she wanted and she never gave a thought to anything else."

"She launched her career quite early for a singer, didn't she?" Gemma asked, remembering the snippets she'd heard from Alison Douglas.

"That was partly Gerald's doing. He plucked her out of the chorus and set her down center-stage, and she had the drive and ambition to meet the challenge, if not the experience." She reached out and broke a corner from a slice of the bread she'd set on the table, then took an experimental nibble. "Just checking," she said, smiling at Gemma. "Quality control." Taking a sip of her tea, she continued, "But you realize that this all happened more than thirty years ago, and there are only a few of us who remember Gerald and Caro before they were leading lights."

Gemma contemplated this for a moment, following Plummy's example and reaching for another slice of bread. "Do they like being reminded that they were ordinary once?"

"I think there is a certain comfort in it."

What had it been like for Julia, Gemma wondered, growing up in her parents' shadow? It was difficult enough under any circumstances to shake off one's parents' influence and become a self-governing individual. She washed her bite of bread down with tea before asking, "And that's how Julia met Connor? Through her parents?"

After a moment's thought, Plummy said, "I believe it was an ENO fund-raising reception. In those days Julia still occasionally attended musical functions. She was just beginning to make her mark as an artist, and she hadn't completely left her parents' orbit." She shook her head. "It took me by surprise from the start—Julia had always preferred the sort of intellectual and arty types, and Con was about as far removed from that as one could imagine. I tried talking to her, but she wouldn't hear a word of it."

"And were they as ill-matched as you thought?"

"Oh yes," she answered with a sigh, swirling the tea in the bottom of her cup. "More so."

When Plummy didn't elaborate, Gemma asked, "Did you know that Connor had been seeing someone?"

She looked up in surprise. "Recently, you mean? A girlfriend?"

"A young woman with a small daughter."

"No. No, I didn't." With the compassion Gemma had begun to expect of her, Plummy added, "Oh, the poor thing. I suppose she will have taken his death quite badly."

The words *unlike Julia* seemed to hang unspoken between them. "She's moved back, you know," said Plummy. "Julia. Into the flat. I told her I didn't think it looked well at all, but she said it was her flat, after all, and she had the right to do whatever she liked with it."

Gemma thought of the upstairs studio, empty of Julia Swann's disturbing presence, and felt an unaccountable sense of relief. "When did she go?"

"This morning, early. She has missed her studio, poor love—I never understood why she let Con stay on in the house. But there's no reasoning with her once she's made up her mind about something."

The exasperated affection in Plummy's voice reminded Gemma of her own mum, who swore that her red-haired daughter had been born stubborn. Not that Vi Walters was one to talk, Gemma thought with a smile. "Was Julia always so headstrong?"

Plummy regarded her steadily for long moment, then said, "No, not always." She glanced at her watch. "Have you finished your tea, dear? Caro should be free by now, and she has another student coming this afternoon, so we'd better sandwich you in between."

"Caro, this is Sergeant James," Plummy announced as she ushered Gemma into the sitting room. Then she withdrew, and Gemma felt the draft of cool air as the door clicked shut.

Caroline Stowe stood with her back to the fire, as had her husband when Gemma and Kincaid had interviewed him two days earlier. She stepped toward Gemma with her hand outstretched. "How nice to meet you, Sergeant. How can I help you?"

Her hand felt small and cool in Gemma's, as soft as a child's. Involuntarily, Gemma glanced at the photograph on the piano. While it had given her a hint of the woman's feminine delicacy, it hadn't begun to express her vitality. "It's just a routine follow-up on the report you gave Thames Valley CID, Dame Caroline," said Gemma, and her own voice sounded harsh in her ears.

"Sit down, please." Dame Caroline moved to the sofa and patted the cushion invitingly. Over white wool trousers she wore a long garnet-colored sweater. The soft cowl neck framed her face, its color the perfect foil for her pale skin and dark hair.

Gemma, who had dressed with particular care that morning, suddenly found her favorite olive silk skirt and blouse as drab as camouflage, and as she sat down she felt awkward and clumsy. A flush of embarrassment warmed her cheeks and she said quickly, "Dame Caroline, I understand from your initial statement that you were at home last Thursday evening. Can you tell me what you did?"

"Of course, Sergeant, if you find it necessary," Caroline said with an air of gracious resignation. "I had dinner with Plummy—that's Vivian Plumley—then we watched something on the telly, I'm afraid I can't remember what. Does it matter?"

"Then what did you do?"

"Plummy made us some cocoa, that must have been around ten o'clock. We talked for a bit, then went to bed." Apologetically, she added, "It was a very ordinary evening, Sergeant."

"Do you remember what time your husband came in?"

"I'm afraid not. I sleep quite soundly, and we have separate beds, so he seldom disturbs me when he comes in late after a performance."

"And your daughter didn't disturb you when she returned in the early hours of the morning?" Gemma asked, wanting to shake Caroline's polished complacency just a bit.

"She did not. My daughter is a grown woman and comes and goes as she pleases. I'm not in the habit of keeping tabs on her whereabouts."

Bull's-eye, thought Gemma. She'd hit a sensitive spot. "I understand from Mrs. Plumley that your daughter has gone back to the flat she shared with Connor. Did you approve of her being on her own again so soon, considering the circumstances?"

Caroline seemed to bite back a response, then sighed. "I thought it rather ill-advised, but then my approval has never had much effect on Julia's actions. And she has behaved very badly over Connor's death from the first." Looking suddenly tired, Caroline rubbed her fingers over her cheekbones, but Gemma noticed that she didn't stretch the skin.

"In what way?" Gemma asked, although she'd had proof enough that Julia wasn't playing the grieving widow to perfection.

Shrugging, Caroline said, "There are things that must be done, and people have certain expectations . . . Julia has simply not met her obligations."

Gemma wondered if Julia would have done what was necessary if she hadn't been sure her parents would step in and take care of everything. The fact that Julia seemed to resent them doing so only served to illustrate the perversity of human nature, and Gemma had begun to think that their relationship might be more perverse than most. She turned a page in her small notebook, running through her questions in her mind. "I believe Connor came here for lunch last Thursday?" At Caroline's nod, she continued, "Did you notice anything unusual about his behavior that day?"

Smiling, Caroline said, "Con was very entertaining, but there was nothing unusual about that."

"Do you remember what you talked about?" Gemma asked, and as she watched Caroline ponder the question, she realized she'd never before seen a woman capable of furrowing her brow prettily.

"Oh, nothing memorable or weighty, Sergeant. Local gossip, Gerald's performance that night—"

"So Connor knew your husband would be in London?"

Looking perplexed, Caroline answered, "Well, of course, Con knew Gerald would be in London."

"Do you know why Connor would have visited the Coliseum that same afternoon?"

"I can't imagine. He certainly didn't say anything to us about going to London—are you saying he visited the theater?"

"According to the porter's sign-in sheet, but no one else admits to seeing him."

"How very odd," Caroline said slowly, and for the first time Gemma sensed her departing from a comfortably rehearsed script. "Of course, he did leave in rather a tiz—"

"What happened?" Gemma felt a prickle of excitement. "You said he hadn't done anything out of the ordinary."

"I don't know that I'd describe it as out of the ordinary. Con was never very much good at sitting still. He excused himself for a moment while Gerald and I were having our coffee. He said he meant to give Plummy a hand in the kitchen, and that's the last we saw of him. A few minutes later we heard his car start up."

"And you thought something had upset him?"

"Well, I suppose we did think it a bit odd that he hadn't told us good-bye."

Gemma turned carefully back through the pages of her notebook, then looked up at Caroline. "Mrs. Plumley said she did the washing up alone. She didn't see Connor again after she left the dining room. Do you think he went upstairs to see Julia? And perhaps they had a row?"

Caroline clasped her hands in her lap, and the shadows shifted on the garnet sweater as she took a breath. "I can't say, Sergeant. If that were the case I'm sure Julia would have said something."

Gemma didn't share her sentiments. "Did you know that Connor had a girlfriend, Dame Caroline? Technically, I suppose she would have been his mistress, since he and Julia were still married."

"A girlfriend? Con?" Caroline said quietly, then as she looked into the fire she added more softly still, "He never said."

Remembering what Kincaid had told her, Gemma said, "Her name is Sharon Doyle, and she has a four-year-old daughter. Apparently it was a fairly serious relationship, and he . . . um, entertained her quite often at the flat."

"A child?" Caroline returned her gaze to Gemma. Her dark eyes had dilated and Gemma saw the fire reflected in their liquid and luminous surface.

The afternoon had drawn in as they talked, and now the fire and the lamps cast a noticeable glow in the quiet room. Gemma could imagine serene hours spent here with music and conversation, or time whiled away on the comfortably worn chintz sofa with a book, but never voices raised in anger. "What if Julia found out about Sharon? Would they have argued over it? Would Julia have liked Connor having another woman in her flat?"

After a long moment, Caroline said, "Julia is often a law unto herself, Sergeant. I can't begin to guess how she would react to a given situation. And why does it matter anyway?" she added wearily. "Surely you don't think Julia had anything to do with Con's death?"

"We're trying to find an explanation for Connor's behavior that last afternoon and evening. He made an unexpected visit to the theater. He also met someone later that evening, after he'd returned to Henley, but we don't yet know who it was."

"What do you know?" Caroline straightened her back and regarded Gemma directly.

"The results of the autopsy didn't tell us much. We're still waiting on some of the forensic reports—all we can do until then is gather information."

"Sergeant, I think you're being deliberately vague," said Caroline, teasing her a little.

Unwilling to be drawn any further, Gemma focused on the first thing that came to mind. She'd been absently examining the paintings Kincaid and Julia had talked about—what had Julia said the painter was called? Flynn? No, Flint. That was it. The rosy bare-breasted women were voluptuous, somehow innocent and slightly decadent at the same time, and the sheen of their satin gowns made Gemma think of the costume fabrics she'd seen that morning at LB House. "I met an old friend of yours today, Dame Caroline. Tommy Godwin."

"Tommy? Good God, what on earth could you possibly want with Tommy?"

"He's very clever, isn't he?" Gemma settled back more comfortably on the sofa and tucked her notebook into her bag. "He told me a lot about the early days, when you were all starting out with the Opera. It must have been terribly exciting."

Caroline's expression softened. She gazed absently into the fire, and after a moment said, "It was glorious. But, of course, I didn't realize quite how special it was, because I had nothing to compare it to. I thought that life could only get better, that everything I touched would turn to gold." She met Gemma's eyes again. "Well, that's the way of it, isn't it, Sergeant? You learn that the charmed times can't last."

The words held an echo of such sorrow that Gemma felt their weight upon her chest. The photographs on the piano pulled at her insistently, but she kept her eyes on Caroline's face. She had no need to look at them—Matthew Asherton's smiling image had burned itself upon her memory. Taking a breath, she said with a daring born out of her own fear, "How do you manage to go on?"

"You protect what you have." Caroline said quietly, vehemently. Then she laughed, breaking the spell. "Tommy wasn't quite so elegant in those days, though you wouldn't think it to look at him now. He shed his background like a snake sloughing off its skin, but he hadn't completed the process. There were still a few rough edges."

Gemma said, "I can't imagine," and they both laughed.

"Tommy was never less than amusing, even at his least polished. We did have some lovely times . . . and we had such vision. Gerald and Tommy and I—we were going to change the face of opera." Caroline smiled fondly.

How could you bear to give it up? thought Gemma. Aloud, she said, "I've heard you sing. I bought a tape of *Traviata*. It's marvelous."

Caroline folded her arms loosely under her breasts and stretched her dainty feet toward the fire. "It is, isn't it? I've always loved singing Verdi. His heroines have a spiritual quality that you don't find in Puccini, and they allow you more room for interpretation. Puccini you must sing exactly as it's written or it becomes vulgar—with Verdi you must find the heroine's heart."

"That's what I felt when I listened to Violetta," Gemma said with delight. Caroline had given definition to her own vaguely formed impressions.

"Do you know the history of *Traviata?*" When Gemma shook her head, Caroline continued. "In Paris in the 1840s there lived a young courtesan named Marie Duplessis. She died on the second of February, 1846, just nineteen days after her twenty-second birthday. Among her numerous lovers in her last year were Franz Liszt and Alexandre Dumas, *fils*. Dumas wrote a play based on Marie's life called *La Dame aux Camélias,* or *Camille*—"

"And Verdi adapted the play as *Traviata.*"

"You've been swotting," said Caroline in mock disappointment.

"Not really, just reading the liner notes. And I didn't know that Violetta was based on a real person."

"Little Marie is buried in the cemetery at Montmartre, just below the church of Sacre Coeur. You can visit her grave."

Gemma found herself unable to ask if Caroline herself had made such a pilgrimage—it came too near the forbidden territory of Matthew's death. She shivered a little at the thought of such waste. Marie Duplessis must have held on to her life with all the passion Verdi wrote into Violetta's music.

A bell rang, echoing in the passage outside the sitting room. The front door—Plummy had said Caroline had another student coming. "I'm sorry, Dame Caroline. I've kept you too long." Gemma slid the strap of her handbag over her shoulder and stood up. "Thank you for your time. You've been very patient."

Caroline rose and once again offered Gemma her hand. "Good-bye, Sergeant."

As Gemma neared the sitting room door, Plummy opened it and said, "Cecily's here, Caro."

As Gemma passed the girl in the hall, she had a brief impression of dark skin and eyes and a flashing shy smile, then Plummy ushered her gently out into the dusk. The door closed and Gemma stood breathing the cool, damp air. She shook her head to clear it, but that made the dawning realization no less uncomfortable.

She had been seduced.

"A message for you, Mr. Kincaid," Tony called out cheerfully from the bar as Kincaid entered the Chequers. "And your room's ready for you." Tony seemed to do everything around the place, and all with the same unflagging good nature. Now he fished a message slip from beneath the bar and handed it to Kincaid.

"Jack Makepeace called?"

"You've just missed him by a few minutes. Use the phone in the lounge if you like." Tony gestured toward the small sitting area opposite the bar.

Kincaid rang High Wycombe CID and shortly Makepeace came on the line. "We've run down a possible lead on your Kenneth Hicks, Superintendent. Rumor from some racing sources has it that he does his drinking in a pub in Henley called the Fox and Hounds. It's on the far side of town, off the Reading Road."

Kincaid had just come through Henley on his way from Reading, and would now have to turn right around and backtrack. He swore under his breath but didn't criticize Makepeace for not contacting him by bleeper or car phone—it wasn't worth the loss of good will. "Anything known about him?"

"No record to speak of—a few juvenile offenses. He's a petty villain from the sound of it, not a serious one. Hand in the till here and there, that sort of thing."

"Description?"

"Five foot eight or nine, nine stone, fairish hair, blue eyes. No available address. If you want to talk to him I guess you'll have to do a spot of drinking at the Fox and Hounds."

Kincaid sighed with resignation at the prospect. "Thanks, Sergeant."

Unlike the pub where he'd lunched in Reading, the Fox and Hounds turned out to be every bit as dreary as he'd imagined. The sparse late afternoon activity centered around the snooker table in the back room, but Kincaid chose the public bar, seating himself at an inadequately wiped plastic-topped table with his back against the wall. Compared to the other customers, he felt conspicuously well groomed in jeans and a fisherman's knit jersey. He sipped the foam from his pint of Brakspear's bitter and settled back to wait.

He'd killed half the pint as slowly as he could when a man came in who fitted Kenneth Hicks's general description. Kincaid watched as he leaned on the bar and said a few low words to the barman, then accepted a pint of lager. He wore expensive-looking clothes badly on his slight frame, and his narrow face had a pinched look that spoke of a malnourished childhood. Kincaid watched over the rim of his pint as the man glanced nervously around the bar, then took a seat at a table near the door.

The sneaky bugger's paranoia would have given him away even if his looks hadn't, thought Kincaid, and he smiled in satisfaction. He drank a little more of his beer, then stood and casually carried his glass across to the other man's table. "Mind if I join you?" he said as he pulled up a stool and sat down.

"What if I do?" the man answered, shrinking back and holding his glass before his body like a shield.

Kincaid could see specks of dandruff mixed with the styling cream that darkened the fair hair. "If you're Kenneth Hicks, you're out of luck, because I want a word with you."

"What if I am? Why should I talk to you?" His eyes shifted from one side of Kincaid's body to the other, but Kincaid had sat between him and the door. The gray light from the front windows illuminated the imperfections of Hicks's face—a patch of pale stubble missed, the dark spot of a shaving cut on his chin.

"Because I asked you nicely," Kincaid said as he pulled his warrant card from his hip pocket and held it open in front of Hicks's face. "Let me see some identification, if you don't mind."

A sheen of perspiration appeared on Hicks's upper lip. "Don't have to. Harassment, that's what that is."

"Oh, I don't think it's harassment at all," Kincaid said softly, "but if you like we'll call in the local lads and have our little chat in the Henley nick."

For a moment he thought Hicks would bolt, and he balanced himself a little better on the stool, his muscles tensing. Then Hicks set his glass down on the plastic table with a thump and wordlessly handed Kincaid his driving license.

"A Clapham address?" Kincaid asked after he had examined it for a moment.

"It's me mum's," Hicks said sullenly.

"But you stay here in Henley, don't you?" Kincaid shook his head. "You really should keep these things current, you know. We like to know where to find you when we want you." He pulled a notebook and pen from his pocket and slid them across the table. "Why don't you write down your address for me before we forget. Make sure you get it right, now," he added as Hicks reluctantly picked up the pen.

"What's it to you?" Hicks asked as he scribbled a few lines on the paper and shoved it back.

Kincaid held his hand out for the pen. "Well, I have a vested interest in staying in touch with you. I'm looking into Connor Swann's death, and I think you know a good deal about Connor Swann. It would be very odd if you didn't, considering the amount of money he paid you every month." Kincaid drank off another half-inch of his pint and smiled at Hicks, whose sallow skin had faded almost to green at the mention of Connor's name.

"I don't know what you're talking about," Hicks managed to squeak, and now Kincaid could smell his fear.

"Oh, I think you do. The way I heard it is that you do some unofficial collecting for a bookie here in town, and that Connor was in over his head—"

"Who told you that? If it was that little tart of his, I'll fix her—"

"You'll not touch Sharon Doyle." Kincaid leaned forward, abandoning his amiable pretense. "And you'd better hope she's not accident prone, because I'll hold you responsible if she so much as breaks a little finger. Have you got that, sunshine?" He waited until Hicks nodded, then said, "Good. I knew you were a bright boy. Now unfortunately, Connor didn't discuss his financial problems with Sharon, so you're going to have to help me out. If Connor owed money to your boss, why did he pay you directly?"

Hicks took a long pull on his lager and fumbled in his jacket pocket until he found a crumpled packet of Benson & Hedges. He lit one with a book of matches bearing the pub's name, and seemed to gather courage as he drew in the smoke. "Don't know what you're talkin' about, and you can't—"

"Connor may not have taken very good care of some parts of his life, but in others he was quite meticulous. He recorded every check he wrote—did you know that, Kenneth? You don't mind if I call you Kenneth, do you?" Kincaid added, all politeness again. When Hicks didn't reply, he continued. "He paid you large amounts on a very regular basis. I'd be curious to see how those amounts tally with what he owed your boss—"

"You leave him out of this!" Hicks almost shouted, sloshing beer on the table. He looked around to see if anyone else had heard, then leaned forward and lowered his voice to a hiss. "I'm telling you, you leave him—"

"What were you doing, Kenneth? A little loan-sharking on the side? Carrying Con's debts with interest? Somehow I don't think your boss would take too kindly to your skimming his clients like that."

"We had a private arrangement, Con and me. I helped him out when he was in trouble, same as he'd have done for me, same as any mates."

"Oh, mates, was it? Well, that puts a different complexion on it entirely. I'm sure in that case Connor didn't mind you making money off his debts." Kincaid leaned forward, hands on the edge of the table, resisting the urge to grab Hicks by the lapels of his leather bomber jacket and shake him until his brains rattled. "You're a bloodsucker, Kenneth, and with mates like you nobody needs enemies. I want to know when you saw Connor last, and I want to know exactly what you talked about, because I'm beginning to think Con got tired of paying your cut. Maybe he threatened to go to your boss—is that what happened, Kenneth? Then maybe the two of you had a little scuffle and you pushed him in the river. What do you think, sunshine? Is that how it happened?"

The bar had begun to fill and Hicks had to raise his voice a little to make himself heard over the increasing babble. "No, I'm telling you, man, it wasn't like that at all."

"What was it like?" Kincaid said reasonably. "Tell me about it, then."

"Con had a couple of really stiff losses, close together, couldn't come up with the ready. I was flush at the time so I covered him. After that it just got to be sort of a habit."

"A nasty habit, just like gambling, and one I'll bet Con got fed up with pretty quickly. Con hadn't written you a check the last few weeks before he died. Was he balking, Kenneth? Had he had enough?"

Perspiration beaded on Hicks's upper lip and he wiped it with the back of his hand. "No, man, the horses had been good to him the last couple of weeks, for a change. He paid off what he owed—we were square, I swear we were."

"That's really heartwarming, just like good little Boy Scouts. I'll bet you shook hands on it, too." Kincaid sipped from his glass again, then said conversationally, "Nice local beer, don't you think?" Before Hicks could reply he leaned across the little table until he was inches from the man's face. "Even if I believed you, which I don't, I think you'd look for some other way to soak him. You seem to know a lot about his personal life, considering your *business* arrangement. Looking for another foothold, were you, Ken? Did you find something out about Connor that he didn't want anyone else to know?"

Hicks shrank back. "Don't know what you're talkin' about, man," he said, then wiped spittle from his lower lip. "Why don't you ask that slut of his what she knows? Maybe she found out hell'd freeze over before he'd marry her." He smiled, showing nicotine-stained teeth, and Kincaid found it no improvement over his sneer. "Maybe she shoved him in the river—did you ever think about that one, Mr. Bloody Know-it-all?"

"What makes you think he wouldn't have married Sharon?"

"Why should he? Get himself stuck with a stupid little cow like that—take on some other bugger's bleedin' kid? Not on your nelly." Sniggering, Hicks pulled another cigarette from the packet and lit it from the butt of the first. "And her with a gob like a fishwife."

"You're a real prince, Kenneth," Kincaid said generously. "How do you know Sharon thought Con intended to marry her? Did she tell you?"

"Too right, she did. Said, 'He'll get shut of you then, Kenneth Hicks. I'll make sure of it.' Stupid—"

"You know, Kenneth, if you'd been the one found floating face-down in the Thames, I don't think we'd have had to look far for a motive."

"You threatening me, man? You can't do that—that's—"

"Harassment, I know. No, Kenneth, I'm not threatening you, just making an observation." Kincaid smiled. "I'm sure you had Connor's best interests at heart."

"He used to tell me things, when he'd had a few, like." Hicks lowered his voice confidentially. "Wife had him by the balls. She crooked her little finger, he'd come running with his tail between his legs. He'd had a hell of a row with her that day, the bitch—"

"What day, Kenneth?" Kincaid said very distinctly, very quietly.

Cigarette frozen halfway to his lips, Hicks stared at Kincaid like a rat surprised by a ferret. "Don't know. You can't prove nothing."

"It was the day he died, wasn't it, Kenneth? You saw Connor the day he died. Where?"

Hicks's close-set eyes shifted nervously away from Kincaid's face and he drew sharply on the cigarette.

"Spit it out, Kenneth. I'll find out, you know. I'll start by asking these nice people here." Kincaid nodded toward the bar. "Don't you think that's a good idea?"

"So what if I did have a couple of pints with him? How was I to know it was different from any other day?"

"Where and when?"

"Here, same as always. Don't know what time," Hicks said evasively, then added as he saw Kincaid's expression, "Twoish, maybe."

After lunch, Kincaid thought. Con had come straight here from Badger's End. "He told you he'd had a row with Julia? What about?"

"Don't know, do I? Nothin' to do with me." Hicks clamped his mouth shut so decisively that Kincaid changed tacks.

"What else did you talk about?"

"Nothin'. We just had a friendly pint, like. Not against the law, is it, havin' a friendly drink with a mate?" Hicks asked, voice rising as if he might be working himself up to hysteria.

"Did you see Connor again after that?"

"No, I never. Not after he left here." He took a last drag on his cigarette and ground it out in the ashtray.

"Where were you that night, Kenneth? From eight o'clock or so on?"

Shaking his head, Hicks said, "None of your friggin' business, is it? I've had enough of your bleedin' harassment. I ain't done nothin', fuckin' filth got no right to keep after me." He shoved his empty glass away and pushed back on his stool, watching Kincaid, the whites of his eyes showing beneath the irises.

Kincaid debated the benefit of pushing him any farther, and decided against it. "All right, Kenneth, have it your way. But stay around where I can find you, just in case we need to have another little visit." Hicks's stool screeched against the floor as he stood up. As he pushed past, Kincaid reached up and sank his fingers into the sleeve of his leather jacket. "If you even think about disappearing, boyo, I'll have the lads after you so fast you won't be able to find a hole big enough to hide your skinny backside. Do we understand each other, mate?"

After a long moment, Hicks nodded and Kincaid smiled and let him go. "There's a good boy, Ken. See you around."

Kincaid turned and watched Hicks scuttle out the door into the street, then he carefully wiped his fingers against his jeans.

CHAPTER
10

Not one to let good beer go to waste, Kincaid drained the last drop of his pint. He considered briefly having another, but the pub's atmosphere didn't encourage lingering.

Out in the street, he sniffed the air curiously. He'd noticed the smell when he arrived in town, but it seemed stronger now. Familiar but elusive . . . tomatoes cooking, perhaps? Finding his car free of sprayed graffiti and still in possession of its wheel covers, Kincaid stood still for a moment and closed his eyes. Hops. Of course it was hops—it was Monday and the brewery was in full operation. The wind must have shifted since he'd arrived at the pub, bringing the rich odor with it. The brewery would be closing soon, as well as most of the shops, he thought as he glanced at his watch—rush hour, such as it was, had begun in Henley.

He'd navigated his way onto the Reading Road, intent on exchanging the day's findings with Gemma back at the Chequers, when the signpost for the Station Road carpark caught his eye. Almost without thinking he found himself making the turn and pulling the car into a vacant slot. From there it was only a few hundred yards' walk down the Station Road to the river. On his right lay the boathouse flats, serene behind their iron fence in the dusk.

Something had been niggling at him—he couldn't swear to the date of the last check Connor had written Kenneth. Kincaid had never finished his interrupted search of Con's desk, and now he let himself into the flat with the key he'd used earlier, intending to have another look at the checkbook.

He stopped just inside the door. Looking around, he tried to pinpoint why the flat felt different. Warmth, for one thing. The central heating had been switched on. Con's shoes had disappeared from beneath the settee. The untidy stack of newspapers on the end table had gone as well, but something even less definable spoke of recent human occupation. He sniffed, trying to place the faint scent in the air. Something tugged at the fringes of his mind, then vanished as he heard a noise above.

He held his breath, listening, then moved quietly toward the stairs. A scrape came, then a thump. Someone moving furniture? He'd only been a few minutes behind Kenneth leaving the pub—had the little sod beat him here, bent on destroying evidence? Or had Sharon come back, after all?

Both doors on the first landing had been pulled to, but before he could investigate, the noise came again from above. He climbed the last flight of steps, carefully keeping his feet to the edge of the treads. The studio door stood open a few inches, not enough to give him a clear view into the room. Taking a breath, he used his fist to slam the door open. He charged into the room as the door bounced against the wall.

Julia Swann dropped the stack of canvases she held in her hands.

"Jesus, Julia, you gave me a fright! What the hell are you doing here?" He stood breathing hard, adrenaline still rushing through his body.

"*I* gave *you* a fright!" She stared at him wide-eyed, holding her balled hand to her chest and flattening her black sweater between her breasts. "You probably just cost me ten years off my life, Superintendent, not to mention damage to my property." She bent to retrieve her paintings. "I might ask you the same question—what are you doing in my flat?"

"It's still under our jurisdiction. I'm sorry I frightened you. I had no idea you were here." Trying to regain a semblance of authority, he added, "You should have notified the police."

"Why should I feel obliged to let the police know I'd come back to my own flat?" She sat on the rolled arm of the chair she used for a prop in her paintings and looked at him challengingly.

"Your husband's death is still under investigation, Mrs. Swann, and he did live here, in case you'd forgotten." He came nearer to her and sat on the only other available piece of furniture, her worktable. His feet dangled a few inches above the floor and he crossed his ankles to stop them swinging.

"You called me Julia before."

"Did I?" Then, it had been instinctive, involuntary. Now he used it deliberately. "Okay, Julia." He drew the syllables out. "So what are you doing here?"

"I should think that would be rather obvious." She gestured around her and he turned, examining the room. Paintings, both the small flower studies and the larger portraits, had been stacked against the walls, and a few had been hung. Dust had vanished from the visible surfaces, and some of the paints and paper familiar to him from her workroom at Badger's End had appeared on the table. She had brought in a large pot plant and placed it near the blue velvet chair—those, along with the faded Persian rug and the brightly colored books in the case behind the chair, formed the still-life tableau he'd seen in several of the paintings at the gallery.

The room felt alive once more, and he finally identified the scent that had eluded him downstairs. It was Julia's perfume.

She had slid down into the depths of the chair and sat quietly smoking with her legs stretched out, and as he looked at her he saw that her eyes were shadowed with fatigue. "Why did you give this up, Julia? It doesn't make any sense."

Studying him, she said, "You look different out of your proper policeman's kit. Nice. Human, even. I'd like to draw you." She stood suddenly and touched her fingers to the angle of his jaw, turning his head. "I don't usually do men, but you have an interesting face, good bones that catch the light well." Just as quickly, she sank into the chair again and regarded him.

He still felt the imprint of her fingers against his skin. Resisting the urge to touch his jaw, he said, "You haven't answered me."

Sighing, she ground the half-smoked cigarette into a pottery ashtray. "I don't know if I can."

"Try me."

"You would have to know how things were with us, toward the end." Idly, she rubbed the nap on the chair arm the wrong way. Kincaid waited, watching her. She looked up and met his eyes. "He couldn't pin me down. The more he tried the more frustrated he got, until finally he started imagining things."

Fastening on the first part, Kincaid asked, "What do you mean, he couldn't pin you down?"

"I was never there for him, not in the way he wanted, not when he wanted . . ." She crossed her arms as if suddenly cold and rubbed her thumbs against the fabric of her sweater. "Have you ever had anyone suck you dry, Superintendent?" Before he could answer, she added, "I can't go on calling you Super-bloody-intendent. Your name's Duncan, isn't it?" She gave his name a slight stress on the first syllable, so that he heard in it a Scots echo.

"What kind of things did Connor imagine, Julia?"

Her mouth turned down at the corners and she shrugged. "Oh, you know. Lovers, secret trysts, that sort of thing."

"And they weren't true?"

"Not then." She lifted her eyebrows and gave him a little flirtatious smile, challenging him.

"You're telling me that Connor was jealous of *you*?"

Julia laughed, and the smile that transformed her thin face moved him in a way he couldn't explain. "It's so ironic, isn't it? What a joke. Connor Swann, everyone's favorite Lothario, afraid his own wife might be messing him about." Kincaid's consternation must have shown, because she smiled again and said, "Did you think I didn't know Con's reputation? I would have to have been deaf, dumb and blind not to." Her mirth faded and she added softly, "Of course, the more I slipped away, the more women he notched on his braces. Was he punishing me? Or was he just looking for what I couldn't give him?" She stared past Kincaid at the window he knew must be darkening.

"You still haven't answered my question," he said again, but this time gently.

"What?" She came back to him from her reverie. "Oh, the flat. I was exhausted, in the end. I ran away. It was easier." They looked at each other in silence for a moment, then she said, "You can see that, can't you, Duncan?"

The words "ran away" echoed in his mind and he had a sudden vision of himself, packing up only the most necessary of possessions, leaving Vic in the flat they had chosen with such care. It had been easier, easier to start over with nothing to remind him of his failure, or of her. "What about your studio?" he said, shutting off the flow of memory.

"I've missed it, but I can paint anywhere, if I must." She leaned back in the chair, watching him.

Kincaid thought back to his earlier interviews with her, trying to put a finger on the change he sensed. She was still sharp and quick, her intelligence always evident, but the brittle nervousness had left her. "It wasn't easy for you, was it, those months you spent at Badger's End?" She stared back at him, her lips parted, and he felt again that frisson along his spine that came with knowing her in a way more intimate than words.

"You're very perceptive, Duncan."

"What about Trevor Simons? Were you seeing him then?"

"I told you, no. There wasn't anyone."

"And now? Do you love him?" A necessary question, he told himself, but the words seemed to leave his lips of their own accord.

"Love, Duncan?" Julia laughed. "Do you want to split philosophical hairs over the nature of love and friendship?" She continued more seriously, "Trev and I are friends, yes, but if you mean am I in love with him, the answer is no. Does it matter?"

"I don't know," Kincaid answered truthfully. "Would he lie for you? You did leave the opening that night, you know. I have an independent witness who saw you go."

"Did I?" She looked away from him, fumbling for the cigarette packet that had slipped under the chair. "I suppose I did, for a bit. It was rather a crush. I don't like to admit it, but sometimes things like that make me feel a little claustrophobic."

"You're still smoking too much," he said as she found the packet and lit another cigarette.

"How much is too much? You're splitting hairs again." Her smile held a hint of mischief.

"Where did you go, when you left the gallery?"

Julia stood up and went to the window, and he twisted around, watching her as she closed the blinds against the charcoal sky. Still with her back to Kincaid, she said, "I don't like bare windows, once it's dark. Silly, I know, but even up here I always feel someone might be watching me." She turned to him again. "I walked along the River Terrace for a bit, had a breath of air, that's all."

"Did you see Connor?"

"No, I didn't," she answered, coming back to her chair. This time she curled herself into it with her legs drawn up, and as she moved the bell of her hair swung against her neck. "And I doubt I was gone more than five or ten minutes."

"But you saw him earlier that day, didn't you? At Badger's End, after lunch, and you had a row."

He saw her chest move with the quick intake of breath, as if she might deny it, but she only watched him quietly for a moment before answering, "It was such a stupid thing, really, such a petty little end note. I was ashamed.

"He came upstairs after lunch, bounding in like a great overgrown puppy, and I lit into him. I'd had a letter that morning from the building society—he'd not made a payment in two months. That was our arrangement, you see," she explained to Kincaid, "that he could stay in the flat as long as he kept up the payments. Well, we argued, as you can imagine, and I told him he had to come up with the money." Pausing, she put out the cigarette she'd left burning in the ashtray, then took another little breath. "I also told him he needed to think about making other arrangements. It was too worrying, about the payments, I mean . . . and things were difficult for me at home."

"And he didn't take that well?" Kincaid asked. She shook her head, her lips pressed together. "Did you give him a time limit?"

"No, but surely he could see that we couldn't go on like that forever . . ."

Kincaid asked the question that had been bothering him from

the beginning. "Why didn't you just divorce him, Julia? Get it over with, make a clean break. This was no trial separation—you knew when you left him that it couldn't be mended."

She smiled at him, teasing. "You of all people should know the law, Duncan. Especially having been through it yourself."

Surprised, he said, "Ancient history. Are my scars still visible?"

Julia shrugged. "A lucky guess. Did your wife file against you?" When he nodded, she continued, "Did you agree to her petition?"

"Well, of course. There was no point going on."

"Do you know what would have happened if you had refused?"

He shook his head. "I never thought about it."

"She would've had to wait two years. That's how long it takes to prove a contested divorce."

"Are you saying that Connor refused to let you divorce him?"

"Got it in one, dear Superintendent." She watched him as he digested this, then said softly, "Was she very beautiful?"

"Who?"

"Your wife, of course."

Kincaid contrasted the image of Vic's delicate, pale prettiness with the woman sitting before him. Julia's face seemed to float between the blackness of her turtlenecked jersey and her dark hair, almost disembodied, and in the lamplight the lines of pain and experience stood out sharply. "I suppose you would say she was beautiful. I don't know. It's been a long time."

Realizing that his rear had gone numb from sitting on the hard table edge, he pushed off with his hands, stretched and lowered himself to the Persian rug. He wrapped his arms around his knees and looked up at Julia, noticing how the difference in perspective altered the planes and shadows of her face. "Did you know about Con's gambling when you married him?"

She shook her head. "No, only that he liked to go racing, and that was rather a lark for me. I'd never been—" She laughed at his expression. "No, really. You think I had this very sophisticated and cosmopolitan upbringing, don't you? What you don't understand is that my parents don't do anything unless it's connected with music." She sighed, then said reflectively, "I loved the colors and the movement, the horses' grace and perfect form. It was only gradually that I began to see that it wasn't just fun for Con, not in the sense it was for me. He'd sweat during the race, and sometimes I'd see his hands tremble. And then I began to realize he was lying to me about how much he'd bet." Shrugging, she added, "After a bit I stopped going."

"But Con kept betting."

"Of course we had rows. 'A harmless pastime' he called it. One he deserved after the pressures at work. But it was only toward the end that it became really frightening."

"Did you bail him out, pay his debts?"

Julia looked away from him, resting her chin on her hand. "For a long time, yes. It was my reputation, too, after all."

"So this row you had last Thursday was old business, in a sense?"

She managed a small smile. "Put that way, yes, I suppose it was. It's so frustrating when you hear yourself saying things you've said a hundred times before—you know it's useless but you can't seem to stop."

"Did he say anything different when he left you? Anything that varied from the normal pattern of these arguments?"

"No, not that I can remember."

And yet he had gone straight to Kenneth. Had he meant to borrow the money for the mortgage? "Did he say anything to you about going to London that afternoon, to the Coliseum?"

Julia lifted her head from her hand, her dark eyes widening in surprise. "London? No. No, I'm sure he didn't. Why should he have gone to the Coli? He'd just seen Mummy and Daddy."

The childish diminutives sounded odd on her lips, and she seemed suddenly young and very vulnerable. "I'd hoped you might tell me," he said softly. "Did you ever hear Connor mention someone called Hicks? Kenneth Hicks?" He watched her carefully, but she only shook her head, looking genuinely puzzled.

"No. Why? Is he a friend?"

"He works for a local bookie, does some collecting for him, among other things. He's also a nasty piece of work, and Connor

166

paid him large amounts of money on a regular basis. That's why I came back, to have another look at Connor's checkbook."

"I never thought of looking through Con's things," Julia said slowly. "I've not even been in the study." She dropped her head in both hands and said through her splayed fingers, "I suppose I was putting off the inevitable." After a moment she raised her head and looked at him, her lips twisting with a mixture of embarrassment and bravado. "I did find some woman's things in the bedroom and in the bath. I've packed them up in a box—I didn't know what else to do with them."

So Sharon had not come back. "Give them to me. I think I can return them to their rightful owner." Although he read the question in her expression, she didn't speak, and they regarded one another in silence. He sat near enough to touch her, and the desire came to him to raise his hand and lay the backs of his fingers against the hollow of her cheek.

Instead, he said gently, "He was seeing someone, you know. A quite steady arrangement, from the sound of it. She has a four-year-old daughter, and Con told her that he would marry her and look after them both, just as soon as you'd let him have a divorce."

For a long moment Julia's face went blank, wiped as clean of expression as a mannequin's, then she gave a strangled laugh. "Oh, poor Con," she said. "The poor, silly bastard."

For the first time since Kincaid had met her, he saw her eyes film with tears.

Gemma finished her second packet of peanuts and licked the salt from the tips of her fingers. Looking up, she saw Tony watching her and smiled a little shamefacedly. "Starving," she said by way of apology.

"Let me have the kitchen fix you something." Tony seemed to have adopted her as his own personal responsibility and was even more solicitous than usual. "We've got lovely pork chops tonight, and a vegetarian lasagna."

Surreptitiously, Gemma glanced at her watch beneath the level of the bar. "I'll wait a bit longer. Thanks, Tony." After leaving

Dame Caroline, she had driven to the pub and carried her case upstairs. Suddenly overcome by a wave of exhaustion, she'd stretched out on top of the duvet in her good clothes and slept deeply and dreamlessly for an hour. She'd awakened feeling cold and a little stiff, but refreshed. After a good wash and brush, she'd changed into her favorite jeans and sweater and gone down to wait for Kincaid.

Tony, polishing glasses at the far end of the bar, still kept an anxious eye on the level of cider in her glass. She had almost decided to let him refill it when he looked toward the door and said, "There's your boss now, love."

Kincaid slid onto the stool beside her. "Has Tony been plying you with drink?" He went on without waiting for an answer, "Good, because I'm going to ply you with food. Sharon Doyle told me that Connor favored the Red Lion in Wargrave—only place the food was up to his standards. I think we should suss it out for ourselves."

"Will you be having a drink before you go, Mr. Kincaid?" asked Tony.

Kincaid looked at Gemma. "Hungry?"

"Famished."

"Then we had better go straight on, Tony."

Tony flapped his dishcloth at them. "Cheerio. Though if you don't mind my saying so," he added in a slightly affronted tone, "their food's no better than ours."

Having lavished reassurances upon Tony, they escaped to the car and drove to Wargrave in silence.

Only when they had settled at a table in the cheerful atmosphere of the Red Lion did Gemma say, "Tony said you had a message from Sergeant Makepeace. What did he want? Where have you been?"

Kincaid, intent on his menu, said, "Let's order first. Then I'll tell you. See anything you fancy? Gratin of haddock and smoked salmon? Prawns in garlic sauce? Chicken breast with red and green peppercorns?" He looked up at her, grinning, and she thought his eyes looked unusually bright. "Con had it right—no shepherd's pie or bangers and mash to be found here."

"Are you sure our expenses will run to this?" Gemma asked.

"Don't worry, Sergeant," he said with exaggerated authority. "I'll take care of it."

Unconvinced, Gemma gave him a doubtful glance, but said, "I'll have the chicken, then. And the tomato and basil soup for starters."

"Going the whole hog?"

"Pudding, too, if I can find room for it." She closed her menu and propped her chin on her hands. He had seated her with her back to the crackling fire and the warmth began to penetrate her sweater. "I feel I deserve it."

The barman came round to them, his pad ready. He had a dish-cloth tucked into his belt, dark, curling hair restrained in a pony-tail, and an engaging smile. "What will you have?"

Kincaid ordered the gratin for himself and added a bottle of American Fumé Blanc. When they had finished the young man said, "Right, then. I'll just turn this in to the kitchen." As he slipped back behind the bar, he added, "My name's David, by the way. Just give me a shout if you need anything else."

Gemma and Kincaid looked at each other, brows raised, then she said, "Do you suppose the service is always this good, or is it just because it's slow tonight?" She looked around the room. Only one other table was occupied—in the far corner a couple sat, heads bent close together.

"I'll bet he has a good memory for customers. After we eat, we'll give it a go."

When David had returned and filled their glasses with chilled wine, Kincaid said, "Tell me."

Gemma related her interview with Tommy Godwin, omitting her rather inglorious arrival. "I'm not sure I buy the bit about his coming into the theater from the front and standing up at the back of the stalls. Doesn't feel quite right."

Their starters came, and as Kincaid tucked into his pâté, he said, "And what about Dame Caroline? Any joy there?"

"It seems their lunch didn't go quite as smoothly as they

claimed at first. Connor excused himself to help with the washing up, but Plummy says he never came in the kitchen, and he left without saying good-bye to Gerald and Caroline." She scraped the last bit of soup from the cup. "I think he must have gone upstairs to Julia."

"He did, and they had a nasty row."

Gemma felt her mouth drop open. She closed it with a snap, then said, "How could you possibly know that?"

"Kenneth Hicks told me, then Julia herself."

"All right, guv," Gemma said, exasperated. "You've got that cat-in-the-cream look. Give."

By the time he'd recounted his day, their main courses had come and they both ate quietly for a few minutes. "What I can't understand," he said as he finished a bite of fish and sipped his wine, "is how a yobbo like Kenneth Hicks managed to hook Connor so thoroughly."

"Money can be a powerful incentive." Gemma deliberated between more braised leeks or more roasted potatoes, then took both. "Why did Julia lie about the row with Connor? It seems innocent enough."

Kincaid hesitated, then shrugged. "I suppose she didn't think it significant. It certainly wasn't a new argument."

Fork halfway to her mouth, Gemma said hotly, "But this wasn't a case of failing to mention something that might or might not have been significant. She deliberately lied. And she lied about leaving the gallery as well." She returned her fork with its speared chicken to her plate, and leaned toward Kincaid. "It's not right the way she's behaved, refusing to take care of the funeral arrangements. What would she have done, let the county bury him?"

"I doubt that very much." Kincaid pushed his plate aside and leaned back a little in his chair.

Although his tone had been mild enough, Gemma felt rebuked. Feeling a flush begin to stain her cheeks, she retrieved her fork, then set it down again as she realized she'd lost her appetite.

Watching her, Kincaid said, "Finished already? What about that pudding?"

"I don't think I can possibly manage it."

"Drink your wine, then," he said, topping up her glass, "and we'll have a word with David."

Gemma bristled at this avuncular instruction, but before she could respond he caught the barman's eye.

"Ready for your sweets?" David said as he reached their table. "The chocolate roulade is heavenly—" As they both shook their heads he continued with hardly a break in stride, "No takers. Cheese, then? The cheese selection is quite good."

"A question or two, actually." Kincaid had opened his wallet. First he showed David his warrant card, then a snapshot of Connor he had begged from Julia. "We understand this fellow was a regular customer of yours. Do you recognize him?"

"Of course I do," answered David, puzzled. "It's Mr. Swann. What do you mean, 'was'?"

"I'm afraid he's dead," Kincaid said, using the standard formula. "We're looking into the circumstances of his death."

"Mr. Swann—dead?" For a moment the young man looked so pale that Kincaid reached out and pulled up a chair from the next table.

"Sit down," said Kincaid. "The mob is not exactly queuing up for service at the bar."

"What?" David folded into the proffered chair as if legless. "Oh, I see what you mean." He gave a wan attempt at a smile. "It's just a bit of a shock, is all. Seems like just the other night he was here, and he was always so . . . larger-than-life. Vital." Reaching out, he touched the surface of the photograph with a tentative fingertip.

"Can you remember what night it was you saw him last?" Kincaid asked quietly, but Gemma could sense his concentrated attention.

David drew his brows together, but said quickly enough, "My girlfriend, Kelly, was working late checkout at the Tesco, didn't finish till half-past nine or thereabouts . . . Thursday. It must have been Thursday." He glanced at them both, expecting approbation.

Kincaid met Gemma's eyes across the table and she saw the flash of victory, but he only said, "Good man. Do you remember what time he came in on Thursday?"

"Late-ish. Must have been after eight." Warming up to his tale,

David continued, "Sometimes he came in by himself, but usually he was with people I thought must be clients of some sort. Not that I eavesdropped on purpose, mind you," he added, looking a bit uncomfortable, "but when you're waiting tables sometimes you can't help but overhear, and they seemed to be talking business."

"And that night?" Gemma prompted.

"I remember it particularly because it was different. He came in alone, and even then he didn't seem his usual self. He was short with me, for one thing. 'Something's really got on his wick,' I thought." Remembering Gemma, he added, "Sorry, miss."

She smiled at him. "Don't mind me."

"Mr. Swann, now, he could put it away with the best of them, but he was always jolly with it. Not like some." David made a face and Gemma nodded sympathetically. As if that had reminded him of his other customers, he glanced at the table in the back, but its occupants were still too engrossed in one another to notice his lack of attention. "Then this other bloke came in, and they took a table for dinner."

"Did they know each other?" Kincaid asked.

"What did—" Gemma interjected, but Kincaid stopped her with a quickly lifted hand.

"Oh, I'm sure they must have done. Mr. Swann stood up as soon as the other bloke came in the door. They went straight to their table after that, so I didn't hear what they said—custom was fairly good that night—but things seemed friendly enough at first."

"And then?" Kincaid said into the moment's pause.

David looked from one to the other, less comfortable now. "I guess you could say they had a heated discussion. Not a shouting match—they didn't really raise their voices, but you could tell they were arguing. And Mr. Swann, well, he always enjoyed the food here, made a point to compliment the cook, that sort of thing." He paused, as if making sure they fully understood the import of what he was about to say. "He didn't even finish his dinner."

"Do you remember what he had?" Kincaid asked, and Gemma knew he was thinking of the still incomplete lab report on the contents of Connor's stomach.

"Steak. Washed down with a good part of a bottle of Burgundy."

Kincaid considered this, then asked, "What happened after that?"

David shifted in his chair and scratched his nose. "They paid their bills—separately—and left."

"They left together?" Gemma asked, clarifying the point.

Nodding, David said, "Still arguing, as far as I could tell." He was fidgeting more obviously now, turning around in his chair to glance at the bar.

Gemma looked at Kincaid, and receiving an almost imperceptible nod, said, "Just one more thing, David. The other man, what did he look like?"

David's smile lit his face. "Very elegant, nice dresser, if you know what I mean. Tall, thin, fairish—"he puckered his brow and thought for a moment—"in his fifties, I should think, but he'd kept himself well."

"Did he pay by credit card?" Kincaid asked hopefully.

Shaking his head and looking genuinely regretful, David said, "Sorry. Cash."

Making an effort to keep the excitement out of her voice, Gemma congratulated him. "You're very observant, David. We seldom get a description half as good."

"It's the job," he said, smiling. "You get in the habit. I put names with the faces when I can. People like to be recognized." Pushing back his chair, he looked questioningly from one to the other. "All right if I clear up now?"

Kincaid nodded and handed him a business card. "You can ring us if you think of anything else."

David had stood and deftly stacked their dirty dishes on his arm when he stopped and seemed to hesitate. "What happened to him? Mr. Swann. You never said."

"To tell you the truth, we're not quite sure, but we are treating it as a suspicious death," said Gemma. "His body was found in the Thames."

The plates rattled and David steadied them with his other hand. "Not along here, surely?"

"No, at Hambleden Lock." Gemma fancied she saw a shadow of relief cross the young man's face, but put it down to the normal human tendency to want trouble kept off one's own patch.

David reached for another dish, balancing it with nonchalant ease. "When? When did it happen?"

"His body was found early Friday morning," Kincaid said, watching David with a pleasant expression that Gemma recognized as meaning his interest was fully engaged.

"Friday morning?" David froze, and although Gemma couldn't be sure in the flickering reflection from the fire, she thought his face paled. "You mean Thursday night . . ."

The front door opened and a large and fairly well-heeled party came in, faces rosy with the cold. David looked from them to the couple in the back, who were finally showing signs of restiveness. "I'll have to go. Sorry." With a flash of an apologetic smile and a rattle of crockery, he hurried to the bar.

Kincaid watched him for a moment, then shrugged and smiled at Gemma. "Nice lad. Might make a good copper. Has the memory for it."

"Listen." Gemma leaned toward him, her voice urgent.

At that moment the two rosy-faced couples, having ordered drinks at the bar, sat down at the next table. They smiled at Gemma and Kincaid in a neighborly fashion, then began a clearly audible conversation among themselves. "Here, David's left us a bill," said Kincaid. "Let's settle up and be on our way."

Not until they had stepped out into the street again was Gemma able to hiss at him, "That was Tommy Godwin." Seeing Kincaid's blank expression, she said, "The man with Connor that night. I'm sure it was Tommy Godwin. That's what I kept trying to tell you," she added testily.

They had stopped on the pavement just outside the pub and stood holding their coat collars up around their throats, a defense against the fog that had crept up from the river. "How can you be certain?"

"I'm telling you, it had to be him." She heard her voice rise in exasperation and made an attempt to level it. "You said yourself that David was observant. His description was too accurate for it to be anyone but Tommy. It's beyond the bounds of probability."

"Okay, okay." Kincaid held up a hand in mock surrender. "But what about the theater? You'll have to recheck—"

The pub door flew open and David almost catapulted into them. "Oh, sorry. I thought I might catch you. Look—" He stopped, as if his impetus had vanished. Still in shirtsleeves, he folded his arms across his torso and stamped his feet a little. "Look—I had no way of knowing, did I? I thought it was just a bit of argy-bargy. I'd have felt a right prat interfering . . ."

"Tell us what happened, David," said Kincaid. "Do you want to go back inside?"

David glanced at the door. "No, they'll be all right for a bit." He looked back at them, swallowed and went on. "A few minutes after Mr. Swann and the other bloke left, I came out for a break. Kelly usually stops by for a drink when she gets off work, and I like to keep an eye out for her—a bird on her own at night, you know. It's not as safe as it used to be." For a moment he paused, perhaps realizing just whom he was lecturing, and Gemma could feel his embarrassment intensify. "Anyway, I was standing just about where we are now, having a smoke, when I heard a noise by the river." He pointed down the gently sloping street. "It was clear, not like tonight, and the river's only a hundred yards or so along." Again he stopped, as if waiting to be drawn.

"Could you see anything?" Kincaid asked.

"The street lamp reflecting off fair hair, and a slightly smaller, darker figure. I think it must have been Mr. Swann and the other bloke, but I couldn't swear to it."

"They were fighting?" Gemma couldn't keep the disbelief from her voice. She found the idea of Tommy Godwin involved in a physical confrontation almost inconceivable.

"Scuffling. Like kids in a school yard."

Kincaid glanced at Gemma, his eyebrows raised in surprise. "What happened then, David?"

"I heard Kelly's car. Loose muffler," he added in explanation. "You can hear the bloody thing for a mile. I went to meet her, and when we came back, they were gone." He scanned their faces anxiously. "You don't think . . . I never dreamed . . ."

"David," said Kincaid, "can you tell us what time this happened?"

He nodded. "Quarter to ten, or near enough."

"The other man," put in Gemma, "would you know him if you saw him again?"

She could see the gooseflesh on his arms from the cold, but he stood still, considering. "Well, yes. I suppose I would. Surely, you don't think he—"

"We might want you to make an identification. Just a matter of routine," Gemma added soothingly. "Can we reach you here? You'd best give us your home address and telephone as well." She passed her notebook to him and he scribbled in it, squinting in the orange glow of the street lamps. "You'd better see to your customers," she said when he'd finished, smiling at him. "We'll be in touch if we need you."

When David had gone, she turned to Kincaid. "I know what you're thinking, but it's not possible! We know he was in London a few minutes after eleven—"

Kincaid touched his fingers to her shoulder, gently turning her. "Let's have a look at the river." As they walked the fog enveloped them, sneaking into their clothes, beading their skin, so that their faces glistened when caught by the light. The pavement ended and their footsteps scrunched on gravel, then they heard the lapping of water against shoreline. "It must be close now," said Kincaid. "Can you smell it?"

The temperature had dropped noticeably as they neared the water, and Gemma shivered, hugging her coat around her. The darkness before them became denser, blacker, and they stopped, straining their eyes. "What is this place?"

Kincaid shone his pocket torch on the gravel. "You can see the wheel ruts where cars have been parked. Forensic will love this."

Gemma turned to him, clamping down on her chattering teeth. "How could Tommy have done it? Even if he'd choked Connor and dumped him in the boot of his car, he would have to have driven like a demon to be in London before eleven o'clock. He couldn't possibly have driven to Hambleden and carried Con's body all that way."

"But," Kincaid began reasonably, "he could have left the body in the boot, driven to London to establish an alibi, and dumped the body later."

"That doesn't make sense. Why go to the theater, the one place that would connect him with the Ashertons, and through them, with Connor? And if he wanted to establish an alibi, why not sign in with the porter? It was only chance that Alison Douglas saw him in Gerald's dressing room, and Gerald certainly hasn't mentioned it." Having forgotten the cold and damp in the heat of her argument, Gemma drew breath for her final salvo. "And even if the rest of it were true, how could he possibly have carried Con's body from the Hambleden carpark to the lock?"

Kincaid smiled his most infuriating smile, the one that meant he found her vehemence amusing. "Well, I guess we had better ask him, hadn't we?"

CHAPTER

11

Alison Douglas protested when Gemma rang her early the next day. "But, Sergeant, how can I possibly ask the ushers to come in this morning when they worked last night? And some of them have other jobs or school."

"Do the best you can. The alternative is having them down to the Yard, which I doubt most of them would be too keen on." Gemma tried to keep the irritation out of her voice. A restless night and a drive back to London in the thick of the commuter traffic had left her feeling shirty, but that was no excuse for taking it out on Alison. And it was not the most reasonable of requests, after all. "I'll be there before noon," she told Alison, ringing off.

Replacing the receiver in its cradle, she surveyed with distaste the paperwork swamping Kincaid's desk. She felt none of her usual satisfaction in having appropriated his office, but rather the same discomfort that had kept her awake into the wee hours. Something had been different about Kincaid last night—at first she had only been aware of a rather feverish quality to his behavior, but as she tossed and turned through the night she came to the conclusion that his responses to her had altered as well. Had she only imagined the easy companionship of the previous evening in London? He had sought her out. Had his delight in her flat and evident enjoyment of her company caused her to drop her barriers a dangerous notch too far?

She shrugged and rubbed her eyes, trying to massage away the fatigue, but she couldn't erase the fleeting thought that the change in Kincaid's manner had something to do with his visit to Julia Swann.

In the end, Alison managed to bring in four of the ushers, and they sat cramped together on folding chairs in her office, looking disgruntled but curious.

Gemma introduced herself, adding, "I'll try not to keep you any longer than necessary. Do any of you know Tommy Godwin, the Wardrobe Manager? Tall, thin, fairish man, very well dressed?" Looking at them, she wasn't hopeful that sartorial elegance had a place in their vocabularies. The three young men were neat but ordinary, and the girl had managed what Gemma recognized as low-budget dressing with a bit of flair. "I want to know if anyone saw him last Thursday evening." The young men glanced sideways at one another from blank faces. Behind them Alison stood with arms crossed, leaning lightly against the wall, and Gemma saw her mouth open slightly in surprise.

Shaking her head slightly at Alison, Gemma waited, letting the silence stretch.

Finally, the girl spoke. "I did, miss." Her voice held a trace of West Indian cadence, probably acquired from parents or other family members who were first-generation immigrants, thought Gemma.

Letting out the breath she'd been unconsciously holding, Gemma said, "Did you? You're sure it was Thursday evening, now? *Pelleas and Melisande*, right?" She hadn't really expected such a positive result, still didn't quite trust it.

"Yes, miss." The girl smiled as if she found Gemma's doubt amusing. "I see all the productions—I can tell which is which."

"Good. I'm glad one of us can." Gemma smiled, silently kicking herself for sounding patronizing. "What's your name?"

"Patricia, miss. I'm a design student—I'm interested in costumes, so sometimes I help out a bit with Wardrobe. That's how I know Mr. Godwin."

"Can you tell me about Thursday evening?"

The girl glanced round at Alison as if seeking permission from the nearest authority. "Go ahead, Patricia, tell the Sergeant. I'm sure it's quite all right," responded Alison.

"Mr. Godwin came into the lobby from the street doors. Usually I stand just inside the auditorium and listen to the performance, but I'd just come back from the Ladies' and was crossing the lobby myself. I called out to him, but he didn't hear me."

Gemma didn't know whether she felt relief or disappointment—if Tommy had been telling the truth about watching the performance, he couldn't have been in Wargrave with Connor. "What did he do then, did you see?"

"Went in the next aisle over. Roland's," she added with a sideways glance at the best-looking of the young men.

"Did you see him?" asked Gemma, turning her attention to him.

He smiled at her, comfortable with the sudden attention. "I can't say for sure, miss, as I don't know him, but I don't remember seeing anyone of that description."

At least he hadn't called her "madame." Gemma returned the smile and turned her attention back to Patricia. "Once you'd gone back to your post in the auditorium, did you see him again?"

The girl shook her head. "The mob started out just after, and I had my hands full."

"Intermission so soon?" asked Gemma, puzzled.

"No." Patricia shook her head more forcefully this time. "Final curtain. I'd only realized I needed to go for a pee"—she sent a quelling glance at the young men—"just in time."

"Final curtain?" Gemma repeated faintly. "I thought you meant he'd come in just after the performance began."

"No, miss. Five minutes, maybe, before the end. Just before eleven o'clock."

Gemma drew in a breath, collecting herself. So it might have been Tommy in the Red Lion after all. "Did you see him later on, Patricia, when you were clearing up?"

"No, miss." Having entered into the spirit of things, she sounded as if she genuinely regretted having nothing more to offer.

"Okay, thanks, Patricia. You've been a great help." Gemma looked at the men. "Anyone else have anything to add?" Receiving the expected negatives, she said, "All right, clear off, then, the lot of you." Patricia trailed out last, looking back a little shyly. "Bright girl," said Gemma as the door closed.

"What is all this about Tommy, Sergeant?" asked Alison, coming to sit on the edge of her desk. She brushed absently at the wrinkles in her brown wool suit. The fabric was the same soft tone as her hair and eyes and made her look, thought Gemma, like a small brown wren.

"Are you quite sure you didn't see him until you went to Gerald's dressing room?"

"I'm positive. Why?"

"He told me he was here in the theater during the entire performance that night. But Patricia's just contradicted that, and she seems a reliable witness."

"Surely you don't think Tommy had anything to do with Connor's death? That's just not possible. Tommy is . . . well, everyone likes Tommy. And not just because he's witty and amusing," Alison said as though Gemma had suggested it."That's not what I mean. He's kind when he doesn't have to be. I know you wouldn't think it from his manner, but he notices people. That girl, Patricia—I imagine he gave her some encouragement. When I first started here I tiptoed around everything, terrified of making a mistake, and he always had a kind word for me."

"I'm sure you're right," said Gemma, hoping to soothe Alison's hostility, "but there is a discrepancy here, and I must follow through on it."

Alison sighed, looking suddenly weary. "I suppose you must. What can I do to help?"

"Think back to those few minutes in Sir Gerald's dressing room. Did you notice anything at all unusual?"

"How can I tell?" asked Alison, her feathers ruffling again. "How can I be sure my recollection's not distorted by what you've told me? That I'm not making something out of nothing?" When Gemma didn't respond, she went on more quietly. "I have been thinking about it. They stopped talking when I came into the room. I felt as if I'd put my foot in—you know?" She looked at

Gemma for confirmation. "Then after that awkward bit, they seemed a bit too hearty, too jolly, if you know what I mean. I think now that's why I only stayed a minute, just long enough to offer the usual congratulations, although I didn't consciously realize it at the time."

"Anything else?" Gemma asked, without too much anticipation.

"No. Sorry."

"That's okay." Smiling at Alison, Gemma made an effort to overcome the lethargy that seemed to be creeping into her limbs. "I will have to talk to him again, and he's proving rather elusive. This morning I've tried his flat, LB House, and here, with no joy. Any suggestions?"

Alison shook her head. "No, he ought to be around."

Seeing the spark of concern in Alison's eyes, Gemma said thoughtfully, "I hope our Mr. Godwin won't prove too difficult to find."

High Wycombe CID had obligingly made room for Kincaid at an absent DI's desk, and there he had spent the morning, going through report after inconclusive report. He stretched, wondering if he should have another cup of dreadful coffee, or give it up and have some lunch.

Duty and coffee were grudgingly in the lead when Jack Makepeace put his head round the door. "Anything?"

Kincaid pulled a face. "Sod all. You've read them. Any word from the team in Wargrave?"

Makepeace grinned evilly. "Two crushed lager cans, some foil gum wrappers, the remains of a dead bird and a half-dozen used condoms."

"A popular parking spot, is it?"

"It marks the beginning of a footpath that runs along the river for a bit, then loops around the churchyard. Parking there isn't strictly legal, but people do it anyway, and I dare say a spot of midnight necking goes on as well." Makepeace fingered his mustache for a moment. "The forensic lads say the gravel's much too soft and messed about for tire casts."

"I expected as much." Kincaid regarded him thoughtfully. "Jack, if the body went in the river at Wargrave, could it have drifted downstream to Hambleden by morning?"

Makepeace was shaking his head before Kincaid had finished. "Not possible. River's too slow, for one thing, and there's Marsh Lock, just past Henley, for another."

Thinking of Julia's brief escape from the gallery, he said, "Then I suppose the same would be true of Henley, if he'd gone in along the River Terrace?"

Makepeace levered his bulk away from the door frame and walked over to the area map on the office wall. He pointed a stubby finger at the twisting blue ribbon representing the River Thames. "Look at all these twists and turns, all making places where a body might catch." Turning back to Kincaid, he added, "I think your body went in within a few hundred yards of where it was found."

Kincaid pushed back the creaky chair, stretched out his legs and laced his fingers behind his neck. "I'm afraid you're right, Jack. I'm just clutching at straws. What about the houses along the river, above the lock? House-to-house turn up anything?"

"Either they were all sleeping like babies by ten o'clock," Makepeace said sarcastically, laying his cheek against the back of his hand, "or they see talking to us as an excuse to trot out their own pet phobias. Remember that flat conversion at the beginning of the weir walkway? Old biddy in one of the riverside flats says she heard voices sometime after the late news finished. When she looked out her window she saw a man and a boy on the walkway. 'Poofters,' she says. 'Queers sinning against the Lord.' And motorcycle hoodlums to boot." Makepeace's eyes crinkled in amusement. "It seems the boy had longish hair and wore leather, and that was good enough for her. Before my PC could get away, she asked him if he'd been saved by Jesus."

Kincaid snorted. "Doesn't make me miss my days on the beat. What about access from south of the river, then? Through the meadows."

"Need a Land Rover, or something with a four-wheel drive. Ground's like glue after all this rain." Makepeace studied

Kincaid's face, then said sympathetically, "Bad luck. Oh"—he patted the file tucked under his left arm—"here's something might cheer you up—final report from pathology." He handed it across to Kincaid. "Spot of lunch?"

"Give me ten minutes," Kincaid said with a wave, then dug into the file.

After a cursory read-through he picked up the phone and eventually managed to reach Dr. Winstead in his lair. "Doctor," he said when he had identified himself, "I know now what time Connor ate—nine, or shortly thereafter. Are you sure he couldn't have died as early as ten?"

"Meat and potatoes, was I right?"

"Steak, actually," Kincaid admitted.

"I'd put it closer to midnight, unless the fellow had stomach acid that would've stripped paint."

"Thanks, Dr. Winnie. You're a dear." Kincaid rang off and contemplated the scattered reports. After a moment he swept them into a pile, pulled up the knot on his tie and went in search of more pleasant prospects.

When Gemma returned to the Yard, she found a message on her desk that read simply, "Tom Godwin called. Brown's Hotel, three o'clock."

She went in search of the duty sergeant. "Was that all, Bert? Are you sure?"

Affronted, he said, "Have you ever known me to make a mistake with a message, Gemma?"

"No, dear, of course not." She patted his grizzled head affectionately. "It's just odd, that's all."

"That's what the gentleman said, verbatim," said Bert, slightly mollified. "The guv'nor wants to see you, by the way."

"Oh, terrific," she muttered under her breath, and received a sympathetic glance from Bert.

"He hasn't eaten anyone since lunch, love."

"Ta, Bert," said Gemma, grinning. "That makes me feel ever so much better."

Still, she went along the corridor in some trepidation. In truth, Chief Superintendent Denis Childs was known to be fair with his staff, but there was something in his pleasant and courteous manner that made her want to confess even imagined misdeeds. His door stood open, as was his policy, and Gemma tapped lightly before entering. "You wanted to see me, sir?"

Childs looked up from a file. He had recently adopted granny-style reading glasses, and they looked so incongruous perched on his massive moon-shaped face that she had to bite her lip to stifle a giggle. Fortunately, he took them off and dangled them daintily from thumb and forefinger. "Sit down, Sergeant. What have you and Kincaid been up to the past few days—tiddlywinks? I've had a prod from the assistant commissioner, wanting to know why we haven't produced the expected brilliant results. Apparently Sir Gerald Asherton has put quite a flea in his ear."

"It's only been four days, sir," Gemma said, stung. "And the pathologist only got round to the PM yesterday. Anyway," she added hurriedly, before Childs could trot out his dreaded maxim—*results, not excuses*—"we have a suspect. I'm interviewing him this afternoon."

"Any hard evidence?"

"No, sir, not yet."

Childs folded his hands across his belly and Gemma marveled, as she always did, that for all his bulk the man radiated such physical magnetism. As far as she knew, he was happily married and used his appeal for nothing more sinister than keeping the typists working to order.

"All the teams are out just now—we've had a regular rash of homicides. But as badly as I need the two of you, I don't think we want to let the AC down, do you, Sergeant? It's always in our best interest to keep the powers-that-be happy." He smiled at her, his teeth blindingly white against his olive skin. "Will you pass that along to Superintendent Kincaid when you talk to him?"

"Yes, sir," Gemma answered, and, taking that as dismissal, beat a hasty and grateful retreat.

★   ★   ★

When Gemma returned to Kincaid's office, bars of sunlight slanted into the room. They looked solid enough to touch, the quality of the light almost viscous. Not quite trusting the phenomenon, she went to the window and peered through the blinds. The sky was indeed clear and as blue as it ever managed with the city smog. She looked from the window to the paperwork, lying haphazardly where she'd left it. The angle of the light across the desk revealed streaks of dust and several perfect fingerprints—smiling, Gemma walked over and wiped them away with a tissue. Remove the evidence—that was the first rule. Then she grabbed her bag from the coat stand and made for the lift before anyone could stop her.

She cut through St. James Park, walking quickly, taking in great breaths of the cool, clear air. The English have an instinct for sunshine, however brief its duration, she thought, like a radar early-warning system. The park was busy with others who had heeded the signal, some walking as quickly as she was, obviously on their way somewhere, others strolling or sitting on benches, and all looking oddly out of place in their business clothes. The trees, which in the past few days' drizzle had looked drab as old washing, showed remnants of red and gold in the sunlight, and pansies and late chrysanthemums made a brave showing in the beds.

She came out into the Mall, and by the time she'd made her way along St. James Street to Piccadilly she could feel her heart beating and warmth in her face. But it was only a few more blocks along Albemarle Street, and her head felt clear for the first time that day.

Although she had timed it accurately, arriving a few minutes early, Tommy Godwin was there before her. He waved at her, looking as at home in the hotel's squashy armchair as he might in his own parlor. She made her way over to him, suddenly aware of her windblown hair and pink cheeks, and of her unfashionably sensible low-heeled shoes.

"Do have a seat, my dear. You look as if you've been exerting yourself unnecessarily. I've ordered for you—I hope you don't mind. Stuffy and old-fashioned as it is"—he nodded at the room, with its wood-paneled walls and crackling fire—"they do a proper tea here."

"Mr. Godwin, this is not a social occasion," Gemma said as severely as she could while sinking into the depths of her chair. "Where have you been? I've been trying to reach you all day."

"I paid a visit to my sister in Clapham this morning. A gruesome but regular family necessity, one which I fear most of us are subject to—unless one has had the good fortune to come into the world via test tube, and even that has ramifications that don't bear thinking of."

Gemma tried to straighten her back against the chair's soft cushion. "Please don't take me round the mulberry bush, Mr. Godwin. I need some answers from you—"

"Can't we have tea first?" he asked plaintively. "And call me Tommy, please." Leaning toward her confidentially, he said, "This hotel was the model for Agatha Christie's *At Bertram's Hotel*—did you know that, Sergeant? I don't believe it's changed much since her day."

Curious in spite of her best intentions, Gemma looked round the room. Some of the little old ladies seated nearby might have been Miss Marple's clones. The faded prints of their dresses (covered by sensibly wooly cardigans), harmonized with the faded blues and violets of their hair rinses, and their shoes—Gemma's comfortable flats weren't even in the same realm of sensibleness as their stout brogues.

What an odd place to appeal to Tommy Godwin, she thought, studying him covertly. She pegged today's navy jacket as cashmere, his shirt was immaculate pale gray broadcloth, his trousers charcoal and his silk tie a discreetly rich navy and red paisley.

As if reading her mind, he said, "It's the prewar aura I can't resist. The Golden Age of British manners—vanished now, much to our loss. I was born during the Blitz, but even during my childhood there were still traces of gentility in English life. Ah, here's our tea," he said as the waiter brought a tray to their table. "I've ordered Assam to go with the sandwiches—I hope that's all right—and a pot of Keemun later with the pastries."

Tea in Gemma's family had run to Tetley's Finest teabags, stewed in a tin pot. Not liking to admit that she had never tasted either, she pounced on his previous remark. "You only think that time must have been perfect because you didn't live it. I imagine the generation between the wars saw Edwardian England as the Golden Age, and probably the Edwardians felt the same way about the Victorians."

"A good point, my dear," he said seriously as he poured tea into her cup, "but there was one great difference—the First World War. They had looked into the mouth of hell, and they knew how fragile our hold on civilization really is." The waiter returned, placing a three-tiered tray on their small table. Finger sandwiches filled the bottom tray, scones the middle, and pastries the top, the crowning touch. "Have a sandwich, my dear," said Tommy. "The salmon on brown bread is particularly nice."

He sipped his tea and continued his lecture, a cucumber sandwich poised in his fingers. "It's fashionable these days to pooh-pooh the Golden Age crime novel as trivial and unrealistic, but that was not the case at all. It was their stand against chaos. The conflicts were intimate, rather than global, and justice, order and retribution always prevailed. They desperately needed that reassurance. Did you know that Britain lost nearly a third of its young men between 1914 and 1918? Yet that war didn't physically threaten us in the same way as the next—it stayed safely on the European Front."

Pausing to down half the cucumber sandwich in one bite, he chewed for a moment, then said sadly, "What a waste it must have seemed, the flower of Britain's manhood lost, with nothing to show for it but some newspaper headlines and politicians' speeches." He smiled. "But if you read Christie or Allingham or Sayers, the detective always got his man. And you'll notice that the detective always operated outside the system—the stories expressed a comforting belief in the validity of individual action."

"But weren't the murders always clean and bloodless?" Gemma asked rather impatiently through a mouthful of sandwich. She'd felt too tired and unsettled to eat lunch, and her walk had left her suddenly ravenous.

"Some of them were in fact quite diabolical. Christie was particularly fond of poisoning, and I can think of no less civilized way to commit murder."

"Are you suggesting that there are civilized methods of murder?" *Such as drowning your victim in a convenient river*, she thought, wondering at the bizarre turn the conversation seemed to be taking.

"Of course not, my dear, only that I've always found the idea of poison especially abhorrent—such suffering and indignity for one person to inflict upon another."

Gemma drank a little more of her tea. She rolled it around on her tongue, deciding she liked the rich, malty taste. "So you prefer your murders quick and clean, do you, Tommy?"

"I don't prefer them any way at all, my dear," he said, glancing up at her as he poured more tea into her cup. He was playing with her, teasing her, she could see it in the suppressed laughter in his eyes.

Time for a little dose of reality, she thought, licking egg salad from her fingertips. "I've always thought drowning would be quite horrible myself. Giving in at last to that desperate need to draw air into the lungs, then choking, struggling, until unconsciousness comes as a blessed relief."

Tommy Godwin sat quite still, watching her, his hands relaxed on the tabletop. What beautiful hands he had, thought Gemma, the fingers long and slender, the nails perfectly kept. She found quite inconceivable the idea of him fighting like a common ruffian, using those hands to choke and squeeze, or perhaps to hold a thrashing body under water.

"You're quite right, my dear," he said softly. "It was tasteless of me to go on that way, but crime novels are rather a hobby of mine." He picked up a watercress sandwich and looked at it a moment before returning it to the plate. The eyes that met hers were a surprisingly dark blue, and guileless. "Do you think poor Connor suffered?"

"We don't know. The pathologist didn't find evidence indicating he'd inhaled river water, but that doesn't rule it out." She let the silence stretch for a heartbeat, then added, "I was hoping you might tell me."

His eyes widened. "Oh, come now, Sergeant. You can't think—"

"You lied to me about attending the opera that night. One of the ushers saw you come in from the street just minutes before the performance ended. And I have a witness who can place you in a pub in Wargrave, having a not-too-friendly dinner with Connor Swann," she said, tendering her bluff with all the authority she could manage.

For the first time since she had met him, Tommy Godwin seemed at a loss for words. As she studied his still face, she saw that most of his attractiveness lay not in his individual features, but in the expression of alert, humorous inquisitiveness that usually animated them. Finally, he sighed and pushed away his empty plate. "I should have known it was no use. Even as a child I was never any good at lying. I had meant to attend the performance that night—that much at least was true. Then I had an urgent message from Connor on my answer phone, saying he needed to see me. I suppose he must have been looking for me when he came to the theater that afternoon."

"He asked you to meet him at the Red Lion?"

As Tommy nodded the waiter brought their second pot of tea. Lifting the pot, Tommy said, "You must try the Keemun, my dear. What would you like with it?"

Gemma had started to shake her head when he said, "Please, Sergeant, do have something. This was to be a special treat for you—I thought hardworking policewomen probably didn't have too many opportunities to take afternoon tea."

She heard Alison's words again, and she found that no matter what else Tommy might have done, she couldn't reject this small act of kindness. "I'll have a scone then, please."

Having taken a scone for himself, he poured tea into her cup from the fresh pot. "Taste your tea. You can put milk in it if you like, but I'd advise you not to."

Gemma did as instructed, then looked up at him in surprise. "It's sweet."

He looked pleased. "Do you like it? It's a north China Congou. The best of the China blacks, I think."

"Tell me about Connor," Gemma said, spreading clotted cream and strawberry jam on her scone.

"There's not much to tell, really. I met him at the Red Lion, as you said, and from the beginning he behaved quite oddly. I'd never seen him like that, although I'd heard stories about the weeks after he and Julia first separated. He had been drinking, but I didn't think he'd had enough to account for his manner. It was . . . I don't know . . . almost hysterical, really."

"Why did he want to see you?"

Tommy washed down a bite of scone with tea. "I found out soon enough. He said he'd decided he wanted his old job back—that he'd had enough of dealing with two-bit, small-town accounts, and he wanted me to intercede for him."

"Could you have done it?" asked Gemma in some surprise.

"Well, yes, I suppose so. I've known the firm's senior partner for years. In fact, it was I who encouraged him to go after the ENO account in the first place." He looked at Gemma over the cup he held cradled in both hands. "It's unfortunate that we can't foresee the consequences of our actions. If I had not done that, Connor would never have met Gerald and Caro, and through them, Julia."

"But you refused Connor's request."

"Politely at first. I told him that my reputation would ride on his performance, and that considering his previous conduct, I didn't feel I could risk it. The truth of the matter is," he added, setting down his cup and looking away from Gemma, "I never liked him. Not the thing to say when one is suspected of foul play, is it, dear Sergeant?" He smiled, teasing her once more, then said reflectively, "I can remember their wedding day quite clearly. It was a June wedding, in the garden at Badger's End—I know you won't have seen it, but it can be quite lovely that time of year. All Plummy's doing, although Julia used to help her quite a bit when she had the time.

"Everyone said how perfect Julia and Connor looked together, and I have to admit they did make a handsome couple, but when I looked at them I saw only disaster. They were completely, utterly unsuited for one another."

"Do stick to the point, Tommy, please," said Gemma, wondering how she could impress the gravity of the situation upon him with her mouth full of scone.

He sighed. "We argued. He became more and more abusive, until finally I told him I'd had enough. I left. That's all."

Moving her plate out of the way, Gemma leaned toward him. "That's not all, Tommy. The barman came out just after you and Connor left the pub. He says he saw you fighting down by the river."

Although she wouldn't have believed that a man with Tommy Godwin's poise and experience could blush, she could have sworn his face turned pink with embarrassment.

There was a moment's pause as he refused to meet her eyes. Finally, he said, "I've not done anything like that since I was at school, and even then I considered any form of physical violence both undignified and uncivilized. It was the accepted way to get on in the world, beating what one wanted out of someone else, and I made a deliberate choice to live my life differently. It got me labeled a pansy and a poofter, of course," he added with a hint of the familiar, charming smile, "but I could live with that. What I couldn't live with was the thought of abandoning my principles.

"When I found myself locked in a ridiculous schoolboy scuffle with Connor, I simply stopped and walked away."

"And he let you?"

Tommy nodded. "I think he'd run out of steam himself by that time."

"Had you parked your car on the gravel by the river?"

"No, I'd found a spot on the street, a block or two up from the pub. Someone may have seen it," he added hopefully. "It's a classic Jaguar, red, quite distinctive."

"And then, after you'd returned to your car?"

"I drove to London. Having agreed to see Con, against my better judgment, I'd spoiled my evening, and I felt he'd rather made a fool of me. I thought I'd try to salvage as much of my original plan as I could."

"Five minutes' worth?" asked Gemma, skeptically.

He smiled. "Well, I did my best."

"And you didn't make a point of stopping by Sir Gerald's dressing room in order to establish an alibi?"

Patiently, he said, "I wanted to congratulate him, as I told you before, Sergeant."

"Even though you hadn't actually seen the performance?"

"I could tell by the audience's response that it had been particularly good."

She searched his face, and he returned her gaze steadily. "You're right, you know, Tommy," she said at last. "You are an awful liar. I suppose you went straight home from the theater?"

"I did, as a matter of fact."

"Is there anyone who can vouch for you?"

"No, my dear. I'm afraid not. And I parked in back of my building and went up in the service lift, so I didn't see anyone at all. I'm sorry," he added, as if it distressed him to disappoint her.

"I'm sorry, too, Tommy." Gemma sighed. Feeling suddenly weary, she said, "You could have put Connor's body in the boot of your car, then driven back to Hambleden after the performance and dumped him in the lock."

"Really? What an extraordinarily imaginative idea." Tommy sounded amused.

Exasperated, she said, "You do realize that we'll have to impound your car so that the forensics team can go over it. And we'll have to search your flat for evidence. And you will have to come down to the Yard with me now and make a formal statement."

He lifted the delicate porcelain teapot and smiled at her. "Well, then you had better finish your tea, my dear Sergeant."

CHAPTER
12

Lunch with Jack Makepeace improved Kincaid's outlook on life considerably. Replete with cheese, pickle and pints of Green King ale, they blinked as they came out into the street from the dim interior of a pub near the High Wycombe nick. "That's a surprise," said Makepeace, turning his face up to the sun. "And I doubt it'll last long—the forecast is for cats and dogs."

The perfect antidote to a morning spent wheel-spinning, thought Kincaid as he felt the faint warmth of the sun against his face, was a good walk. "I think I'll take advantage of it," he said to Makepeace as they reached the station. "You can reach me if anything comes up."

"Some people have all the luck," Makepeace answered good-naturedly. "It's back to the salt mines for the likes of me." He waved and disappeared through the glass doors.

Kincaid made the short drive from High Wycombe to Fingest, and on reaching the village he hesitated for a moment before turning into the pub's carpark. Although the vicarage looked mellow and inviting in the afternoon sun and the vicar was certainly the authority on local walks, he decided it was much too likely he'd end up spending the rest of the afternoon being comfortably entertained in the vicar's study.

In the end, Tony proved as useful and accommodating on the matter of walks as he had about everything else. "I've just the thing," he said, retrieving a book from the mysterious recesses under the bar. "Local pub walks. Three and a half miles too much for you?" He eyed Kincaid measuringly.

"I think I can just about manage that," Kincaid said, grinning.

"Fingest, Skirmett, Turville, and back to Fingest. All three villages are in their own valleys, but this particular walk avoids the steepest hill. You might get a bit mucky, though."

"Thanks, Tony. I promise not to track up your carpets. I'll just go and change."

"Take my compass," Tony called out as Kincaid turned away, producing it from the palm of his hand like a conjurer. "It'll come in handy."

At the top of the first long climb, some thoughtful citizen had placed a bench on which the winded walker could sit and enjoy the view. Kincaid took brief advantage of it, then toiled on, through woods and fields and over stiles. At first the vicar's brief history rolled through his mind, and as he walked he imagined the progression of Celts, Romans, Saxons and Normans settling these hills, all leaving their own particular imprint upon the land.

After a while the combination of fresh air, exercise and solitude worked its magic, and his mind returned freely to the question of Connor Swann's death, sorting the facts and impressions that he had gathered so far. The pathologist's evidence made it highly unlikely that Tommy Godwin had killed Connor outside the Red Lion in Wargrave. He might, of course, have knocked Connor unconscious and killed him a couple of hours later after returning from London—but like Gemma, Kincaid could come up with no logical scenario for the later removal of the body from the car to the lock.

Dr. Winstead's report also meant that Julia could not have killed Con during her brief absence from the gallery, and David's statement placing Connor in Wargrave until at least ten o'clock made it impossible for her to have met him along the River Terrace and made an assignation for later. Kincaid shied away from the feeling of relief that this conclusion brought him, and forced himself to consider the next possibility—that she had met Connor much later and that Trevor Simons had lied to protect her.

So caught up was he in these ruminations that he failed to see the cowpat until he had put his foot in it. Swearing, he wiped his trainer as best he could on the grass. Motive was like that, he mused as he walked on more carefully—sometimes you just couldn't see it until you fell into it. Hard as he tried, he couldn't come up with a likely reason why Julia would have wanted to kill Con, nor did he believe that having had one row with him that day, she would have agreed to meet him later in order to have another.

Had that lunchtime argument with Julia been the trigger for Connor's increasingly odd behavior during the rest of that day? Yet it was only after he had left Kenneth that Con had visibly deviated from an expected pattern. And that brought Kincaid to Kenneth—where had Kenneth been on Thursday evening, and why had asking him about his movements sent him from reluctant cooperation into complete and obstinate withdrawal? As he pictured Kenneth, huddled in his bomber jacket as if it were armor, he remembered the female witness Makepeace had mentioned. "A boy in leather," she'd said . . . Kenneth was slightly built and Makepeace had described him as five foot eight or nine. Next to Connor he might easily have been mistaken for a boy. It was certainly a possibility worth pursuing.

The woods enclosed him again as he left Skirmett. He walked in a dim and soundless world, his footfalls absorbed by the leaf mold. Not even birdsong broke the stillness, and when he stopped, staring after a flash of white that might have been a deer bounding away, he could hear the rush of his own blood in his ears.

Kincaid walked on, following the next tendril that shot out from the amoebic mass of speculation—if Connor had driven away from the Red Lion after his scuffle with Tommy Godwin, where had he gone? Sharon Doyle's face came into his mind— she, like Kenneth, had become belligerent when Kincaid had pushed her about her movements later that evening.

As he came into Turville he looked northwest, toward Northend, up the hill where Badger's End lay hidden under the dark canopy of the beeches. What had brought Julia back to that house, as if drawn by an unseen umbilical cord?

He stopped at the Northend turning and frowned. Some thread ran through this case that he couldn't quite grasp—he felt it move away whenever he approached it too closely, like some dark underwater creature always swimming just out of reach.

Nestled among Turville's cluster of cottages, The Bull and Butcher beckoned, but Kincaid declared himself immune to the temptation of Brakspear's ales and pushed on into the fields again.

He soon came out onto the road that led to Fingest. The sun had dropped beneath the tops of the trees, and the light slanted through the boles, illuminating dust motes and flickering on his clothes like a faulty film projector.

By the time the now-familiar twin-gabled tower of Fingest church came into view, Kincaid found he had made two decisions. He would ask Thames Valley to pick up Kenneth Hicks, and then they'd see how well Hicks's bravado held up in an interview room in the local nick.

And he would pay another visit to Sharon Doyle.

When Kincaid returned to the Chequers, a bit muddy as Tony had predicted and feeling pleasantly tired from his walk, there was still no word from Gemma regarding her progress with Tommy Godwin. He rang the Yard and left a message for her with the duty sergeant. As soon as she finished in London she was to join him again. He wanted her in on the interview with Hicks. And considering Kenneth's obvious dislike of women, Kincaid thought with a smile, maybe she should conduct it.

In Henley, Kincaid left the car near the police station and walked down Hart Street, his eyes on the tower of the church of St. Mary the Virgin.

Square and substantial, it anchored the town around it like the hub of a wheel. Church Avenue lay neatly tucked in the tower's shadow, facing the churchyard as if it were its own private garden. A plaque set into the stonework informed him that the row of almshouses had been endowed by John Longland, Bishop of Lincoln, in 1547, and rebuilt in 1830.

The cottages were unexpectedly charming, built of a very pale green-washed stucco, with bright blue doors and lace curtains in every window. Kincaid knocked at the number Sharon Doyle had given him. He heard the sound of the television, and faintly, the high voice of a child.

He had raised his hand to knock again when Sharon opened the door. Except for the unmistakable golden corkscrew curls, he would hardly have recognized her. She wore no makeup, not even lipstick, and her bare face looked young and unprotected. The tarted-up clothes and high heels were gone—replaced by a faded sweatshirt, jeans and dirty trainers, and in the few days since he had seen her she seemed visibly thinner. To his surprise, she also seemed rather pathetically glad to see him.

"Superintendent! What are you doing here?" A sticky and disheveled version of the child in the wallet photo Kincaid had seen slipped up beside Sharon and wrapped herself around her mother's leg.

"Hullo, Hayley," said Kincaid, squatting at her eye level. He looked up at Sharon and added, "I came to see how you were getting on."

"Oh, come in," she said as if making an effort to recall her manners, and she stepped back, hobbled by the child clinging to her like a limpet. "Hayley was just having her tea, weren't you, love? In the kitchen with Gran." Now that she had Kincaid in the sitting room, she seemed to have no idea what to do with him, and simply stood there stroking the child's tangle of fair curls.

Kincaid looked around the small room with interest. Doilies and dark furniture, fringed lampshades and the smell of lavender wax, all as neat and clean as if they had been preserved in a museum. The sound of the television was only a bit louder than it had been when he stood outside, and he surmised that the cottage's interior walls must be constructed of thick plaster.

"Gran likes the telly in the kitchen," Sharon said into the silence. "It's cozier to sit in there, close by the range."

The front room might have been the scene of some long-ago courtship, thought Kincaid. He imagined young lovers sitting

199

stiltedly on the horsehair chairs, then remembered that these cottages had been built for pensioners, and any wooing must have been done by those old enough to know better. He wondered if Connor had ever come here.

Diplomatically, he said, "If Hayley would like to go in with Gran and finish her tea, perhaps you and I could go outside and have a chat."

Sharon gave Kincaid a grateful glance and bent down to her daughter. "Did you hear what the superintendent said, love? He needs to have a word with me, so you go along in with Gran and finish your tea. If you eat up all your beans and toast, you can have a biscuit," she added cajolingly.

Hayley studied her mum as if gauging the sincerity of this pledge.

"I promise," said Sharon, turning her and giving her a pat on the bottom. "Go on now. Tell Gran I'll be along in a bit." She watched the little girl disappear through the door in the back of the room, then said to Kincaid, "Just let me get a cardy."

The cardy turned out to be a man's brown wool cardigan, a bit moth-eaten, and ironically reminiscent of the one Sir Gerald Asherton had worn the night Kincaid met him. Seeing Kincaid's glance, Sharon smiled and said, "It was my granddad's. Gran keeps it for wearing about the house." As she followed Kincaid out into the churchyard, she continued, "Actually, she's my great-gran, but I never knew my real gran. She died when my mum was a baby."

Although the sun had set in the few minutes Kincaid had been inside the house, the churchyard looked even more inviting in the soft twilight. They walked to a bench across the way from the cottages, and as they sat down Kincaid said, "Is Hayley always so shy?"

"She's always chattered like a magpie, from the day she learned to talk, even with strangers." Sharon's hands lay loosely in her lap, palms turned up. They might have been disembodied, so unanimated were they, and Kincaid noticed that since he'd seen her last, the small pink nails had been bitten to the quick. "It's only since I told her about Con that she's been like this." She looked up at

Kincaid in appeal. "I had to tell her, didn't I, Mr. Kincaid? I couldn't let her think he just scarpered, could I? I couldn't let her think he didn't care about us."

Kincaid gave the question careful consideration before answering. "I think you did the right thing, Sharon. It would be hard for her now, regardless, and in the long run I'm sure it's better to tell the truth. Children sense when you're lying, and then they have that betrayal to deal with as well as the loss."

Sharon listened intently, then nodded once when he'd finished. She studied her hands for a moment. "Now she wants to know why we can't see him. My auntie Pearl died last year and Gran took her to the viewing before the funeral."

"What did you tell her?"

Shrugging, Sharon said, "Different people do things different ways, that's all. What else could I say?"

"I imagine she wants some concrete evidence that Con is really gone. Perhaps you could take her to see his grave, afterward." He gestured at the graves laid out so neatly in the green grass of the churchyard. "That should seem familiar enough to her."

She turned to him again, her hands clenching convulsively. "There's not been anyone to talk to, see? Gran doesn't want to know about it—she disapproved of him anyway—"

"Why was that?" asked Kincaid, surprised that the woman would not have been pleased at a better prospect for her great-granddaughter.

"Marriage is marriage in the eyes of the Lord," mimicked Sharon, and Kincaid had a sudden clear vision of the old lady. "Gran's very firm in her beliefs. It made no difference that Con wasn't living with *her*. And as long as Con was married I had no rights, Gran said. Turned out she knew what she was on about, didn't she?"

"You must have girlfriends you can talk with," said Kincaid, as there seemed no helpful answer to the last question.

"They don't want to know, either. You'd think I'd got leprosy or something all of a sudden—they act like they're afraid it might rub off on them and spoil their fun." Sharon sniffed, then added more softly, "I don't want to talk to them about Con, anyway. What we had was between us, and it doesn't seem right to air it like last week's washing."

"No, I can see that."

They sat quietly for a few minutes as the lights began to come on in the cottages. Indistinct shapes moved behind the net curtains, and every so often a pensioner would pop out from one door and then another, putting out milk bottles or picking up papers. It made Kincaid think of those elaborate German clocks, the kind in which the little people bob cheerfully in-and-out as the hour chimes. He looked at the girl beside him, her head again bent over her hands. "I'll see you get your things back, Sharon. *She* would want you—" Bloody hell, now he was doing it. "Mrs. Swann would like you to have them," he corrected himself.

Her response, when it came, surprised him. "Those things I said, the other night . . . well, I've been thinking." In the fading light he caught a quick flash of her eyes before she looked away from him again. "It wasn't right, what I said. You know. About her . . ."

"About Julia having killed Connor, is that what you mean?"

She nodded, picking idly at a spot on the front of her sweatshirt. "I don't know why I said it. I wanted to hit at someone, I guess." After a moment she continued in a tone of discovery, "I think I wanted to believe she was as awful as Con said. It made me feel better. Safer."

"And now?" Kincaid asked, and when she didn't answer he continued, "You had no reason for making those accusations? Con never said anything that made you think Julia might have threatened him?"

Shaking her head, she said so softly that he had to lean close to catch it, "No." She smelled of Pears soap, and the good, clean ordinariness of it suddenly squeezed at his throat.

The twilight deepened, and from some of the cottage windows came the blue flicker of televisions. Kincaid imagined the pensioners, all women that he had seen, having their evening meals early so that they could settle down in front of the box, uninterrupted, isolated from themselves as well as one another. He gave a tiny shudder, shaking off the wave of melancholy that threatened him, like a dog coming out of water. Why should he begrudge them their comfort, after all?

Beside him, Sharon stirred and pulled the cardigan a little closer about her. Rubbing his hands together to warm them, he turned to her, saying briskly, "One more thing, Sharon, and then you'd better go in before you catch a chill. We have a witness who's certain he saw Connor at the Red Lion in Wargrave after he left you that night. Con met a man who fits the description of Tommy Godwin, an old friend of the Ashertons. Do you know him, or did you ever hear Con mention him?"

He could almost hear her thinking as she sat beside him in the dark, and he thought that if he looked closely enough he would see her brow furrowed in concentration. "No," she said eventually, "I never did." She turned to him, pulling her knee up on the bench so that she could face him directly. "Did they . . . were they having a row?"

"According to the witness, it was not a particularly friendly meeting. Why?"

She put her hand to her mouth, nibbling at the nail of her index finger. Nail-biting was a form of self-mutilation that had never tempted Kincaid, and it always made him wince for the damaged flesh. He waited, lacing his own fingers together to stop himself from pulling her hand away from her mouth.

"I thought it was me made him angry," she said in a rush. "He came back that night. He wasn't pleased to see me—he wanted to know why hadn't I gone back to Gran's, like I said." She touched Kincaid's sleeve. "That's why I didn't say anything before. I felt such a bloody fool."

Kincaid patted her hand. "Why hadn't you gone home?"

"Oh, I did. But Gran's bridge finished early—one of the old ladies felt a bit ill—so I came back. I was sorry I'd left in a huff before. I thought he'd be glad to see me and we could—" She gulped, unable to go on, but what she had hoped was painfully clear to Kincaid without any further elaboration.

"Was he drunk?"

"He'd had a few, but he wasn't proper pissed, not really."

"And he didn't tell you where he'd been or who he'd seen?"

Sharon shook her head. "'E said, 'What are you doing here?' and walked past me like I was a piece of bloody furniture or something."

"Then what? Tell me bit by bit, everything you can remember."

Closing her eyes, she thought for a moment, then began obediently, "He went into the kitchen and fixed himself a drink—"

"Not to the drinks trolley?" asked Kincaid, remembering the plethora of bottles.

"Oh, that was just for show. Company. Con drank whiskey and he always kept a bottle on the kitchen counter," she said, then continued more slowly. "He came back into the sitting room and I noticed he kept rubbing at his throat. 'Are you all right?' I asked him. 'You're not feeling ill, love?' But he didn't answer. He went upstairs into the study and closed the door."

"Did you follow him?" Kincaid asked when she lapsed into silence.

"I didn't know what to do. I'd started up the stairs when I heard him talking—he must have rung someone." She looked at Kincaid and even in the dim reflected light he could see her distress. "He was laughing. That's what I couldn't understand. Why would he laugh when he'd hardly said boo to me?

"When he came downstairs again, he said, 'I'm going out, Shar. Lock up when you leave.' Well, I'd had enough by that time, I can tell you. I told him to lock his own bloody door—I wasn't hanging about to be treated like a bloody tart, was I? I told him if he wanted to see me he could pick up the sodding phone and ring me, and I'd think about it if I hadn't anything better to do."

"What did Connor say to that?"

"'E just stood there, his face all blank, like he hadn't heard a word I said."

Kincaid had heard Sharon in full fury, and he thought Connor must have been very preoccupied indeed. "And did you? Leave, I mean?"

"Well, I had to, hadn't I? What else was I to do?"

LEAVE THE GRAVE GREEN

"The scene definitely called for a grand exit," said Kincaid, smiling.

Sharon smiled back a little reluctantly. "I slammed the bloody door so hard I ripped my nail right off. Hurt like hell, too."

"So you didn't actually see him leave the flat?"

"No. I stood about for a minute. I guess I still hoped he'd come after me, say he was sorry. Silly cow," she added bitterly.

"You weren't silly at all. You had no way of explaining Con's behavior—in your place I think I'd have done exactly the same."

She took a moment to absorb this, then said haltingly, "Mr. Kincaid, do you know why Con said those things . . . why he treated me like that?"

Wishing he had some comfort to give her, he said, "No," then added with more certainty than he felt, "but I'm going to find out. Come on, let's get you inside. Your gran'll have the police out after you."

Her smile was as weak as his little joke, and manufactured simply to please him, he felt sure. As they reached the cottage door, he asked, "What time was it when you left Con, Sharon? Do you remember?"

She nodded at the massive tower behind them. "Church clock struck eleven just as I came round the Angel."

After he left Sharon, it seemed the most natural thing in the world to Kincaid that he should continue down the hill and along the river to Julia's flat. He would collect Sharon's things while he was thinking of it, and while he was there he'd question Julia again about her movements after the gallery closed that night.

Or so said the rational, logical part of his mind. Some other part stood back and watched the machinations of the first, an amused and taunting spectator. Why didn't he admit he hoped he might sit with her, watching the warm lamplight reflect from the shining curve of her hair? Or admit that he wanted to see again the way her lips curved up at the corners when she found something he said amusing? Or that his skin still remembered the touch of her fingers against his face?

205

"Bollocks!" Kincaid said aloud, banishing the spectator to the recesses of his mind. He needed to clear up a few points, that was all, and his interest in Julia Swann was purely professional.

The wind that earlier cleared the sky had died at sunset, leaving the evening still and hushed, waiting expectantly. Lights reflecting on the water's surface made it look ice-solid, and as he passed the Angel pub and walked along the embankment, he felt the chill air hovering over the river like a cloud.

As he came opposite Trevor Simons's gallery, he saw Simons come out the door. Hurriedly crossing the street, Kincaid found him still bent over the latch. He touched his arm. "Mr. Simons. Having a bit of trouble with your lock?"

Simons jumped, dropping the heavy key ring he'd held in his hand. "Christ, Superintendent, but you gave me a fright." He stooped to retrieve the keys and added, "It does stick a bit, I'm afraid, but I've got it now."

"On your way home?" Kincaid said pleasantly, wondering even as he asked if Simons's itinerary included a visit to Julia. Now that she was reinstalled in the flat just down the road, they would have no more need of furtive meetings in the workshop behind the gallery.

Simons stood a little awkwardly, holding his keys in one hand and a portfolio in the other. "Yes, actually. Did you need to see me?"

"There were one or two things," Kincaid answered, making a decision as he spoke. "Why don't we go across the road and have a drink?"

"It won't take more than half an hour?" Simons looked at his watch. "We're going out for a meal tonight. My wife's sent the children to friends—it's more than my life's worth to be late."

Kincaid hastened to reassure him. "We'll just nip across to the Angel. I promise we won't be long."

They found the pub busy, but it was a sedate crowd—made up, judged Kincaid, mostly of professional people having a quick drink before making their way home after work.

"Nice place," Kincaid said as they settled comfortably at a table by one of the windows overlooking the river. "Cheers. I admit I've developed rather a taste for Brakspear's Special." Tasting his beer, he watched his companion curiously. Simons had sounded a bit embarrassed about his dinner engagement, yet it had the ring of truth. "Sounds as though you and your wife have quite a romantic evening planned," Kincaid said, fishing.

Simons looked away, his earlier discomfort more evident. The silver in his thick brown hair caught the light as he ran a hand through it. "Well, Superintendent, you know what women are like. She'll be very disappointed if I don't participate with enthusiasm."

A boat motored slowly under the Henley Bridge, its port and starboard lights gleaming steadily. Kincaid idly pushed his beer mat back and forth with one finger, then looked up at Simons. "Did you know that Julia's moved back into her flat?"

"Yes. Yes, I did. She rang me yesterday." Before Kincaid could respond, Simons said more forcefully, "Look, Superintendent. I took your advice the other day. I told my wife about . . . what happened with Julia." Simons's fine-boned face looked drawn with exhaustion, and as he sipped from his whiskey and water, his hand trembled slightly.

"And?" Kincaid said when he didn't continue.

"She was shocked. And hurt, as you can imagine," Simons said quietly. "I think that the damage won't be easy to repair. We've had a good marriage, probably better than most. I should never have been so careless of it."

"You sound as though you don't mean to continue things with Julia," Kincaid said, knowing it was none of his business, and that his investigation hardly justified crossing the boundary of good manners.

Simons shook his head. "I can't. Not if I mean to mend things with my wife. I've told Julia."

"How did she take it?"

"Oh, she'll be all right." Simons smiled with the same gentle, self-deprecating humor Kincaid had seen before. "I was never more than a passing fancy to Julia, I'm afraid. I've probably saved her the bother of having to say, 'Sorry, old dear, but it was only a bit of a lark.'"

It occurred to Kincaid that Simons, like Sharon Doyle, was probably glad of a nonpartisan ear, and he pushed his advantage. "Were you in love with her?"

"I'm not sure 'love' and 'Julia' exist in the same vocabulary, Mr. Kincaid. I've been married almost twenty years—to me love means darned socks and 'whose turn is it to take out the rubbish, darling?'" Grinning, he drank a little more of his whiskey. "It may not be exciting, but you know where you are—" He sobered suddenly. "Or at least you should, unless one of you behaves like an ass.

"I was infatuated with Julia, fascinated, entranced; but I'm not sure one could ever get close enough to love her."

As much as Kincaid disliked the necessity, he dug in, his voice suddenly harsh. "Were you infatuated enough to lie for her? Are you sure she didn't leave the gallery when the party finished that night? Did she tell you that she had to see someone? That she'd be back in an hour or two?"

The pleasant humor vanished from Trevor Simons's face. He finished his whiskey and set his glass down deliberately, carefully, in the exact center of its mat. "She did not.

"I may be an adulterer, Superintendent, but I'm not a liar. And if you think Julia had anything to do with Connor's death, I can tell you you're barking up the wrong tree. She was with me from the time we closed up the gallery until daybreak. And having burned my bridges, so to speak, by confessing to my wife, I'll testify to that in court if I must."

CHAPTER
13

Kincaid rang the bell and waited. He rang again, shifting his weight a bit from foot to foot and whistling under his breath. No sound came from inside the flat, and he turned away, feeling an unexpected stab of disappointment.

The sound of the door opening stopped him. When he turned back he found Julia looking at him silently, registering neither pleasure nor dismay at his presence. She lifted the wineglass she held in a mock salute. "Superintendent. Is this a social call? You can't join me if you're going to play the heavy."

"My, my," he said, taking in the faded red jersey she wore over black leggings, "an outbreak of color. Is this significant?"

"Sometimes one has to abandon one's principles when one hasn't done laundry," she answered rather owlishly. "Do come in—what will you think of my manners? Of course," she added as she stepped back into the sitting room, "it might be my concession to mourning."

"A reverse statement?" Kincaid asked, following her into the kitchen.

"Something like that. I'll get you a glass. The wine's upstairs." She opened a cupboard and stood up on her toes, stretching to reach a shelf. Kincaid noticed that she wore thick socks but no shoes, and her feet looked small and unprotected. "Con arranged everything in the kitchen to suit himself," she said, snagging a glass. "And it seems whenever I want anything it's always just out of reach."

Kincaid felt as if he'd barged in on a party in progress. "Were you expecting someone? There's no need for me to interrupt—I only wanted a quick word with you, and I thought I'd pick up Sharon Doyle's things as well."

Julia turned around and stood with her back against the counter, looking up at him, holding both glasses against her chest. "I wasn't expecting a soul, Superintendent. There's not a soul to expect." She chuckled a little at her own humor. "Come on. We had graduated from 'Superintendent,' hadn't we?" she added over her shoulder as she led him back through the sitting room. "I suppose I'm the one backsliding."

She wasn't more than a bit tipsy, Kincaid decided as he climbed the stairs after her. Her balance and coordination were still good, although she moved a little more carefully than usual. As they passed the first landing he glimpsed the tumbled, unmade bed through the bedroom's open doorway, but the study door still stood tightly shut.

When they reached the studio he saw that the lamps were lit and the blinds drawn, and it seemed to him that the room had acquired another layer of Julia's personality in the twenty-four hours since he'd seen it last. She had been working and a partially finished painting was pinned to the board on her worktable. Kincaid recognized the plant from the rambles of his Cheshire boyhood—speedwell, the gentian-blue flowers along the pathside that were said to "speed you well" upon your journey. He also remembered his dismay in discovering that its beauty could not be held captive—the delicate blooms wilted and died within minutes of picking.

The rest of the table's surface held open botanical texts, crumpled papers and several used glasses. The room smelled of cigarette smoke, and very faintly of Julia's perfume.

She padded across the Persian carpet and sank to the floor in front of the armchair, which she used as a backrest. Beside the chair were Julia's ashtray, close to overflowing, and an ice bucket holding a bottle of white wine. She filled Kincaid's glass. "Sit down, for heaven's sake, Duncan. You can't hold a funeral celebration standing up."

Kincaid lowered himself to the floor and accepted his drink. "Is that what we're doing?"

"With a bloody good Cap d'Antibes, too. Con would have liked a wake, don't you think? He was all for Irish tradition." Tasting what remained of her wine, she made a face. "Warm." She refilled her glass, then lit a cigarette. "I'm going to cut down, I promise," she said in anticipation of Kincaid's protest, smiling.

"What are you doing, barricading yourself up here like this, Julia? The rest of the house doesn't look like anyone's been in it." He examined her face, deciding that the shadows under her eyes were more pronounced than they had been the day before. "Have you eaten anything?"

Shrugging, she said, "There were still some bits and pieces in the fridge. Con's sort of bits, of course. I would have settled for bread and jam. I suppose I hadn't realized," she paused to draw on her cigarette, "that it would have become Con's house. Not mine. Yesterday I spent most of the day cleaning, but it didn't seem to make any difference—he's everywhere." She made a circular gesture with her head, indicating the studio. "Except here. If he ever came up here, he left no traces."

"What makes you want to eradicate him so thoroughly?"

"I told you before, didn't I?" She knitted her brow and gazed at him over the rim of her glass, as if she couldn't quite remember. "Con was a first-class shit," she said without heat. "A drinker, a gambler, a womanizer, a lout with a load of Irish blarney that he thought would get him anything he wanted—why would I want to be reminded of him?"

Kincaid raised a skeptical eyebrow and sipped his wine. "Can we attribute this to Con, too?" he asked, tasting its crisp delicacy against the roof of his mouth.

"He had good taste, and he was surprisingly adept at finding a bargain," Julia admitted. "A legacy of his upbringing, I would imagine."

Kincaid wondered if Connor's attraction to Sharon Doyle stemmed from his upbringing as well—a spoiled only son of a doting mum might have considered devotion his due. He hoped that Con had also seen her value.

Uncannily echoing his thoughts, Julia said, "The mistress—what did you say she's called?"

"Sharon. Sharon Doyle."

Julia nodded, as if it fit an image in her mind. "Blond and a little plump, young, not very sophisticated?"

"Have you seen her?" Kincaid asked, surprised.

"Didn't need to." Julia's smile was rueful. "I only imagined my antithesis," she said, having a little difficulty with the consonants. "Look at me."

Kincaid found it all too easy to oblige. Framed in the dark bell of her hair, her face revealed humor and intelligence in equal measure. He said, teasing her, "I'll only follow your hypothesis so far. Are you suggesting I should regard you as ancient and world-weary?"

"Well, not quite." This time she gave him the full benefit of her grin, and Kincaid thought again how odd it seemed to see Sir Gerald's smile translated so directly onto her thin face. "But you do see what I mean?"

"Why should Connor have wanted someone as unlike you as he could find?"

She hesitated a moment, then shook her head, shying away from it. "This girl—Sharon—how is she taking it?"

"I'd say she's coping, just."

"Do you think it would help if I spoke to her?" She ground out her cigarette and added more lightly, "I've never quite been sure of the proper protocol in these situations."

Kincaid sensed how vulnerable Sharon would feel in Julia's presence, and yet she had no one with whom she could share her grief. He had seen stranger alliances formed. "I don't know, Julia. I think she'd like to attend Connor's funeral. I'll tell her she's welcome, if you like. But I wouldn't expect too much."

"Con will have told her horror tales about me, I'm sure," Julia said, nodding. "It's only natural."

Regarding her quizzically, Kincaid said, "You're certainly feeling magnanimous tonight. Is it something in the air? I just had a word with Trevor Simons and he was in the same frame of mind." He paused, swallowing a little more of his wine, and when Julia didn't respond, he went on, "He's says he's willing to swear under oath that you were together the entire night, regardless of the damage to his marriage."

She sighed. "Trev's a decent sort. Surely it won't come to that?" Wrapping her arms around her calves, she rested her chin on her knees and looked at Kincaid steadily. "You can't really think I killed poor Con, can you?" When Kincaid didn't answer she lifted her head and said, "*You* don't think that, do you, Duncan?"

Kincaid ran the evidence through his mind. Connor had died between the closing of the gallery show and the very early hours of the morning, the time for which Trevor Simons had given Julia a cast-iron alibi. Simons was a decent sort, as Julia had so aptly put it, and Kincaid had disliked goading him, but he felt more certain now than ever that he would not have compromised himself by lying for Julia.

But even as he set out these facts, he knew that they had little to do with what he felt. He studied her face. Could one see guilt, if one had the right skills, the right information? He had sensed it often enough, and his rational mind told him the assessment must be based on a combination of subliminal cues—body language, smell, shadings in the voice. But he also knew that there was an element to it that transcended the rational—call it a hunch, or a feeling, it didn't matter. It was based on an innate and inexplicable knowledge of another human being, and his knowledge of Julia went bone-deep. He was as certain of her innocence as his own.

Slowly, he shook his head. "No. I don't think you killed Connor. But someone did, and I'm not sure we're getting any closer to it." His back had begun to ache and he stretched, recrossing his legs. "Do you know why Connor would have had dinner with Tommy Godwin the night he died?"

Julia sat up straight, her eyes widening in astonishment. "Tommy? Our Tommy? I've known Tommy since I was this high." She held out a hand, toddler height. "I can't imagine anything less likely than the two of them having a social get-together. Tommy never quite approved of Con, and I'm sure he made it clear. Very politely, of course," she added fondly. "If Con had meant to see Tommy, surely he would have said?"

"According to Godwin, Con wanted his old job back, and thought he might help."

Julia shook her head. "That's piffle. Con had a screaming nervous breakdown. The firm wouldn't have considered it." Her eyes were peat-dark, and guileless.

Kincaid closed his eyes for a moment, in hopes that removing her face from his sight would allow him to gather his thoughts. When he opened them again he found her watching him. "What did Connor say that day, Julia? It seems to me that his behavior only became out of the ordinary after he left you at lunchtime. I think you've not quite told me the whole truth."

She looked away from him, fumbling for her cigarettes, then pushed the packet away and stood up, as graceful as a dancer. Moving to the table, she unscrewed the top of a paint tube and squeezed a drop of deep blue color onto her palette. Choosing a fine brush, she dabbed a little of the color onto the painting. "Can't seem to get the bloody thing quite right, and I'm tired of looking at it. Maybe if I—"

"Julia."

She stopped, paintbrush frozen in midair. After a long moment, she rinsed the brush and placed it carefully beside the drawing, then turned to him. "It began ordinarily enough, just the way I told you. A little row about money, about the flat." She came back to the arm of the chair.

"Then what happened?" He moved closer to her and touched her hand, urging her on.

Julia captured his hand between her palms and held it tightly. She looked down, rubbing the back of his hand with her fingertips. "He begged me," she said so softly Kincaid had to strain to hear. "He literally got down on his knees and begged me. Begged me to take him back, begged me to love him. I don't know what set him off that day. I'd thought he had pretty well accepted things."

"What did you tell him?"

"That it was no use. That I meant to divorce him as soon as the two-year limit had passed, if he still refused to cooperate." She met Kincaid's eyes. "I was perfectly beastly to him, and it wasn't his fault. None of it was."

"What are you talking about?" Kincaid said, startled enough to forget for a moment the sensation of her fingers against his skin.

"It was all my fault, from the very beginning. I should never have married Con. I knew it wasn't fair, but I was in love with the idea of getting married, and I suppose I thought we'd muddle through somehow." She laughed, letting go his hand. "But the more he loved me, the more he needed, the less I had to give. In the end there was nothing at all." Softly, she added, "Except pity."

"Julia," Kincaid said sharply, "you were not responsible for Connor's needs. There are people who will suck you dry, no matter how much you give. You couldn't—"

"You don't understand." She slipped from the arm of the chair, moving restlessly away from him, then turned back as she reached the worktable. "I knew when I married Con I couldn't love him. Not him, not anyone, not even Trev, who hasn't asked for much except honesty and affection. I can't, do you see? I'm not capable."

"Don't be absurd, Julia," Kincaid said, pushing to his feet. "Of course you—"

"No." She stopped him with the one flat word. "I can't. Because of Matty."

The despair in her voice banished his anger as quickly as it had come. He went to her and drew her gently to him, stroking her hair as she laid her head against his shoulder. Her slender body fit into the curve of his arms as easily as if it had always been there, and her hair felt as silky as feathers against the palm of his hand. She smelled faintly, unexpectedly, of lilacs. Kincaid took a breath, steadying himself against the wave of dizziness that swept over him, forcing himself to concentrate on the matter at hand. "What has Matty to do with it, Julia?"

"Everything. I loved him, too, you see, but that never seemed to occur to anyone . . . except Plummy, I suppose. She knew. I was ill, you know . . . afterward. But it gave me time to think, and it was then I decided that nothing would ever hurt me like that again." She pulled away from him just enough to look up into his face. "It's not worth it. Nothing is."

"But surely the alternative—a lifetime of emotional isolation—is worse?"

215

She came back into his arms, resting her cheek in the hollow of his shoulder. "It's bearable, at least," she said, her voice muffled, and he felt her breath, warm through the fabric of his shirt. "I tried to explain it to Con that day—why I could never give him what he wanted . . . a family, children. I had nothing to go by, you see, no blueprint for an ordinary life. And a child—I could never take that risk. You do you see that, don't you?"

He saw himself with uncomfortable clarity, curling up like a wounded hedgehog after Vic had shattered his safe and comfortable existence. He had protected himself from risk as surely as Julia. But she, at least, had been honest with herself, while he had used work, with the convenient demands of a cop's life, as an excuse for not making emotional commitments. "I do see it," he said softly, "but I don't agree with it."

He rubbed her back, gently kneading the knotted muscles, and her shoulder blades felt sharp under his hands. "Did Connor understand?"

"It only made him more angry. It was then I was beastly to him. I said—" She stopped, shaking her head, and her hair tickled Kincaid's nose. "Horrid things, really horrid. I'm so ashamed." Harshly, she added, "It's my fault he's dead. I don't know what he did after he left Badger's End that day, but if I hadn't sent him away so cruelly—" She was crying now, her words coming in hiccuping gulps.

Kincaid took her face in his hands and wiped the tears from her cheeks with his thumbs. "Julia, Julia. You don't know that. You can't know that. You were not responsible for Connor's behavior, or for his death." He looked down at her, and in her tousled hair and tear-streaked face he saw again the child of his vision, alone with her grief in the narrow white bed. After a moment he said, "Nor were you responsible for Matthew's death. Look at me, Julia. Do you hear me?"

"How can you know that?" she asked fiercely. "Everyone thought . . . Mummy and Daddy never forgave—"

"Those who knew and loved you never held you responsible, Julia. I've spoken to Plummy. And the vicar. You're the one who has never forgiven yourself. That's too heavy a burden for anyone to carry for twenty years. Let it go."

For a long moment she held his gaze, then he felt the tension drain from her body. She returned her head to his shoulder, slipped her arms around his waist and leaned against him, letting him support her weight.

Thus they stood, quietly, until Kincaid became aware of every point where their bodies made contact. For all her slenderness, her body seemed suddenly, undeniably solid against his, and her breasts pressed firmly against his chest. He could hear his blood pounding in his ears.

Julia gave a hiccuping sigh and raised her head a little. "I've gone and made your shirt all soggy," she said, rubbing at the damp patch on his shoulder. Then she tilted her head so that she could look into his face and added, her voice husky with suppressed laughter, "Does Scotland Yard always render its services so . . . enthusiastically?"

He stepped back, flushing with embarrassment, wishing he had worn less-revealing jeans rather than slacks. "I'm sorry. I didn't mean—"

"It's all right," she said, drawing him to her again. "I don't mind. I don't mind at all."

CHAPTER
14

He woke to the sound of Tony's voice. "Morning tea, Mr. Kincaid," he said as he tapped on the door and entered. "And a message for you from Sergeant Makepeace at High Wycombe. Something about catching the bird you wanted?"

Kincaid sat up and ran a hand through his hair, then accepted the cup. "Thanks, Tony," he said to Tony's departing back. So they had found Kenneth Hicks and brought him in. They wouldn't be able to hold him long without cause. He should have checked in last night—hot tea sloshed onto his hand as awareness came flooding into his still groggy brain.

Last night. Julia. Oh, bloody hell. What have I done.? How could he have been so unprofessional? With the thought came the memory of Trevor Simons's words, "I never meant to do it. It was just . . . Julia," and of his own rather supercilious comments about the man's loss of judgment.

He closed his eyes. Never, in all his years on the job, had he crossed that line, hadn't even thought, really, that he needed to protect himself from the temptation. Yet even in his self-reproach he found that there was a part of him that felt no remorse, for their union had been clean and healing, a solace for old wounds and a destruction of barriers too long held.

It was not until he entered the Chequers' dining room and saw Gemma seated alone at a table that he remembered the message he'd left for her yesterday. When had she arrived, and how long had she waited for him?

Sitting down across from her, he said, "You're an early bird," with as much aplomb as he could manage. "We'll need to get on to High Wycombe as soon as we can. They're holding Kenneth Hicks for questioning."

Gemma answered him without a trace of her usual morning cheeriness. "I know. I've spoken to Jack Makepeace already."

"Are you all right, Gemma?"

"Headache." She nibbled without much enthusiasm on a piece of dry toast.

"Tony pour you one drink too many?" he said, attempting to humor her, but she merely shrugged. "Look," he said, wondering if the flush of guilt he felt were visible, "I'm sorry about last night. I was . . . delayed." She must have rushed here from London and waited for him, might even have been worried about him, and he had sent no word. "I should have rung you. It was thoughtless of me." Tilting his head, he studied her, measuring her mood. "Shall I grovel some more? Would a bed of hot coals do?"

This time she smiled and he gave an inward sigh of relief. Searching for a change of subject, he said, "Tell me about Tommy Godwin." Just then his breakfast arrived, and he tucked into eggs and bacon while Gemma gave him a brief recounting of her interview.

"I took a statement, and I've had the forensics lads go over his flat and car."

"I saw Sharon Doyle again, and Trevor Simons," he said through a mouthful of toast. "And Julia. Connor went home again after his scuffle with Tommy, Gemma. It looks as though Tommy Godwin's out of the frame unless we can prove he met Con again later. He did ring someone from the flat, though—problem is, we've no earthly idea who it was."

Julia. There had been a familiarity, an unconscious intimacy, in the way Kincaid said her name. Gemma tried to concentrate on her driving, tried to ignore the certainty that was growing in the pit of her stomach. Surely she was imagining things? And what if it were true? Why should it matter so much to her if Duncan Kincaid had formed a less-than-professional relationship with a suspect in a murder investigation? It was common enough—she'd seen it happen with other officers—and she'd never thought he was infallible. Had she?

"Grow up, Gemma," she said under her breath. He was human, and male, and she should never have forgotten that even gods sometimes have feet of clay. But those reminders made her feel no less miserable, and she was thankful when the High Wycombe roundabouts claimed all her attention.

"I've had Hicks warming up nicely for you the last half-hour," Jack Makepeace said in greeting when they found him in his office. He shook their hands, and Gemma thought he gave hers an extra little squeeze. "Thought it would do him a world of good. Too bad he didn't quite manage to finish his breakfast." Makepeace winked at Gemma. "He's made his phone call—his mum, or so he says—but the cavalry's not come to the rescue."

Having been briefed earlier on the telephone by Makepeace, Kincaid had brought Gemma up to date in the car and suggested that she begin the interview. "He doesn't care for women," Kincaid said as Makepeace left them at the nondescript door of Room A. "I want you to upset his balance a bit, prime him for me."

One interview room seldom differed much from another— they could be expected to meet some variation of small and square, and to smell of stale cigarette smoke and human sweat, but when Gemma entered the room she swallowed convulsively, fighting the instinctive urge to cover her nose. Unshaven and all too obviously unbathed, Kenneth Hicks reeked of fear.

"Christ," Kincaid muttered in Gemma's ear as he came in behind her. "We should've brought masks." He coughed, then added at full volume as he pulled out a chair for Gemma, "Hullo, Kenneth. Like the accommodations? Not quite up to the Hilton, I'm afraid, but then what can you do?"

"Go fuck yourself," Hicks said succinctly. His voice was nasal, and Gemma pegged his accent as South London.

Kincaid shook his head as he sat down beside Gemma, facing Hicks across the narrow laminated table. "I'm disappointed in you, Kenneth. I thought you had better manners. We'll just record our little conversation," he said, pushing the switch on the tape recorder. "If you don't mind, of course. You don't mind, do you, Kenneth?"

Gemma studied Kenneth Hicks while Kincaid nattered pleasantly on and fiddled with the recorder. Hicks's narrow, acne-spotted face seemed permanently stamped with a surly expression. In spite of the warmth of the room, he had kept on a black leather bomber jacket, and he rubbed nervously at his nose and chin as Kincaid's patter continued. There seemed something vaguely familiar about him, and Gemma frowned with frustration as it hovered on the fringe of her mind.

"Sergeant James will be asking you a few questions," Kincaid said, pushing his chair back from the table a bit. He folded his arms and stretched out his legs, as if he might catnap through the interview.

"Kenneth," she said pleasantly, when they had completed the recorded preliminaries, "why don't you make it easy for everyone and tell us exactly what you were doing the night Connor Swann was killed?"

Hicks darted a glance at Kincaid. "I already told the other bloke, the one as brought me in here. Big ginger-haired berk."

"You told Sergeant Makepeace that you were drinking with friends at the Fox and Hounds in Henley until closing, after which you continued the party in the friends' flat," said Gemma, and the sound of her voice brought Hicks's eyes back to her. "Is that right?" she added a little more forcefully.

"Yeah, that's right. That's just like I told him." Hicks seemed to gain a little confidence from her recital. He relaxed in his chair and stared at Gemma, letting his eyes rest for a long moment on her breasts.

She smiled sweetly at him and made a show of consulting her notebook. "Thames Valley CID took statements last night from the friends you named, Kenneth, and unfortunately none of them seems to remember you being there at all."

Hicks's skin turned the color of the room's nicotine-stained walls as the blood drained from his face. "I'll kill 'em, the friggin' little shits. They're lying their bloody heads off." He looked from Gemma to Kincaid, and, apparently finding no reassurance in their expressions, said a little more frantically, "You can't do me for this. I never saw Con after we had that drink at the Fox. I swear I didn't."

Gemma flipped another page in her notebook. "You may have to, unless you can come up with a little better accounting of your movements after half-past ten. Connor made a telephone call from his flat around then, and afterward said he meant to go out."

"Who says he did?" asked Hicks, with more shrewdness than Gemma had credited him.

"Never mind that. Do you want to know what I think, Kenneth?" Gemma asked, leaning toward him and lowering her voice confidentially. "I think Connor rang you and asked you to meet him at the lock. You argued and Connor fell in. It could happen to anybody, couldn't it, Ken? Did you try to help him, or were you afraid of the water?" Her tone said she understood and would forgive him anything.

"I never!" Hicks pushed his chair back from the table. "That's a bleedin' lie. And how the bleedin' hell am I supposed to have got there without a car?"

"Connor picked you up in his car," Gemma said reasonably, "and afterward you hitched a ride back to Henley."

"I didn't, I tell you, and you can't prove I did."

Unfortunately, Gemma knew from Thames Valley's reports that he was correct—Connor's car had been freshly washed and vacuumed and forensics had found no significant traces. "Then where were you? Tell the truth this time."

"I've told you already. I was at the Fox, then at this bloke's. Jackie—he's called Jackie Fawcett."

Kincaid recrossed his ankles lazily and spoke for the first time since Gemma had begun. "Then why wouldn't your mates give you a nice, tidy alibi, Kenneth? I can see two possibilities—the first is that you're lying, and the second is that they don't like you, and I must say I don't know which I think is the more likely. Did you help out other friends the same way you helped Connor?"

"Don't know what you're on about." Hicks pulled a battered cigarette pack from the pocket of his jacket. He shook it, then probed inside it with thumb and forefinger before crumpling it in disgust.

Gemma took up the thread again. "That's what you argued about, isn't it, Kenneth? When you met Con after lunch, did you tell him he had to pay up? Did he agree to meet you later that evening? Then when he turned up without the money, you fought with him," she embroidered as she went along.

An element of pleading crept into Hicks's voice. "He didn't owe me nothin', I told you." He kept his eyes fixed anxiously on Kincaid, and Gemma wondered what Kincaid had done to put the wind up him like that.

Straightening up in his chair, Kincaid said, "So you're telling me that Con paid you off, and yet I happen to know that Con was so hard up he couldn't make the mortgage on the flat. I think you're lying. I think you said something to Connor over that little social pint at the Fox that sent him over the edge. What was it, Kenneth? Did you threaten to have your boss call out his muscle?" He stood up and leaned forward with his hands on the table.

"I never threatened him. It wasn't like that," Hicks squeaked, shrinking away from Kincaid.

"But he did still owe you money?"

Hicks looked at them, sweat beading on his upper lip, and Gemma could see him calculating which way to turn next. *Rat in a trap*, she thought, and pressed her lips together to conceal her satisfaction. They waited in silence, until finally Hicks said, "Maybe he did. So what? I never threatened him like you said."

Moving restlessly back and forth in the small space before the table, Kincaid said, "I don't believe you. Your boss was going to take it out of your skin if you didn't come up with the ready—I don't believe you didn't use a little persuasion." He smiled at Hicks as he came near him again. "And the trouble with persuasion is that sometimes it gets out of hand. Isn't that so, Kenneth?"

"No. I don't know. I mean—"

"Are you saying that it wasn't an accident? That you intended to kill him?"

"That's not what I meant." Hicks swallowed and wiped his hands on his thighs. "I only made him a suggestion, a proposition, like."

Kincaid stopped pacing and stood very still with his hands in his pockets, watching Hicks. "That sounds very interesting, Kenneth. What sort of proposition?"

Gemma held her breath as Hicks teetered on the edge of confession, afraid any move might nudge him in the wrong direction. Listening to the ragged cadence of his breathing, she offered up a silent little incantation to the god of interviews.

Hicks spoke finally, with the rush of release, and his words were venomous. "I knew about him from the first, him and his hoity-toity Ashertons. You would've thought they were the bleedin' Royals, the way he talked, but I knew better. That Dame Caroline's just a jumped-up tart, no better than she should be. And all the fuss they made over that kid what drowned, well, he wasn't even Sir Gerald's kid, was he, just a bleedin' little bastard." Matty. He was talking about Matty, Gemma thought, trying to make sense of it.

Kincaid sat down again, pulling his chair up until he could rest his elbows on the table. "Let's start over from the beginning, shall we, Kenneth?" he said very quietly, very evenly, and Gemma shivered. "You told Connor that Matthew Asherton was illegitimate, have I got that right?"

Hicks's Adam's apple bobbed in his skinny throat as he swallowed and nodded, then looked in appeal at Gemma. He'd got more than he bargained for, she thought, wondering suddenly what Kincaid might have done if she hadn't been in the room and the tape recorder running.

"How could you possibly know that?" Kincaid asked, still soft as velvet.

"'Cause my uncle Tommy was his bleedin' dad, that's how."

★   ★   ★

In the silence that followed, Kenneth Hicks's ragged, adenoidal breathing sounded loud in Gemma's ears. She opened her mouth, but found she couldn't quite formulate any words.

"Your uncle Tommy? Do you mean Tommy Godwin?" Kincaid said finally, not quite managing to control his surprise.

Gemma felt as if a giant hand were squeezing her diaphragm. She saw again the silver-framed photograph of Matthew Asherton— the blond hair and the impish grin on his friendly face. She remembered Tommy's voice as he spoke of Caroline, and she wondered why she had not seen it before.

"I heard him telling me mum about it when the kid drowned," said Hicks. He must have interpreted the shock in their faces as disbelief, because he added on a rising note of panic, "I swear. I never said nothin', but after I met Con and he went on about them, I remembered the names."

Gemma felt a wave of nausea sweep over her as the corollary sank in. "I don't believe you. You can't be Tommy Godwin's nephew, it's just not possible," she said hotly, thinking of Tommy's elegance, and of his courteous patience as she'd taken him through his statement at the Yard, but even as she resisted the idea, she felt again that odd sense of familiarity. Could it be something in the line of the nose, or the set of the jaw?

"You go to Clapham and ask me mum, then. She'll tell you soon enough—"

"You said you made Connor a proposition," Kincaid dropped the words into Hicks's protest like stones in a pool. "Just what was it, exactly?"

Hicks rubbed his nose and sniffed, shifting away from eye contact with them.

"Come on, sunshine, you can tell us all about it," Kincaid urged him. "Spit it out."

"Well, the Ashertons have got to be pretty stinking with it, haven't they, what with their titles and all. Always in the newspapers, in the gossip sections. So I figured they'd not like it put about that their kid was wrong side of the blanket, like."

The intensity of Kincaid's anger seemed to have abated. "Do I take it that you suggested to Connor that he should blackmail his own in-laws?" he asked, regarding Hicks with cool amusement. "What about your own family? Did it occur to you that this might damage your uncle and your mother?"

"He wasn't to say I was the one told him," Hicks said, as if that absolved him of any culpability.

"In other words, you didn't care how it might affect your uncle as long as it couldn't be traced back to you." Kincaid smiled. "Very noble of you, Kenneth. And how did Connor react to your little proposition?"

"He didn't believe me," said Hicks, sounding aggrieved. "Not right away. Then he thought about it a bit and he started to get all strung up. He said how much money was I thinking about, and when I told him 'start with fifty-thousand quid and we'd split it, we could always ask for more later,' he bloody laughed at me. Told me to shut my friggin' face and if I ever said another word about it, he'd kill me." Hicks blinked his pale lashes and added, as if he still couldn't quite believe it, "After everything I did for him!"

"He really didn't understand why Connor was angry with him," Kincaid said to Gemma as they stood at the zebra crossing separating High Wycombe Station from the carpark where they had left Gemma's Escort. "He's more than a few bricks short of a load in the morals department, is our Kenneth. I imagine it's only the fact that he's such a 'timorous wee beastie' that's kept him to petty villainy—although I think the comparison does an injustice to the poor mouse," he added, brushing at the sleeve of his sport jacket.

It was one of his favorites, Gemma noticed with the detachment that had overtaken her, a fine blue-and-gray wool that brought out the color of his eyes. Why was he waffling on as if he'd never come across a small-time crook before?

The oncoming traffic came to a halt and they crossed on the stripes. Kincaid glanced at his watch as they reached the opposite pavement. "I think we can manage a word with Tommy Godwin before lunch if we drive like the hounds of hell are after us. In fact," he said as they reached the car and Gemma dug the Escort's keys out of her bag, "since it looks as though we may not need to come back here, we'd better pick up our things and get my car back to London as well."

Without a word, Gemma started the engine as he slid in beside her. She felt as though a kaleidoscope inside her head had shifted, jumbling the pieces so that they no longer made a recognizable pattern.

Kincaid touched her arm. "Gemma, what is it? You've been like this since breakfast. If you really don't feel well—"

She turned toward him, tasting salt where she had bitten the inside of her lip. "Did you believe him?"

"Who, Kenneth?" asked Kincaid, sounding a bit puzzled. "Well, you have to admit, it does make sense of things that—"

"You haven't met Tommy. Oh, I can believe that Tommy was Matthew's dad," she conceded, "but not the rest of it. It's a cock-and-bull story if I ever—

"Just improbable enough to be true, I'm afraid," said Kincaid. "And how else could he have found out about Tommy and Matthew? It gives us the missing piece, Gemma—motive. Connor confronted Tommy over dinner that night with what he'd found out, and Tommy killed him to keep him quiet."

"I don't believe it," Gemma said stubbornly, but even as she spoke little slivers of doubt crept into her mind. Tommy loved Caro, and Julia. You could see that. And Gerald he spoke of with respect and affection. Had protecting them been enough reason for murder? But even if she could swallow that premise, the rest still didn't make sense to her. "Why would Connor have agreed to meet him at the lock?"

"Tommy promised to bring him money."

Gemma stared blindly at the drizzle that had begun to coat the windscreen. "Somehow I don't think that Connor wanted money," she said with quiet certainty. "And that doesn't explain why Tommy went to London to see Gerald. It can't have been to establish an alibi, not if Connor was still alive."

"I think you're letting your liking for Tommy Godwin affect your judgment, Gemma. No one else has a shred of motive. Surely you can see—"

The anger that had been building in her all morning broke like a flash flood. "You're the one that's blind," she shouted at him. "You're so besotted with Julia Swann that you won't consider that she might be implicated in Connor's death, when you know as well as I do that the husband or wife is most likely to be involved in a spouse's murder. How can you be sure Trevor Simons isn't lying to protect her? How do you know she didn't meet Connor before his dinner with Tommy, before the gallery opening, and arrange to meet him later that night? Maybe she thought a scandal involving her family would damage her career. Maybe she wanted to protect her parents. Maybe . . ." She ran down, her fury quickly spent, and sat waiting desolately for the inevitable backlash. This time she had really crossed over the line.

But instead of giving her the dressing-down she expected, Kincaid looked away. In the silence that followed she could hear the swishing of tires on the damp pavement, and a faint ticking that seemed to be inside her own head. "Perhaps you're right," he said finally. "Perhaps my judgment can't be trusted. But unless we come up with some concrete physical evidence, it's all I have to go on with."

They made the journey back to London in separate cars, meeting again at Kincaid's flat as they had arranged. The drizzle had followed them, and Kincaid drew the tarp over the Midget before locking it. As he climbed into Gemma's car he said, "You really must do something about your tires, Gemma. The right rear is as bald as my granddad's head." It was an often-repeated nag, and when she didn't rise to the bait, he sighed and continued, "I rang LB House on the mobile phone. Tommy Godwin didn't come in today, said he was unwell. Didn't you say his flat was in Highgate?"

Gemma nodded. "I have the address in my notebook. It's quite near here, I think." A formless anxiety settled over her as she drove, and it was with relief that she spotted the block of flats. She left the car in the circular drive and hopped out, jiggling her foot in impatience as she waited for Kincaid to lock his side of the car and catch her up at the building entrance.

"Christ, Gemma, is there a fire no one bothered to tell me about?" he said, but she ignored the barb and pushed through the frosted-glass doors. When they presented their identification to the doorman, he scowled and grudgingly directed them to take the lift to the fourth floor.

"Nice building," Kincaid said as they rose creakingly in the lift. "It's been well maintained, but not overly modernized." The fourth-floor foyer, tiled in a highly polished black-and-white geometric design, bore him out. "Deco, if I'm not mistaken."

Gemma, searching for the flat number, had only been listening with half an ear. "What?" she asked, knocking at 4C.

"Art Deco. The building must date from between—"

The door swung open and Tommy Godwin regarded them quizzically. "Mike rang me and said the Bill were paying another call. Very disapproving he was, too. I think he must have had unfortunate dealings with the law in a previous existence." Godwin wore a paisley silk dressing gown and slippers, and his usually immaculate blond hair stood on end. "You must be Superintendent Kincaid," he said as he ushered them into the flat.

Having assured herself that Tommy hadn't gone and put his head in the oven or something equally silly, Gemma felt irrationally angry with him for having worried her. She followed slowly behind the men, looking about her. A small, sleek kitchen lay to her left, done in the same black and white as the foyer. To her right, the sitting room carried on the theme, and through its bank of windows she could see a gray London spread before her. All the lines of the furniture were curved, but without fussiness, and the monochromatic color scheme was accented by a collection of pink frosted glass. Gemma found the room restful, and saw that its gentle order fit Tommy like a second suit of clothes.

A Siamese cat posed on a chair beneath the window. Paws tucked under her chest, she regarded them with unblinking sapphire eyes.

"You're quite right, Superintendent," Tommy said as she joined them, "these flats were built in the early thirties, and they were the ultimate in advanced design for their day. They've held up remarkably well, unlike most of the postwar monstrosities. Sit down, please," he added as he seated himself in a fan-shaped chair that complemented the swirling design on his dressing gown. "Although I must say, I think it must have been a bit nerve-racking during the war, as high above the city as we are. You'd have felt like a sitting duck when the German bombers came over. A chink in the blackout and—"

"Tommy," Gemma interrupted severely, "they said at LB House that you weren't well. What is it?"

He ran a hand through his hair, and in the clear gray light Gemma saw the skin beginning to pouch a little under his eyes. "Just a bit under the weather, Sergeant. I must admit that yesterday rather took its toll." He stood and went to the drinks cabinet against the wall. "Will you have a little sherry? It's appropriately near lunchtime, and I'm sure Rory Allyn always accepted a sherry when he was interrogating suspects."

"Tommy, this isn't a detective novel, for heaven's sake," said Gemma, unable to contain her exasperation.

He turned to look at her, sherry decanter poised in one hand. "I know, my dear. But it's my way of whistling in the dark." The gentleness of his tone told her that he acknowledged her concern and was touched by it.

"I won't refuse a small one," said Kincaid, and Tommy placed three glasses and the decanter on a small cocktail tray. The glasses were sensuously scalloped in the same delicate frosted pink as the fluted lampshades and vases Gemma had already noticed, and when she tasted the sherry it seemed to dissolve on her tongue like butter.

"After all," said Tommy as he filled his own glass and returned to his chair, "if I'm to take the blame for a crime I didn't commit, I might as well do it with good grace."

"Yesterday you told me you'd been to Clapham to visit your sister." Gemma paused to lick a trace of sherry from her lip, then went on more slowly. "You didn't tell me about Kenneth."

"Ah." Tommy leaned against the chair back and closed his eyes. The light etched lines of exhaustion around his mouth and nose, delineated the pulse ticking in his throat. Gemma wondered why she hadn't seen the gray mixed in with the gold at his temples. "Would you admit to Kenneth, given a choice?" Tommy said, without moving. "No, don't answer that." He opened his eyes and gave Gemma a valiant attempt at a smile. "I take it you've met him?"

Gemma nodded.

"Then I can also assume that the whole sordid cat is out of the bag."

"I think so, yes. You lied to me about your dinner with Connor. There wasn't any question of him going back to his old job. He confronted you with what Kenneth had told him." This seemed to be her day for making accusations, she thought, finding that she took Tommy's deception personally, as if she'd been betrayed by a friend.

"A mere taradiddle, my dear—" Catching Gemma's expression he stopped and sighed. "I'm sorry, Sergeant. You're quite right. What do you want to know?"

"Start from the beginning. Tell us about Caroline."

"Ah, you mean from the very beginning." Tommy swirled the sherry in his glass, watching it reflectively. "I loved Caro, you see, with all the blind, single-minded recklessness of youth. Or perhaps age has nothing to do with it . . . I don't know. Our affair ended with Matthew's conception. I wanted her to leave Gerald and marry me. I would have loved Julia as my own child." Pausing, he finished his sherry and returned the glass to the tray with deliberate care. "It was a fantasy, of course. Caro was beginning a promising career, she was comfortably ensconced at Badger's End with the backing of the Asherton name and money. What had I to offer her? And there was Gerald, who has never behaved less than honorably in all the years I've known him.

"One makes what adjustments one must," he said, smiling at Gemma. "I've come to the conclusion that great tragedies are created by those who don't make it through the adjustment stage. We went on. As 'Uncle Tommy' I was allowed to watch Matty grow up, and no one knew the truth except Caro and me.

"Then Matty died."

Kincaid set his empty glass on the cocktail tray, and the click of glass against wood sounded loud as a shot in the silent room.

Gemma gave him a startled glance—so focused had she been on Tommy that for a moment she had forgotten his presence. Neither of them spoke, and after a moment, Tommy continued.

"They shut me out. Closed ranks. In their grief Caro and Gerald had no room for anyone else's. As much as I loved Matty, I also saw that he was an ordinary little boy, with an ordinary little boy's faults and graces. The fact that he was also extraordinarily gifted meant no more to him than if he'd had an extra finger or been able to do lightning calculus in his head. Not so, Gerald and Caro. Do you understand that? Matty was the embodiment of their dreams, a gift God had sent them to mold in their own image."

"So how did Kenneth come into this?" asked Gemma.

"My sister is not a bad sort. We all have our crosses—Kenneth is hers. Our mother died while she was still at school. I was barely making ends meet at the time and wasn't able to do much for her, so I think she married Kenneth's dad out of desperation. As it turned out, he stayed around just long enough to produce his son and heir, then scarpered, leaving her with a baby to look after as well as herself."

Gemma saw an echo of her own marriage in Tommy's account of his sister, and she shuddered at the thought that in spite of all her efforts, her own little son might turn out to be like Kenneth. It didn't bear thinking of. She finished her sherry in one long swallow, and as the warmth spread to her stomach and suffused her face, she remembered she'd gone without breakfast that morning.

Tommy shifted in his chair and smoothed the fold of his dressing gown across his lap. The cat seemed to take that as an invitation, leaping easily up and settling herself under his hands. His long, slender fingers stroked her chocolate-and-cream fur, and Gemma found she could not force herself to see those hands wrapped around Connor's throat. She looked up and met Tommy's eyes.

"After Matty died," he said, "I went to my sister and poured out the whole story. There was no one else." Clearing his throat, he reached for the decanter and poured himself a little more sherry. "I don't remember that time very clearly, you understand, and I've just been piecing things together myself. Kenneth can't have been more than eight or nine, but I think he was born a sneak—possessive of his mother, always hiding and eavesdropping on adult conversations. I had no idea he was even in the house that day. Can you imagine how shocked I was when Connor told me what he had heard, and who had told him?"

"Why did Connor come to you?" asked Kincaid. "Did he ask for money?"

"I don't think Connor knew what he wanted. He seemed to have got it into his head that Julia would have loved him if it hadn't been for Matty's death, and that if Julia had known the truth about Matty, things would have been different between them. I'm afraid he wasn't very coherent. 'Bloody liars,' he kept saying, 'They're all bloody hypocrites.'" Tommy laced his fingers together and sighed. "I think Con had bought the Asherton family image lock, stock and barrel, and he couldn't bear the disillusionment. Or perhaps he just needed someone to blame for his own failure. They had hurt him and he had been powerless, unable to nick even their armor. Kenneth put the perfect weapon into his waiting hands."

"Couldn't you have stopped him?" Kincaid asked.

Tommy smiled at him, undeceived by the casual tone. "Not in the way you mean. I begged him, pleaded with him to keep quiet, for Gerald's and Caro's sake, and for Julia's, but that only seemed to make him angrier. In the end I even tussled with him, much to my shame.

"When I walked away from Connor I had made up my mind what to do. The lies had gone on long enough. Connor was right, in a sense—the deception had warped all our lives, whether we realized it or not."

"I don't understand," said Kincaid. "Why did you think killing Connor would put an end to the deception?"

"But I didn't kill Connor, Superintendent," Tommy said flatly, weariness evident in the set of his mouth. "I told Gerald the truth."

CHAPTER

15

Gemma started the Escort's engine and let it idle while Kincaid buckled himself into the passenger seat. She had been silent all the way from Tommy's flat down to the car. Kincaid glanced at her, feeling utterly baffled. He thought of the usual free give-and-take of their working relationship, and of dinner at her flat just a few nights ago, when they had shared such easy intimacy. At some level he had been aware of her special talent for forming bonds with people, but he had never quite formulated it. She had welcomed him into her warm circle, made him feel comfortable with himself as well as her, and he had taken it for granted. Now, having seen the rapport she'd developed with Tommy Godwin, he felt suddenly envious, like a child shut out in the cold.

She swatted at a spiraling wisp that had escaped her braid and turned to him. "What now, guv?" she said, without inflection.

He wanted urgently to repair the damage between them, but he didn't quite know how to proceed, and other matters needed his immediate attention. "Hold on a tick," he said, and dialed the Yard on the mobile phone. He asked a brief question and rang off. "According to forensics, Tommy Godwin's flat and car were as clean as a whistle." Feeling his way tentatively, he said, "Perhaps I was a bit hasty in my conclusions about Tommy. That's more your style," he added with a smile, but Gemma merely went on regarding him with a frustratingly neutral expression. He sighed and rubbed his face. "I think we'll have to see Sir Gerald again, but first let's have something to eat and see where we are."

As Gemma drove he closed his eyes, wondering how he might mend their relationship, and why the solution to this case continued to elude him.

They stopped at a café in Golders Green for a late lunch, having rung Badger's End and made sure that Sir Gerald would see them whenever they arrived.

Much to Kincaid's satisfaction, Gemma ate her way steadily through a tuna sandwich without any of the reluctance she'd shown at breakfast. He finished his ham-and-cheese, then sipped his coffee and watched Gemma as she polished off a bag of crisps. "I can't make sense of it," he said when she had reached the finger-licking stage. "It can't have been Gerald whom Con phoned from the flat. According to Sharon, Con made that call at a little after half-past ten, when Gerald was busy conducting a full orchestra."

"He might have left a message," said Gemma, wiping her fingertips with a paper napkin.

"With whom? Your porter would have remembered. Alison what's-her-name would have remembered."

"True." Gemma tasted her coffee and made a face. "Cold. Ugh." She pushed her cup away and folded her arms on the tabletop. "It would make much more sense if Sir Gerald rang Con after Tommy had left."

According to Tommy, Gerald had expressed neither shock nor outrage at his revelation. He gave Tommy a drink, as if nothing out of the ordinary had occurred, then said as if to himself, "The worm ate Arthur's empire from the inside, too, as he always knew it would." Tommy had left him sitting slumped in his makeup chair, glass in hand.

"What if the call Sharon overheard had nothing to do with Connor's murder? We have no proof that it did." Kincaid drew speculative circles on the tabletop with the damp end of his spoon. "What if Con didn't follow Sharon out of the flat? He didn't tell her he meant to leave right away."

"You mean that if Gerald had rung him after Tommy left, he

might still have been there? And he might have agreed to meet him at the lock?" continued Gemma with a spark of interest.

"But we've no proof," said Kincaid. "We've no proof of anything. This entire mess is like a pudding—as soon as you sink your teeth into it, it slides away."

Gemma laughed, and Kincaid gave thanks for even a small sign of a thaw.

By the time they reached Badger's End, the drizzle had evolved into a slow and steady rain. They sat for a moment in the car, listening to the rhythmic patter on roof and bonnet. Lamps were already lit in the house, and they saw a flick of the drape at the sitting room window.

"The light will be gone soon," said Gemma. "The evenings draw in so early in this weather." As Kincaid reached for the door handle, she touched his arm. "Guv, if Sir Gerald killed Connor, why did he want us in on it?"

Kincaid turned back to her. "Maybe Caroline insisted. Maybe his friend, the assistant commissioner, volunteered us, and he didn't think he should protest." Sensing her discomfort, he touched her fingers and added, "I don't like this, either, Gemma, but we have to follow it through."

They dashed for the house under the cover of one umbrella, and stood huddled together on the doorstep. They heard the short double ring as Kincaid pushed the bell, but before he could lift his finger, Sir Gerald opened the door himself. "Come in by the fire," he said. "Here, take your wet things off. It's beastly out, I'm afraid, and not likely to get any better." He shepherded them into the sitting room, where a fire blazed in the grate, and Kincaid had a moment's fancy that it was never allowed to go out.

"You'll need something to warm you inside as well as out," said Sir Gerald when they were established with their backs to the fire. "Plummy's making us some tea."

"Sir Gerald, we must talk to you," said Kincaid, making a stand against the tide of social convention.

"I'm sorry Caroline's out," said Gerald, continuing in his

hearty, friendly way as if there were nothing the least bit odd about their conversation. "She and Julia are making the final arrangements for Connor's funeral."

"Julia's helping with the funeral?" asked Kincaid, surprised enough to be distracted from his agenda.

Sir Gerald ran a hand through his sparse hair, and sat down on the sofa. It was his spot, obviously, as the cushions had depressions that exactly matched his bulk, like a dog's favorite old bed. Today he wore another variation of the moth-eaten sweater, this time in olive green, and what seemed to be the same baggy corduroys Kincaid had seen before. "Yes. She seems to have had a change of heart. I don't know why, and I'm too thankful to question it," he said, and gave them his engaging smile. "She came in like a whirlwind after lunch and said she'd made up her mind what should be done for Con, and she's been putting us through our paces ever since."

It would seem that Julia had made peace with Con's ghost. Kincaid pushed the thought of her aside and concentrated on Gerald. "It's you we wanted to see, sir."

"Have you found something?" He sat forward a bit and scanned their faces anxiously. "Tell me, please. I don't want Caroline and Julia upset."

"We've just come from Tommy Godwin, Sir Gerald. We know why Tommy came to see you at the theater the night Connor died." As Kincaid watched, Gerald sank back into the sofa, his face suddenly shuttered. Remembering the comment Sir Gerald had made to Tommy, Kincaid added, "You knew that Tommy was Matthew's father all along, didn't you, sir?"

Gerald Asherton closed his eyes. Under the jut of his eyebrows, his face looked impassive, remote and ancient as a biblical prophet's. "Of course I knew. I may be a fool, Mr. Kincaid, but I'm not a blind fool. Have you any idea how beautiful they were together, Tommy and Caroline?" Opening his eyes, he continued, "Grace, elegance, talent—you would have thought they'd been made for one another. I spent my days in terror that she would leave me, wondering how I would anchor my existence without her. When things seemed to fizzle out between them with Matty's conception, I thanked the gods for restoring her to me. The rest didn't matter. And Matty . . . Matty was everything we could have wanted."

"You never told Caroline you knew?" put in Gemma, disbelief evident in her tone.

"How could we have gone on, if I had?"

It had started, thought Kincaid, not with outright lies but with a denial of the truth, and that denial had become woven into the very fabric of their lives. "But Connor meant to wreck it all, didn't he, Sir Gerald? You must have felt some relief when you heard the next morning that he was dead." Kincaid caught Gemma's quick, surprised glance, then she moved quietly to stand by the piano, examining the photographs. He left the fire and sat in the armchair opposite Gerald.

"I must admit I felt some sense of reprieve. It shamed me, and made me all the more determined to get to the bottom of things. He was my son-in-law, and in spite of his sometimes rather hysterical behavior, I cared for him." Gerald clasped his hands and leaned forward. "Please, Superintendent, surely it can't benefit Connor for all this past history to be raked over. Can't we spare Caroline that?"

"Sir Gerald—"

The sitting room door opened and Caroline came in, followed by Julia. "What a perfectly horrid day," said Caroline, shaking fine drops of water from her dark hair. "Superintendent. Sergeant. Plummy's just coming with some tea. I'm sure we could all do with some." She slipped out of her leather jacket and tossed it wrong-side-out over the sofa back, before sitting beside her husband. The deep red silk of the jacket's lining rippled like blood in the glow from the fire.

Kincaid met Julia's eyes and saw pleasure mixed with wariness. It was the first time he had seen her with her mother, and he marveled at the combination of contrast and similarity. It seemed to him as if Julia were Caroline stretched and reforged, edges sharpened and refined, with the unmistakable stamp of her father's smile. And in spite of her tough mannerisms, her face was as transparent to him as his own, while he found Caroline's unreadable.

"We've been to Fingest church," said Julia, speaking to him as if there were no one else in the room. "Con's mum would have insisted on a Catholic funeral and burial, with all the trappings, but it didn't matter the least bit to Con, so I mean to do what seems right to me." She crossed the room to warm her hands by the fire. Dressed for the outdoors, she wore a heavy oiled-wool sweater still beaded with moisture, and her cheeks were faintly pink from the cold. "I've been round the churchyard with the vicar, and I've picked a gravesite within a stone's throw of Matty's. Perhaps they'll like being neighbors."

"Julia, don't be irreverent," said Caroline sharply. Turning to Kincaid, she added, "To what do we owe the pleasure of your company, Superintendent?"

"I've just been telling Sir Gerald—"

The door swung open again as Plummy came through with a laden tea tray. Julia went immediately to her aid, and together they arranged the tea things on the low table before the fire. "Mr. Kincaid, Sergeant James." Plummy smiled at Gemma, looking genuinely pleased to see her. "I've made extra, in case you've not had a proper lunch again." She busied herself pouring, this time into china cups and saucers rather than the comfortable stoneware mugs they'd used in the kitchen.

Refusing the offer of freshly toasted bread, Kincaid accepted tea reluctantly. He looked directly at Gerald. "I'm sorry, sir, but I'm afraid we must go on with this."

"Go on with what, Mr. Kincaid?" said Caroline. She had taken her cup from Plummy and returned to perch on the arm of the sofa, so that in spite of her small stature she seemed to hover protectively over her husband.

Kincaid wet his lips with a sip of tea. "The night Connor died, Dame Caroline, Tommy Godwin visited your husband in his dressing room at the Coliseum. He told Sir Gerald that he had just had a very unpleasant encounter with Connor. Although Connor was a little drunk and not terribly coherent, it eventually became clear that he had discovered the truth about Matthew's parentage, and was threatening to make his knowledge public with as much attendant scandal as possible." Kincaid paused, watching their faces. "Connor had discovered, in fact, that Matthew was Tommy's son, not Gerald's."

Sir Gerald had sunk into the sofa cushions again, eyes closed, his hand only loosely balancing the cup on his knee.

"Tommy and Mummy?" said Julia. "But that means Matty . . ." She subsided, her eyes wide and dark with shock. Kincaid wished he could have softened it for her somehow, wished he could comfort her as he had yesterday.

Vivian Plumley also watched the others, and Kincaid saw in her the perpetual observer, always on the edge of the family but not privy to its deepest secrets. She nodded once and compressed her lips, but Kincaid couldn't tell if her expression indicated distress or satisfaction.

"What utter nonsense, Superintendent," said Caroline. She laid her hand lightly on Gerald's shoulder. "I won't have it. You've overstepped the bounds of good manners as well as—"

"I am sorry if it distresses you, Dame Caroline, but I'm afraid it is necessary. Sir Gerald, will you tell me exactly what you did after Connor left you that night?"

Gerald touched his wife's hand. "It's all right, Caro. There can't be any harm in it." He roused himself, sitting forward a little and draining his teacup before he began. "There's not much to tell, really. I'd had quite a stiff drink with Tommy, and I'm afraid I kept on after he left. By the time I left the theater I was well over the limit. Shouldn't have been driving, of course, very irresponsible of me, but I managed without mishap." He smiled, showing healthy, pink gums above his upper teeth. "Well, almost without mishap. I had a bit of a run-in with Caro's car as I was parking mine. It seems my memory misled me by a foot or so as to its position, and I gave the paintwork a little scrape on the near side. It must have been close on one o'clock when I wobbled my way up to bed. Caro was asleep. I knew Julia was still out, of course, as I hadn't seen her car in the drive, but she's long past having a curfew." He gave his daughter an affectionate look.

"But I thought I heard you come in around midnight," said Plummy. She shook her head. "I just opened my eyes and squinted at the clock—perhaps I misread it."

Caroline slipped from the arm of the sofa and went to stand with her back to the fire. "I really don't see the point to this, Superintendent. Just because Connor was obviously disturbed does not mean we should be subjected to some sort of fascist grilling. We've already been over this once—that should be enough. I hope you realize that your assistant commissioner will hear about your irrational behavior."

She stood with her hands clasped behind her back and her feet slightly apart. In her black turtleneck, with fitted trousers tucked inside soft leather riding boots, she looked as though she might have been playing a trouser role in an opera. With her chin-length dark hair and in those clothes, she could easily pass for a boy on the verge of manhood. Her color was a little high, as befitted the hero/heroine under trying circumstances, but her voice, as always, was perfectly controlled.

"Dame Caroline," said Kincaid, "Connor may have been emotionally distraught, but he was also telling the truth. Tommy admitted it, and Sir Gerald has confirmed it as well. I think it's time—" He caught a movement out of the corner of his eye. Caroline's jacket slid from the back of the sofa to the cushion with a rustling sound, the soft black leather as fluid as running water.

An odd sensation came over him, as if he had suddenly receded down a tunnel, distorting both his hearing and his vision. Blinking, he turned again to Caroline. Rearrange a few insignificant pieces in the pattern, and the whole thing shifted, turning on itself and popping into focus, clear and sharp and irrefutable. It amazed him now that he hadn't seen it all from the beginning.

They were all watching him with various degrees of concern. Smiling at Gemma, who had frozen with her cup poised midway in the air, he set his own empty cup firmly upon the table. "It wasn't the doorbell you heard that night, Mrs. Plumley, it was the telephone. And it wasn't Gerald you heard coming in a few minutes after midnight, but Caroline.

"Connor rang this number from the flat a little before eleven o'clock. I think it likely that he was looking for Julia, but it was Caroline who answered the phone." Kincaid rose and went to stand against the piano, so that he could face Caroline directly. "He couldn't resist baiting you, could he, Caroline? You were the architect of the deception he felt had cost him his happiness, after all.

"You thought you could calm him down, make him see reason, so you said you'd meet him. But you didn't want him making a scene in a public place, so you suggested somewhere you wouldn't be overheard—what could have been more natural than your favorite walk along Hambleden Lock?

"You dressed quickly, I imagine in something quite similar to the things you're wearing just now, and put on your leather jacket. The night was cold and damp, and it's a good brisk walk from the carpark to the river. You slipped quietly out of the house, making sure not to wake Plummy, and when you reached the river you waited for Con at the beginning of the weir."

He shifted his position a bit, putting his hands in his trouser pockets. They all watched him, as mesmerized as if he were a conjurer about to pull a rabbit from a hat. Julia's eyes looked glazed, as if she were unable to assimilate a second shock so soon after the first.

"What happened then, Caroline?" he asked. Closing his eyes, he pictured the scene as he spoke. "You walked along the weir, and you argued. The more you tried to reason with Con, the more difficult he became. You reached the lock, crossing over it to the far side, and there the paved path ends." He opened his eyes again and watched Caroline's still, composed face. "So you stood with Connor on the little concrete apron just upstream of the sluicegate. Did you suggest turning back? But Con was out of control by that time, and the argument disintegrated into—"

"Please, Superintendent," said Sir Gerald, "you really have gone too far. This is all absurd. Caro couldn't kill anyone. She's not physically capable—just look at her. And Con was over six feet tall and well built . . ."

"She's also an actress, Sir Gerald, trained to use her body on the stage. It may have been something as simple as stepping aside

243

when he rushed at her. We'll probably never be certain of that, or know what actually killed Connor. From the results of the post-mortem I think it likely he had a laryngospasm—his throat closed from the shock of hitting the water, and he died from suffocation without ever drawing water into his lungs.

"What we do know," he said, turning back to Caroline, "is that help was less than fifty yards away. The lockkeeper was at home, he had the necessary equipment and expertise. And even had he not been available, there were other houses just a bit farther along the opposite bank of the river.

"Whether Connor's fall into the river was an accident, or self-defense, or a deliberate act of violence, the fact remains that you are culpable, Dame Caroline. You might have saved him. Did you wait what seemed a reasonable time for him to come up again? When he didn't surface, you walked away, drove home and climbed back into bed, where Gerald found you sleeping peacefully. Only you were a bit more flustered than you thought, and didn't quite manage to leave your car exactly as it had been."

Caroline smiled at him. "That's quite an amusing fiction, Mr. Kincaid. I'm sure the chief constable and your assistant commissioner will find it most entertaining as well. You have nothing but circumstantial evidence and an overactive imagination."

"That may be true, Dame Caroline. We will have forensics go over your car and your clothes, however, and there's the matter of the witness who saw a man and, she assumed, a boy wearing a leather jacket on the weir walkway—she may recognize you in an identity parade.

"Whether or not we can build a case against you that will hold up in court, those of us here today will know the truth."

"Truth?" said Caroline, at last allowing her voice to rise in anger. "You wouldn't know truth if it came up and bit you, Mr. Kincaid. The truth is that this family will stand together, as we always have, and you can't touch us. You're a fool to think—"

"Stop it! Just stop it, all of you." Julia rose from the sofa and stood shaking, her hands clenched and her face drained of color. "This has gone on long enough. How can you be such a hypocrite,

Mummy? No wonder Con was furious. He'd bought your load of rubbish and taken on my share of it, too." She paused for a breath, then said more evenly, "I grew up hating myself because I never quite fit into your ideal circle, thinking that if I'd only been different, better somehow, you would have loved me more. And it was all a lie, the perfect family was a lie. You warped my life with it, and you would have warped Matty's, too, if you'd been given a chance."

"Julia, you mustn't say these things." Sir Gerald's voice held more anguish than when he'd defended his wife. "You've no right to desecrate Matthew's memory."

"Don't talk to me about Matty's memory. I'm the only one who really grieved for Matty, the little boy who could be rude and silly, and sometimes had to sleep with his light on because he was frightened of his dreams. You only lost what you wanted him to be." Julia looked at Plummy, who still sat quietly on the edge of her seat, her back straight as a staff. "I'm sorry, Plummy, that's unfair to you. You loved him—you loved both of us, and honestly.

"And Tommy—as ill as I was I remember Tommy coming to the house, and now I can understand what I only sensed then. He sat with me, offering what solace he could, but you were the only one who might have comforted him, Mummy, and you wouldn't see him. You were too busy making high drama of your grief. He deserved better."

In two lightning steps, Caroline crossed the space that separated her from Julia. She raised her open hand and slapped her daughter across the face. "Don't you dare speak to me like that. You don't know anything. You're making a fool of yourself with this ridiculous scene. You're making fools of us all, and I won't have it in my house."

Julia stood her ground. Even though her eyes filled with tears, she neither spoke nor lifted a hand to touch the white imprint on her cheek.

Vivian Plumley went to her and put an arm gently around her shoulders. She said, "Maybe it's time someone made a scene, Caro. Who knows what might have been avoided if some of these things had been said long ago?"

Caroline stepped back. "I only meant to protect you, Julia, always. And you, Gerald," she added, turning to him.

Wearily, Julia said, "You've protected yourself, from the very beginning."

"We were all right as we were," said Caroline. "Why should anything change?"

"It's too late, Mummy," said Julia, and Kincaid heard an unexpected note of compassion. "Can't you see that?"

Caroline turned to her husband, hand out in a gesture of supplication. "Gerald—"

He looked away.

In the silence that followed, a gust of wind blew a spatter of rain against the window, and the fire flared up in response. Kincaid met Gemma's eyes. He nodded slightly and she came to stand beside him. He said, "I'm sorry, Dame Caroline, but I'm afraid you'll need to come with us to High Wycombe and make a formal statement. You can come in your own car, if you like, Sir Gerald, and wait for her."

Julia looked at her parents. What judgment would she pass on them, wondered Kincaid, now that they had revealed themselves as all too fallibly human, and flawed?

For the first time Julia's hand strayed to her cheek. She went to Gerald and briefly touched his arm. "I'll wait for you here, Daddy," she said, then she turned away and left the room without another glance at her mother.

When they had rung High Wycombe and organized the preliminaries, Kincaid excused himself and slipped out of the sitting room. By the time he reached the top landing he had to catch his breath, and he felt a welcome ache in his calves. He tapped lightly on the door of Julia's studio and opened it.

She stood in the center of the room, holding an open box in her arms and looking about her. "Plummy's cleaned up after me, can you tell?" she said as he came in.

It did look uncharacteristically clean and lifeless, as if the removal of Julia's attendant clutter had stripped it of its heart.

"There's nothing left I need, really. I suppose what I wanted was to say good-bye." She gestured around the room with her chin. The mark of her mother's hand stood out clearly now, fiery against the pale skin of her cheek. "I won't be back here again. Not in the same way. This was a child's refuge."

"Yes," said Kincaid. She would move on now, into her own life. "You'll be all right."

"I know." They looked at one another and he understood that he would not see her again, that their coming together had served its purpose. He would move on now as well, perhaps take a leaf from Gemma's book—she had been hurt, as he had, but she had put it behind her with the forthright practicality he so admired.

After a moment, Julia said, "What will happen to my mother?"

"I don't know. It depends on the forensic evidence, but even if we turned up something fairly concrete, I doubt we'll make anything stiffer than involuntary manslaughter stick."

She nodded.

Near to the eaves as they were, the sound of the rain beating against the roof came clearly, and the wind rattled the windows like a beast seeking entrance. "Julia, I'm sorry."

"You mustn't be. You only did your job, and what you knew was right. You couldn't violate your integrity to protect me, or my family. There's been enough of that in this house," she said firmly. "Are you sorry about what happened with us, as well?" she added, with a trace of a smile.

Was he sorry? For ten years he had kept his emotions safely, tightly reined, until he had almost forgotten how it felt to give another person access. Julia had forced his hand, made him see himself in the mirror of her isolation, and what he found frightened him. But probing beyond the fear, he felt a new and unexpected sense of freedom, even of anticipation.

He smiled back at Julia. "No."

CHAPTER
16

"We should have taken the Midget," Kincaid said testily as Gemma pulled the Escort up in front of the Carlingford Road flat.

"You know as well as I do that the bloody thing leaks in the rain," she retorted, glaring at him. She felt as miserable and bedraggled as a cat forced into the bath, and he wasn't much of an improvement. As she watched, a rivulet of water trickled down his forehead from his matted hair.

He wiped it away with the back of his hand, then burst out laughing. "Gemma, look at us. How can you be so stubborn?"

After what seemed an interminable session at High Wycombe, they had started back to London on the M40, only to have a puncture before they reached the North Circular Road. Gemma had pulled over to the verge and plunged out into the driving rain, refusing his help in changing the tire. He had stood in the rain, arguing with her while she worked, so that in the end they were both soaked to the skin.

"It's too late to collect Toby tonight," he said. "Come in and get some dry things on before you catch your death, and have something proper to eat. Please."

After a moment, she said, "All right," but the words she'd meant to be acquiescent came out grudging and sullen. Her bad temper seemed to be out of control, feeding on itself, and she didn't know how to break the cycle.

They didn't bother with umbrellas as they crossed the road to Kincaid's building—how could they get any more wet, after all?—and the pellets of water stung against her skin.

When they reached the flat, Kincaid went straight to the kitchen, leaving a dripping trail on the carpet. He pulled an already uncorked bottle of white wine from the fridge and poured two glasses. Handing her one, he said, "Start on this. It will warm you up from the inside. Sorry I haven't anything stronger. And in the meantime I'll get you something dry to put on."

He left her standing in the sitting room holding her glass, too wet to sit down, too exhausted to sort out her own feelings. Was she angry with him because of Julia? She had felt a communion between them, an understanding that excluded her, and the strength of her reaction dismayed her.

She tasted the wine, then drank half the glass. Chill in her mouth, it did seem to generate some warmth in her middle.

Or was she angry with Caroline Stowe for having taken her in, and Kincaid merely happened to be the nearest available target?

Perhaps it was just the waste of it all that made her feel like chucking something.

Sid uncurled himself from his nest on the sofa, stretching, and came to her. He elongated his sleek body as he rubbed around her ankles and butted his head against her legs. She bent to scratch him in the soft spot under his chin, and his throat began to vibrate under her fingertips. "Hullo, Sid. You've got the right idea tonight—warm and dry. We should all be so lucky."

She looked around the familiar and comfortable room. Light from the lamps Kincaid had switched on spilled out in warm pools, illuminating his collection of brightly colored London transport posters. The coffee table held a haphazard pile of books and an empty mug, and the sofa a crumpled afghan rug. Gemma felt a sudden pang of longing. She wanted to feel at home here, wanted to feel safe.

"I didn't know about underthings," said Kincaid, returning from the bedroom carrying a stack of folded clothes with a big fluffy towel on the top. "I suppose you'll have to make do." He deposited the jeans and sweatshirt on the sofa and draped the towel around her shoulders. "Oh, and socks. I forgot socks."

Wiping her face with one end of the towel, Gemma began fumbling with her sodden braid. Her fingers were too numb with cold to work properly, and she felt tears of frustration smart behind her eyelids.

"Let me help," he said gently. He turned her around and deftly worked loose the braid, combing her hair out with his fingers. "Now." Rotating her until she faced him again, he began rubbing her head with the towel. His hair stood on end where he had scrubbed at it, and his skin smelled warm and damp.

The weight of his hands against her head seemed to physically crumble her defenses, and she felt her legs go limp and boneless, as if they could no longer support her weight. She closed her eyes against the faintness, thinking *too much wine, too quickly,* but the sensation didn't pass. Reaching up, she put a hand over his, and a buzz ran through her like electric current as their skin made contact.

He stopped his toweling of her hair, looking at her with concern. "Sorry," he said. "Did I get carried away?"

When she managed to shake her head, he let the towel slide to her shoulders and began gently rubbing her neck and the back of her head. She thought disjointedly of Rob—he had never looked after her like this. No one had. And nowhere in her calculations had she reckoned with the power of tenderness, irresistible as gravity.

The pressure of his hand on the back of her head brought her a stumbling step forward, against him, and she gasped with shock as his weight pressed her icy clothes to her skin. She turned her face up, and of its own volition her hand reached for him, cupping the back of his damp head, pulling his mouth down to meet hers.

Drowsily, Gemma raised herself on one elbow and looked at him, realizing she'd never seen him asleep. His relaxed face seemed younger, softer, and the fan of his eyelashes made dark shadows on his cheeks. His eyelids fluttered for an instant, as if he were dreaming, and the corners of his mouth turned up in the hint of a smile.

She reached out to smooth the unruly chestnut hair from his brow and froze. Suddenly, in that small act of intimacy, she saw the enormity, the absurdity, of what she had done.

She drew her hand back as if stung. Oh dear God, what had she been thinking of? What on earth had possessed her? How could she face him at work in the morning, say, "Yes, guv, no, guv, right-oh, guv," as if nothing had happened between them?

Her heart racing, she slid carefully from the bed. They'd left a trail of wet clothes across the bedroom, and as she disentangled hers from the jumble she felt tears fill her eyes. She swore under her breath. *Silly, bloody fool.* She never cried. Even when Rob had left her, she hadn't cried. Shivering, she pulled on damp panties, slipped her soggy jumper over her head.

She had done what she'd sworn she'd never do. As hard as she'd worked to earn her position, to be considered an equal, a colleague, she'd shown herself no better than any tart who slept her way up the ladder. A wave of dizziness swept over her as she stepped into her skirt and she swayed.

What could she do now? Ask for a transfer? Everyone would know why—she might as well wear a sign and save them speculating. Resign? Give up her dreams, let all her hard work turn to dust in her fingers? How could she bear it? Oh, she would have sympathy and a plausible excuse—too hard a life for a single mum, a need to spend more time with her son—but she would know how badly she had failed.

Kincaid stirred and turned, freeing an arm from the covers. Staring at him, she tried to memorize the curve of his shoulder, the angle of his cheek, and her heart contracted with longing and desire. She turned away, afraid of her own weakness.

In the sitting room she squelched her bare feet into her shoes and gathered up her coat and bag. The dry jeans and sweater he'd brought her still lay neatly folded on the sofa, and the towel he'd used to dry her hair lay crumpled on the floor. She picked it up and held its soft nap against her cheek, imagining that it smelled faintly of shaving soap. With exaggerated care she folded it and placed it beside the clothes, then let herself quietly out of the flat.

When Gemma reached the street door, she found the rain still coming down in relentless sheets, a solid wall of water. She stood for a moment, watching it. In her traitorous mind she imagined running back up the stairs and into the flat, shedding her clothes and climbing back into bed beside his sleeping form.

She pushed open the door, stepped slowly out into the rain and crossed the road, making no effort to shield herself. The dim outline of the Escort was familiar, comforting even. Scrabbling for the handle like one blind, she wrenched the door open and half fell into the driver's seat. She wiped her streaming face with her hands and started the engine.

The radio blared into life and instead of hitting the off switch, she reflexively jammed a tape into the player. Caroline Stowe's voice filled the car as Violetta sang her last aria, begging for life, for love, for the physical strength to match her courageous will.

Gemma put her head down against the steering wheel and wept.

After a moment she mopped her face with some tissues and put the car into gear, and when the music finished the only sound was the drumming of the rain against the roof.

The soft click of a door penetrated Kincaid's consciousness. He struggled toward the surface of sleep, but it clung to him tenaciously, dragging him down again into its cotton-wool depths. His body felt boneless, warmly lethargic, and his eyelids seemed to have acquired surplus weight. Rousing himself enough to tuck his exposed arm under the covers, he felt the sheet cool and empty beside him. He blinked. Gemma. She must have gone to the loo—women always had to go to the loo—or perhaps to the kitchen for a glass of water.

He smiled a little at his own stupidity. What he wanted, needed, had been right under his nose all along and he'd been too blind to see it. Now he felt as if his life had come round full circle, complete, and he imagined the pattern of their days together. Work, then home, and at day's end he would find sanctuary beside her, entangling himself in the curtain of her coppery hair.

Kincaid stretched his arm across her pillow, ready to enfold her when she returned. The rain beat steadily against the windowpane, counterpoint to the warmth of the room. With a sigh of contentment, he drifted once again into sleep.